I0763412

BLOOD OATH

A PARANORMAL REVERSE HAREM ROMANCE

CURSED LEGACIES
BOOK 1

MORGAN B LEE

Cover Design: Okay Creations

No AI was used in the creation of this book.

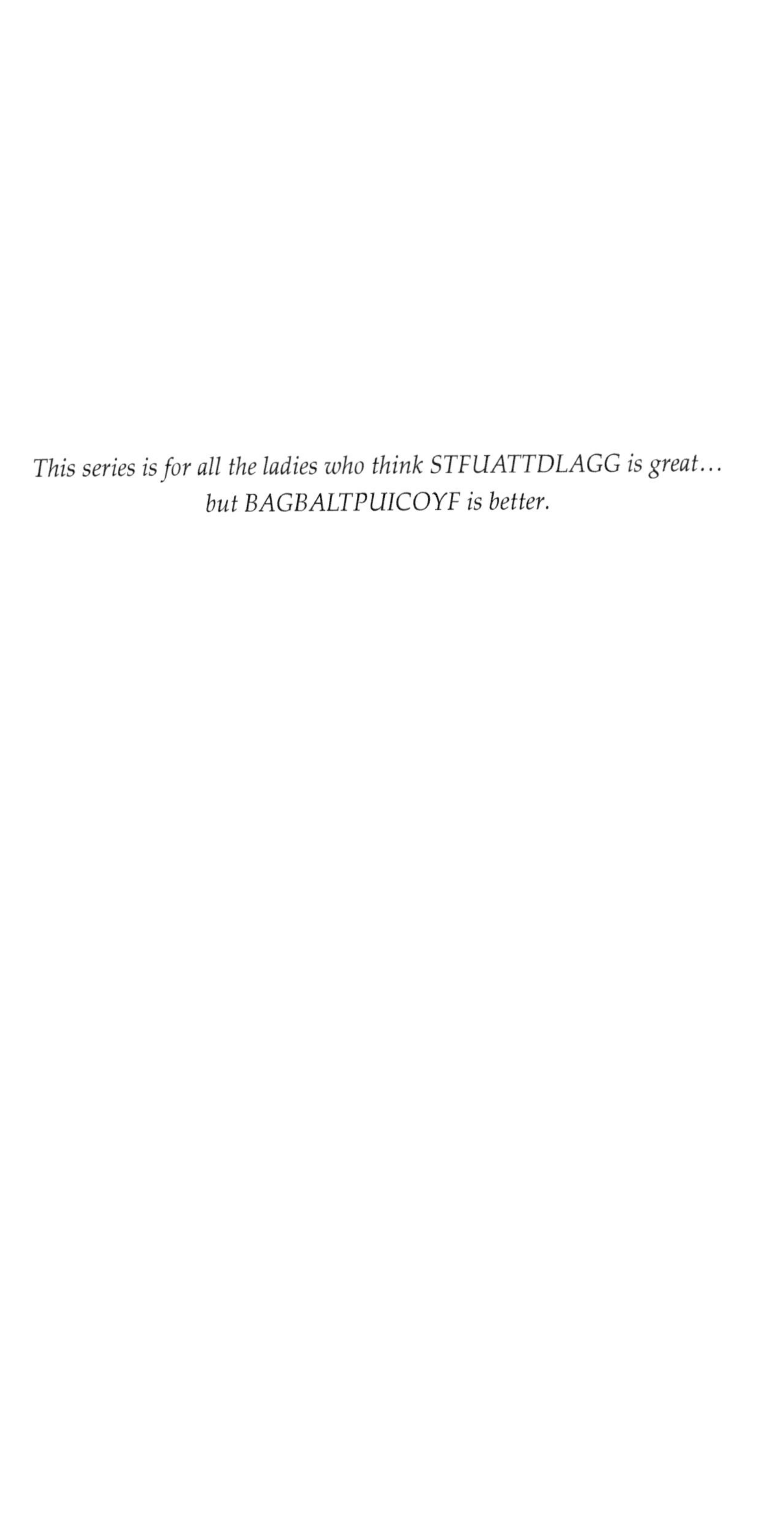

This series is for all the ladies who think STFUATTDLAGG is great…
but BAGBALTPUICOYF is better.

READ BEFORE YOU READ

This series is a dark academy paranormal why-choose/reverse harem romance, meaning the leading lady ends up with more than one fated mate. It gets spicy and kinky, but starts off slow. Mind the cliff.

Series trigger ~~check~~list:

- attempted SA of main character (brief and the perpetrator is quickly unalived)
- BDSM
- death (on page)
- death of main character (don't worry, it doesn't stick)
- strong language
- female dominant/switch
- group sex scenes (no M/M)
- graphic violence
- loss of a loved one (past tense)
- mentions of childhood abuse
- PTSD
- somnophilia (with prior consent given)
- stalking (of FMC by MMC)
- torture

Never fear, this series will have an HEA. Enjoy, lovelies <3

1

MAVEN

LEPIDOPTERY IS A BEAUTIFULLY MORBID HOBBY.

I come to this conclusion after several minutes of staring at the extensive collection of gossamer butterfly wings pinned to the wall behind the faculty member's desk. He's been making one-sided small talk the entire time, unaware of my growing appreciation for impaling insect corpses up in such a macabre display.

He laughs at one of his own jokes and raises his bushy eyebrows at me expectantly. When I offer no change in expression, he clears his throat, tapping one finger against a file resting on the mahogany desk in front of him.

"Well, now that introductions are out of the way, I suppose we should get down to business. Welcome to Everbound University, Miss Oakley. I've read all your student records, and it seems you are what we would call an atypical caster—the magic in your blood manifested of its own accord despite your completely human pedigree. There aren't many atypical casters, so I'm sure this world is probably all a bit overwhelming for you," he smiles apologetically.

You have absolutely no fucking idea.

He goes on, opening my file. "It says here that after you manifested your magic a week ago, you immediately turned yourself in to the proper authorities. As required by law, they, in turn, registered you to attend this semester, although we only have a month left. Turning yourself in must have been difficult, but you should be proud. I'm sure that if you work hard and watch your back, you will thrive here at Everbound University."

His smile is sickeningly optimistic.

My attention drifts back to the dead bugs on the wall. "The headmaster. Where is he?"

That catches him by surprise. "Professor Hearst? I'm not sure how much you know about the world of legacies, Miss Oakley, but I'm sure even the humans teach about the Immortal Quintet in their schools. They're an integral part of history between humans and legacies, and they put the Divide in place to protect the mortal world. Professor Hearst is a member of that vital quintet and, as such, had some important business to attend to that required him to leave Everbound. Until further notice, *I* am the interim headmaster—Mr. Gibbons, at your service."

Damn it.

As usual, I refuse to let emotion of any kind show on my face as I look out the window of the ornate office. He's right about one thing: this atmosphere is entirely foreign to me. Two stories below us, stone courtyards illuminated in bright winter morning light give way to the expansive training fields on this side of Everbound Castle.

Because of course legacies are mandated to study in a gods-damned castle.

It's fitting—a bunch of descendants of monsters housed in a gothic behemoth surrounded by thick forest, miles away from the nearest human civilization. Every inch of this place radiates prestige with an undertone of danger, like a rose perched at the tip of a bloodied knife.

On second thought, maybe I will enjoy this place after all.

Mr. Gibbons clears his throat. "You've undoubtedly heard the rumors about how dangerous Everbound University is. I'm afraid those rumors are true. We are preparing legacies to become weapons to protect the mortal world, and while we try to enforce a *no-killing* rule for unmatched legacies, sometimes they do get carried away, and..." He shrugs uncomfortably. "At any rate, we send out emergency notifications in the event of a student's severe injury or untimely death. Who should I list as your emergency contact?"

"Leave it blank."

"Are you certain?"

I meet his gaze. "Depends. Are you a necromancer?"

He rears back, almost choking. "Of *course* not!"

"Then I'm certain."

"Good gods," he huffs. "Why would you even ask such a thing?"

It's amusing how scandalized he is that I even dared bring up necromancy. He rearranges the two papers in my file several times before rising from his chair with a haughty sniff.

"Miss Oakley, the Nether and all things pertaining to it are *not* to be spoken of lightly. It is a parasitic hellhole full of the worst horrors imaginable, and the only things keeping it from gaining a foothold in this world are the Divide and the blood, sweat, and sacrifice of us legacies. Only mere weeks ago, a surge of shadow fiends escaped and slaughtered hundreds of innocent humans in a small town in Maine. Just think of *that* before talking about the creatures there with such levity again."

Touchy subject.

I study the office around me once again, memorizing the setup. The other faculty offices likely have a similar layout, so it's valuable information.

"Is that the reason Headmaster Hearst left?"

Mr. Gibbons shakes his head as he puts my file away, withdrawing an envelope that appears to be overfilled with my student ID, introductory papers, and a key.

"That's not our business, but I'm sure he'll be back by the end of the semester for First Placement in about a month."

One month here. I can do that.

"Now, then, about your dorm room. You'll be rooming with a lion shifter in the upper northeast wing. She'll be—"

"I requested a private dorm."

"They're all occupied at the moment. But that shouldn't inconvenience you much, considering that the Seeking is in two weeks. At that time, so many legacies will be moving to the quintet apartments that I'm sure something will open up for you by then." Then he tips his head. "Do you know what the Seeking is?"

Right. The Seeking. When the gods reveal which quintet a legacy is meant to belong with.

In other words, total bullshit.

I opt to ignore the question entirely, since I couldn't care less about their precious Seeking. If everything goes smoothly, I'll be done with Everbound quickly.

"I'll pay extra for any private room."

He sighs heavily. "Legacies may be in the minority compared to humans, Miss Oakley, but there are still enough attending this semester that we truly are out of private spaces. I'm afraid you're quite stuck with this roommate for the time being—and the no-killing rule is especially strict about roommates. So play nice."

Make me.

I learned long ago, in the most brutal ways possible, that playing nice with others is an excellent way to get killed. I would very literally rather spend the next two weeks enduring Chinese water torture than chumming it up with someone here, but telling that to him is of little use.

If I want my own space, I'll just have to drive this new *roommate* of mine away. It's just a matter of getting creative.

"Fine. Are we done?" I ask, standing.

He stands, too, but looks over my baggy clothing and leather-gloved hands with a wary expression.

"Before you leave, you should know how *precarious* your first few weeks here will likely be. I cannot stress enough just how different our world is from the human one you were raised in. Legacies are extremely competitive, Miss Oakley—especially after quintets rankings begin after the Seeking since that is when the no-killing rule is lifted. Here, it truly is survival of the fittest—or rather, the most powerful. We are descended from monsters, so you could say a thirst for bloodshed comes with the territory. So if one's magic is on the weaker side, as it tends to be with atypical casters like you..."

Gibbons pauses, scratching one bushy brow. "Well, the highest-ranked legacies here will probably overlook you completely since they won't perceive you as a threat. But the less powerful ones will see you as someone to best in order to secure their social standing. Just remember that legacies are far more monstrous than humans often realize. You will need to watch your back at all times, as we faculty members will not be able to protect you."

"Forced to come here. Unlikely to survive. Got it."

I grab the overstuffed envelope from his desk and leave the room without another word, ignoring how he calls out a final *good luck* after me. His office and several other faculty offices are in a small hallway branching off the massive entry hall of Everbound Castle. This entire place is a gothic maze, but I start in the general direction of the upper northeast wing, where he said my dorm would be.

The halls aren't crowded since most legacies are in their classes, but there are still clusters of students here or there. I pass a couple of vampires sitting on a stone bench, latched onto one another's necks as they moan and feed. Sirens with silky voices are giggling and gossiping in a group as they pass. They pay me no heed—no one does, because I keep my head down and slip through the crowd at just the right speed to blend in perfectly.

Finally, I turn down an empty corridor. All along the right is a row of tall vaulted windows overlooking Everbound Forest.

But I only make it a few steps before a door directly to my left bursts open, and a trio of completely naked people tumble out onto the floor. There's one girl—a fae, judging by her pointed ears and luminescent purple hair—and two guys, one of whom has blood oozing down the side of his neck from two puncture marks. He doesn't seem concerned about it staining the untied robe hanging around his shoulders.

The other man laughs uproariously, stands, brushes himself off, and returns to the dorm room...

Which is full of a raging orgy.

Choruses of moans and gasps fill the space. A handful of legacies down alcohol off to one side of the sensually lit room. Everyone present is nude and completely uninhibited. Near the doorway, a vampire sinks his teeth into the neck of what appears to be a succubus. She moans and bounces faster on the lap of another man.

It's all a blur of tangled limbs, kissing, fucking, and…

Touching.

My breathing doesn't feel steady, and that all-too-familiar prickle courses over my skin, my neck breaking out into a cold sweat.

"You new here, sweetheart?"

That draws my attention back to the guy with the bleeding neck standing in front of me. The fae girl has already rejoined the others, and when she shuts the door behind her, it leaves me alone in the hall with him. He doesn't bother tying his robe, and he's eyeing me with a carnal gleam in his eye, even though my clothes completely obscure what my body looks like.

"Very," I reply. "Excuse me."

I try to step around him, but he blocks my path with a wide smile. Two colors of lipstick are smeared around his mouth, down his chest, and all over his junk. From the way he's eyeing me, it's not hard to tell he's sizing me up to get a feel for how strong or weak of a legacy I am. I suppose the interim headmaster was right about needing to watch my back right off the bat.

"Not so fast. Why're you here so late in the semester? You an asscaster?" When I say nothing, he grins. "That's what we call atypical casters. Because their magic is total ass."

Again, I try to sidestep him. Again, he gets in the way.

"Whoa there. You need a crash course, sweetie. Wanna join us? Collins' orgies are always the best. Or if you're not into group scenes, I'm more than ready to give you the best one-on-one welcome you could possibly ask for."

I look pointedly down at his flaccid, lipstick-and-sex-juice-covered dick. "Hard pass. Besides, your little soldier obviously didn't get the *more-than-ready* memo."

I finally manage to step around him, assuming he'll give up on harassing me and return to the mosh pit of sex. Instead, he keeps pace with me, eyeing the area where my sweatshirt obscures my chest as he licks his lips.

"This prissy, robotic virgin thing you've got going? Yeah, you're an asscaster, all right. But I've got a knack for guessing people's undiscovered kinks, and I get the feeling that once I peel all those stuffy layers off of you, you'll be my sweet little submissive cock-sucker just begging for dick."

Gag me with a knife.

I'm not going to waste more time with this prick by going into all the many ways he's dead wrong. "Not interested."

I turn again and begin ascending a half-hidden narrow staircase toward the second floor, but in a blur, the idiot is standing a few stairs up from me, so now his disgusting, still-wet cock is at eye level. He leers down.

"Didn't ask if you were. See, you've got me curious, and I hate being curious. I can tell just by looking you're a one-fuck cunt, so I'll leave you alone afterward. Come on, give it a taste. You'll love it."

That's it. My patience has officially run out.

I look him in the eye and speak clearly so his single functioning brain cell will understand. "You don't want to test me. Move."

He throws his head back on a sharp laugh. "Poor thing, do you *actually* think you could handle me? I'm a vampire. You're basically a human. The least powerful legacy of all time is still a hundred times more threatening than an asscaster. Go on, give it your best shot. I wanna see you snap."

Trust me, you don't.

He slowly descends the stairs, his appetite shifting from my body to the side of my neck. "Maybe I'll cut you a deal, New Girl. Suck me off without fighting, and I'll only drink a pint. Keep playing hard to get, and it'll be your fault when I drain you dry."

I want to roll my eyes at how deluded this guy is, but then he reaches down to cup my jaw, his other hand slipping behind me to squeeze my ass.

Time jolts, sending my stomach careening. For one fraction of a second after my body registers his touch on my face, my limbs go numb, and I can't breathe. The drag of his unwanted bare skin against mine is like a scalding razor running across a frayed nerve, raw and unbearable.

I snap.

Instincts kick in hard and fast, my body going into auto drive as I knock his arm to one side while pulling my favorite small dagger from one of my concealed sleeve pockets. By the time the vamp even realizes I've moved, the dagger is already jammed up between his ribs, twisting into his heart deep enough that the tips of my fingers sink into the new hole in his chest that's already gushing blood.

Good thing my gloves are black, so the stain won't show.

He gasps and staggers into the wall as every vein in his body bulges through his quickly blackening skin. It's an agonizing sensation. I would know.

"Th—this isn't an oak stake," he chokes, desperately trying to claw the dagger out. Unfortunately for him, he only has about ten seconds left before his vampire strength is sapped away with the remainder of his life force. "W—what is—"

"Adamantine. With some very fun tweaks."

I wrench the dagger out, and he cries out in pain, slumping to the floor. As he starts to spasm uncontrollably, I use his bathrobe to wipe off my blade, giving him a bored look that belies the residual panic pumping through my system from his touch.

"Congratulations. You got to see me snap."

The vampire's eyes widen just before he goes utterly still.

My veins fill with a familiar buzz. For the first time since arriving here, the corners of my lips curl up slowly. Slipping the dagger back into its hidden pocket in my sleeve, I continue up the stairs.

These legacies don't have to worry about me not being monstrous enough for this place.

They have no idea what they just let in.

2

MAVEN

The moment I enter my new dorm, a shrill squeal assaults my eardrums.

"*Oh my gods!* You're here!"

A tall legacy jumps up from the pillow-filled bed on the right side of the dorm, dressed in a fuzzy blue crop top sweater and shiny yoga pants. My attention immediately goes to her hair. Light as straw and naturally as curly as corkscrews, it creates a pale halo around her head.

It looks exactly like Lillian's hair.

She beams at me and holds out her hand to shake. "I'm Kenzie. Lion shifter. Artist. Slut extraordinaire. I'm kidding about that last one—I'm just a normal slut. In a good way. Damn, is your hair naturally that dark? It's so pretty! What House are you in? What's your name?"

I glance down at her hand, sliding my own into my pockets. "Maven."

"Nice to meet ya, Maven. Can I call you May? I'm gonna call you May. Did you just get here? Where are your things?" She glances into the hallway behind me with a frown.

"I pack light." As in, everything I currently own is on my person.

"Well, then, it's a good thing I'm a terrible student because I'm *so* down to play hooky the rest of the day so we can go buy you all the essentials. We could hit up one of the university stores here, but honestly, the drive to Halfton is so worth it because they have the most darling little boutique there, and we could get some boba tea—"

Gods. Does she even breathe between words?

Tuning her out, I walk past her to observe the undecorated left side of the room which is now mine. It's small, just one twin bed with a desk at the foot of it and a dresser under the window. It's soothingly bare and simple, especially compared to Kenzie's very busy, very *artsy* side of the room.

When she sees me eyeballing one of the many erotic paintings on display where two abstract women are literally melting together, she practically preens. "Yep, I'm helplessly raunchy. I'm usually inspired to paint after a very memorable sexual experience."

"That's a lot of paintings."

"Did I not make the *slut* thing clear? I'm very open about it."

"Most legacies seem to be," I muse, thinking of the orgy I'd passed.

She tips her head, curls falling to the side. "Compared to what? Humans?" Then she gasps hard. "Oh! Did you grow up around humans? What was that like? I think they're so fascinating, but obviously, my moms and dads were against me having human friends growing up. I mean, us legacies are all supposed to keep to our own kind until we're graduated, bonded, and considered legal in the eyes of the human government, blah blah blah."

She waves off all the legality talk and grins. "But I know some legacy families are a lot friendlier with humans anyway! Is that how you grew up? What are your parents like?"

"Dead."

That shuts her up. Her face falls. "Oh. I—I'm sorry. I put my foot in my mouth a lot."

Easy to do when it always seems to be flapping open.

I was already planning on getting rid of whatever roommate I ended up with, so finding out I'm stuck for two weeks with this energetic chatterbox should motivate me further. I should be plotting to stuff her pillow with bundles of spider eggs or something equally entertaining.

Instead, my attention slides back to her hair. And her eyes. They're like Lillian's, too—a bright, happy blue. Their personalities seem similar.

She'll probably be so fucking annoying as a roommate, but it feels too much like I'm looking at a younger, taller version of Lillian, so I decide to hold off on the spider eggs.

For now.

Walking to the window on my side of the room, I close the thick, dark curtains to make the bright lighting less harsh on my eyes. I'll need to blend in here until Headmaster Hearst returns. Which means I'll attend my classes and draw absolutely no attention to myself. Keeping my head down is the best strategy.

If I have to endure Kenzie as a roommate until the Seeking, I should at least get an idea of how dangerous she is as a legacy.

"So. You're a lion shifter."

She nods, but her smile is less bright as she perches on the side of her bed. "Yeah, well…I'm supposed to be. I mean, I *am*, because I can sense my inner lioness, but my curse…" She makes a face and then leans towards me in a conspiratorial whisper. "I know it's taboo for legacies to reveal their curses, but mine is *really* obvious—so I'll just tell you since everyone else already knows. I can't shift until my curse is broken."

Ah, yes. The curse.

I've heard plenty about it, including the fact that the curse affects each legacy differently. Typically the stronger the legacy, the stronger their curse.

The gods put the Legacy Curse in place decades ago to ensure balance and peace since legacies have a long and gloriously bloody history of nearly destroying the world through warfare. Long story short, Everbound University has been the mandatory two-year graduate school for legacies for over a century. They come here to study, train, and determine how they fit into the hierarchy of the Four Houses based on their strength and power.

But mostly, legacies come here to find their missing pieces. Because the only way legacies can break their curses and reach their full potential is through binding their souls in a quintet pieced together from members of all Four Houses.

A matching set of monstrous soulmates, if you will. Hand-selected by the gods themselves.

What a crock of bullshit.

"Anyway," Kenzie's entire face lights up again. "It's fine because the Seeking is only two weeks away! Can you believe it? I'm so fucking stoked. I've been waiting my entire life to find out who I'll be matched with. Isn't it so exciting?"

"Thrilling," I mutter.

She tips her head. "I just realized something. Why are you so late to Everbound? I mean, we're only a month away from the end of the semester."

"Long story."

She tries to hide her disappointment at my non-answer. "Got it. Well, then…hey! Want a tour of Everbound? I would love to be a tour guide. Not just for you—for anyone. I wish legacies could have boring, run-of-the-mill jobs like tour guiding because I think it's my true calling in life. I know things about this place that even the headmaster can't imagine. Dead-ass, if you ever have a random question about this place or anyone here, I'm your girl because I've made the gossip mill my little bitch."

The corner of my lips twitch. So far, she's not as annoying as I expected. She might even be…tolerable.

"A tour would be useful," I decide.

"Yes! Let's go now so we have plenty of time to do move-in shopping for you."

Kenzie is buzzing with excitement as we leave the dorm, but as we walk down the corridor, she tries to loop her arm with mine. I sidestep away from the contact.

She gives me a curious look, but then she earns her first real brownie points as a roommate when she gets it, no questions asked, and gives me a thumbs-up.

"Not a touchy person. No worries. So, where to first? One of the two massive libraries? The dining hall? Ballroom? Courtyards?" Before I can get a word in, she waves her hand. "Who am I kidding? Let's start with the entry, and I'll show you everything!"

Too late, I realize we're descending the same stairwell I took earlier. We both stop on the steps at the scene below us: two faculty members scrubbing blood off the stone steps.

But the vampire's corpse? It's nothing but charcoal.

I tip my head curiously when I note that they're also cleaning up scorch marks and smoke all over the walls. It looks like a fire went out of control, consuming anything that wasn't solid stone.

Kenzie gives me an *oh yikes* look before clearing her throat. "Uh… what happened here?"

One of the faculty members glances at us with a huff. "We'd love to know that too. Looks like a fire elemental lost control, or it was a fire spell or something like that. Whoever did it was a spoiled brat and left it for us to clean up."

I almost snort out loud.

But I *am* curious who lit this area on fire. I had nothing to do with that.

Finally, we slip past them and make our way down another passage, and Kenzie whispers, "Oof. I mean, it's not the first time I've seen shit like that here, but still. I wonder who that was. It's pretty sad that they bit the dust when they might've been just two weeks away from meeting their soul mates. What a bad time to go."

Whoever that vampire was *supposedly* "destined" to end up with, I did them a favor.

Kenzie shows me the key places at Everbound for the next hour and a half. Everbound is a maze of Gothic architecture that's remained relatively untouched despite modern times. Aside from the Wi-Fi, electric lighting, and plumbing, walking around the university is like stepping back in time several hundred years. The vaulted stone archways, winding stairways, gargoyles, chandeliers, multi-room libraries with domed glass ceilings, and sliding ladders for reaching the upper shelves…

I admit it. This place is impressive.

Just as we're stepping outside into one of the courtyards filled with marble statues, a deafening roar fills the air. I go stock still and wait for it to die out. I've never heard a sound like this before. It's nothing like a normal animal's call. It's powerful, hair-raising, vibrating through the air and echoing over the nearby forest.

And then a massive golden dragon soars into view.

For a moment, I can only stare incredulously as the creature's wings beat the air, creating a strong wind that rustles everything around us. The beast lands in one of the training fields nearby, and I can feel the ground tremble from all the way over here. Its wingspan is staggering, scales gleaming. It folds away its impressive wings and snorts blue fire into the air…and then, in two blinks of the eye, he shifts into a man.

Dragon shifter.

I can't see him clearly from here, but I can tell he's a huge, naked mass of solid, tanned muscles. A few other legacies—presumably shifters—jog up and slap him on the back. Shifters are extremely comfortable with nudity, from what I've heard. All of them are shorter than he is, even though shifters tend to be taller than all other legacies.

"What a drama king," Kenzie scoffs, shaking her head. "I wonder what set him off today."

"You know him?"

"Oh, yeah! Everyone knows him. You're looking at Baelfire Decimus, the youngest son of the revered Decimus family. You've heard of them at least, right?"

"No."

Kenzie is surprised. "Really? Well, they're basically the last branch of dragon shifters in existence, and as their youngest son, Baelfire basks in a *ridiculous* amount of attention. Although that's also probably because he's a rizz master."

I face her. "A what now?"

"You know. Rizz. Cha*ris*ma. He's a people person," she amends when I clearly don't get it. Then she wags her brows. "Not to mention his looks. Crazy handsome, don't you think?"

Hard to tell from so far away. I watch as he laughs with his fellow shifters, throwing an arm around two of them at once.

"Huge. I pity the vagina of anyone he takes to bed."

Kenzie throws her head back and cackles. "Yeah, well, don't tell him that. He's already got a dragon-sized ego. Come on, I'll show you the grand dining hall. Did you get a map of where your classes are tomorrow? Because if you want, I can help you find them—"

"Kenzie!"

We both look over at two girls approaching. Before they get close enough, Kenzie grumbles under her breath and whispers to me, "Watch out. These girls are highly ranked. Nice, but *way* too competitive. It's better to stay under their radar."

They stop in front of us, and the redhead on the left looks over me sharply. "Never seen this one around. She new here?"

I don't miss that she addresses Kenzie and not me, as if I'm just a vague presence she hasn't deemed with person status yet.

"Oh—yeah, this is Maven. I'm just showing her around. We're roommates."

The other girl is tall with dark skin, a nose ring, and short purple hair. "House?"

She's demanding the answer from me. A small part of me is tempted to flip her the bird to show how little I care about her "high rank" status, but Kenzie is right. I don't want any attention, so for the next two weeks, I'll be nothing but a quiet, shy wallflower.

"Arcana," I say quietly.

The girl grunts, and they both turn back to Kenzie like I no longer exist. Fascinating. They really do care about their power games, don't they?

"So," the redhead grins. "Tea time. Decimus lost control earlier. Went from zero to dragon in the blink of an eye—I saw it myself! He barely made it out of the castle in time, and rumor has it he lit an entire hallway on fire and killed someone they haven't been able to identify."

Kenzie glances at me with raised brows, clearly coming to the same conclusion I have that the dragon shifter must have been the one to set fire to that stairwell. "Oh, shit. What made him so mad?"

"Who knows? I get that you shifters have intense emotions and all, but gods, he's on another level." She sighs, clearly thinking that's attractive.

"And you wanna hear something else?" Nose Ring leans closer to whisper. "We overheard some siphons talking, and rumor has it that the Nightmare Prince was spotted in Halfton."

At that, Kenzie's mouth drops open. "What? No way. No one has seen him for a couple of years, not since he slaughtered an entire courtroom full of humans during that whole sex trafficking debacle and pissed off the Legacy Council *and* the human government. Why the fuck would he be in this area?"

"Maybe he's going to the Seeking," the redhead suggests.

"Yeah, right. He's never been to a Seeking, not even when he attended Everbound years ago," the other girl cuts in, rolling her eyes.

Kenzie says something else, and they keep talking, but I find my thoughtful interest drawn back to where the dragon shifter is still chatting with other shifters far in the distance.

Apparently, powerful legacies draw too much attention. These girls prove that if I want to blend into the shadows and be forgotten during my time here, I'll need to avoid people like him at all costs. I can't have the gossips watching me like a hawk.

"...and Crane absolutely humiliated the professor before leaving class. Of course, he didn't get in trouble for it—who the hell is stupid enough to face off with the Garnet Wizard's apprentice? Gods, I wish I could school my professors like that," one of the girls is saying when I tune back in.

"Especially Mr. Frost," the other agrees with a groan. "So cold and stuck up, but *so* fucking gorgeous."

"I see you with the whole student-teacher kink," Kenzie laughs.

"Sue me! We all have what we like. Don't you have a thing for vamps? I mean—other than that asshole bully who's always making your life hell," the redhead adds with an eye roll.

That gets my attention. Especially since it seems to make Kenzie uncomfortable. She quickly brushes it off with a laugh, makes some excuse about us needing to be somewhere, and gingerly takes my elbow to lead me away.

Once we're out of earshot, I pull my elbow back, adjusting the sleeve even though she didn't touch my skin.

"Shit—sorry. I forgot about the no-touching thing," she says, still looking distracted.

No one is around, so I stop and face her. "A vampire is bullying you?"

She wrinkles her nose and tries to wave away the question. "Gah. It's nothing. He's just…no, really, it's nothing. I'm fine."

Just like Lillian, she's incapable of hiding her real emotions. They all play out on her face, and right now, I can tell she's genuinely upset at even just the mention of this guy. Almost on the verge of tears, even.

Which makes me clench my hands. It's always the nice ones like her who pretend they're fine when someone is making their life miserable. I had to put up with it whenever it happened to Lillian, but I don't have to now. I've only just met Kenzie, and I don't want her to think we're bonding—or, gods forbid, *friends*—but I decide that once I learn the name of this asshole, I'll pay him a visit.

Maybe I'll brew a hex just for him.

But asking more questions about it right now will only upset her more, and I would literally rather pry my nails off with bamboo shoots than be around someone on the verge of tears.

So, to distract her, I mutter, "Touching through clothes isn't completely unbearable."

Kenzie blinks. "Oh. Okay, that's good to know. So I can hug you as long as you're wearing, like, a super puffy jacket?"

Yikes. "No hugging. Ever."

She laughs as we start in the direction of the dining hall. "Fine,

fine. I guess now I also know you're a caster—you said House of Arcana, right?"

"Yes."

"Are you like a super powerful caster? Skilled with all kinds of magic and stuff?"

With any other legacy, I'd be on edge, but there's not an ounce of guile on Kenzie's face. She's genuinely just curious, not deciding whether she should try to kill me in my sleep.

"Nope." That's not even a lie.

She breathes out a puff of air. "Damn. I was hoping you were secretly clairvoyant and you could tell me if I'll get matched with someone at the Seeking. It's all I can think about. Gods, I just want the next two weeks to be over so I can find out who I get to be with."

I hum in reply, but I couldn't give two fucks about the upcoming ceremony. I'm far more interested in my mission here. Which reminds me…

"Where can I buy ingredients for potions?"

"Oh, that'll be at the university store. It carries a lot of stuff, but if you need specific ingredients, you can actually order them on the app lickety-split—or so my caster friends have said," she chatters, back to her usual cheeriness. Then she frowns. "Speaking of which, I don't have your number yet. Here."

She pulls out her cell phone and hands it to me. I stare at it for a long moment, trying to figure out what to do with the rectangle, and finally, I hand it back to her.

"My phone broke. I haven't gotten a new one," I lie.

She looks scandalized. "Seriously? Okay, we are so going to Halfton today. We're getting you all the things, and you can tell me all about humans. Now come on, I'm famished."

3

MAVEN

Two Weeks Later

Knock, knock. "Maven? Are you here?"

I don't bother responding since Kenzie has already burst into our dorm room. She blinks in surprise at where I sit on the floor, surrounded by charred plant remains and a ring of smoke.

The smoke dissipates as I discreetly move my hands behind my back so she won't see my blackened fingertips. I offer no expression.

"Oh! Sorry, I didn't mean to fuck up your…aromatherapy?" She glances at the other withered plants on the desk at the foot of my four-poster bed. Then she shrugs it off. "Smells good in here. A bit overpowering for my nose, but I still like it."

For the last two weeks, I've avoided any and all attention at Everbound University. My routine is set in stone: wake up, go to classes, speak only when spoken to, brew potions, keep my head down, and return to my dorm to bide my time.

I've gone to Halfton with Kenzie a few times, and I occasionally explore Everbound Forest. But otherwise, I have carefully kept to myself to avoid any chance of running into high-profile legacies.

My reputation as a forgettable nobody is solid.

And for the last two weeks, Kenzie hasn't asked any more prying questions. It's why we've become comfortable acquaintances, and I've all but retired my spider-egg-pillow idea. She now calls me her bestie and makes me binge-watch steamy Regency romance shows with her. Meanwhile, I put a limp dick hex on the asshole vampire who was bullying her.

Basically, being stuck in the same room as her has not been the worst arrangement.

Except for when she barges into our room like this without warning. That's no good, but at least she didn't see anything.

"So? What do you think of my outfit for the Seeking? I was going for sexy and stunning with a dash of inappropriate."

She twirls, showing off the shimmering gold bodycon dress that clings to her. That's in addition to the strappy platform heels and fishnets. It's a statement that I'm not surprised she pulls off—though why she keeps coming to me for fashion advice, I'll never know.

"You are both inappropriately stunning and stunningly inappropriate," I confirm.

Kenzie squeals. "This is it. Today is the day we've been waiting for. In less than an hour, we'll know which other legacies we'll be bound to for the rest of our lives!"

She skips to the window on my side of the room and tries to throw open the black curtains. When she remembers that I spelled them permanently shut, she gives up and sits next to me, tapping her long, newly manicured nails against the wooden floor.

"Are you nervous? Gods, I am so nervous. I wonder if I'm going to be a keeper. What if I wind up in a quintet with ugly people? Or —" She gasps and gives me the most horrified look. "Shit, what if I have no matches?"

From everything I've learned since arriving, that does happen.

The gods may decide that a quintet still has missing pieces, such as legacies not yet at the university. Those quintets graduate without being bound to each other, meaning their curses go unbroken. Most incomplete quintets return yearly for the Seeking, living on a prayer and a hope.

In other words, quintets with age gaps get the shaft.

"I don't want to wait," Kenzie growls, clearly thinking about the same thing I am. She rolls onto her back, stretching like a cat and sighing at my ceiling. "I just want all my people at once. Is that too much to ask? I want two or three gorgeous guys and at least one sexy girl, and then we can all break our curse together and skip to the good part, where we get on with life, have lots of kinky, mind-blowing sex, and live happily ever after. Doesn't that sound perfect?"

I won't tell Kenzie this, but I don't believe in happily ever after. Not for me, anyway.

Am I a pessimist?

Yes. I find it keeps me from being disappointed.

Then Kenzie frowns and props herself up to look at my side of the room. Her side of the dorm is pretty much empty now, all her bright decorations, erotic paintings, and other belongings packed neatly into boxes stacked by her stripped four-poster bed.

My half of the room is almost as bare as the day I arrived. I did buy things like black sheets and blankets and gray pots for my plants, but I don't see the point of decorating when I plan to leave soon. The only evidence of my space being inhabited are the potted plants on my desk that get their light from a gentle sunlight spell and the white pillow on the dark bed.

"Hang on. Why haven't you packed your stuff up yet, May? You know we'll move in with our quintet members immediately after the Seeking, right?"

"If I get matched to a quintet, I'll move my stuff later."

It's a lie. I'm not budging.

"Suit yourself." She gets to her feet. "Now come on! Get ready so we can get to the Seeking early."

"I'm ready."

Her eyes drop to my baggy, shape-concealing clothes that are so dark green they're nearly black. "Uh…not to be a bitch, but do you remember how I bought you a pretty, lacy, emerald-green dress when we went shopping two weeks ago?"

"Yes. I love it." I'll never wear it here, where I'm carefully crafting my reputation for being a frumpy, forgettable nobody, but I do love it.

"But...you're not wearing it."

"Very astute observation."

Kenzie rolls her eyes at me and then grins. "Well, all right. You know I think you're pretty in anything—but promise that even after we're super busy with our new quintets, you'll make the time to have a girl's night with me, and we'll both get dressed up for a night on the town."

"I promise." It's an easy compromise because I won't have a quintet.

I plan to reject any matches I get.

Me tying my soul with four other people? Not going to happen. It wouldn't end well for any of us. It's more than likely that I'll be the one to get no matches today. Fingers crossed.

"Great! Then come on, let's go."

I grab my favorite pair of black leather gloves from the top drawer of my dresser and slip them on as I follow Kenzie out of my room. I always wear gloves. But right now, they're especially useful because my fingertips are still charred, and I won't have the time to make up a healing balm until later.

The moment we step into the large courtyard, we're thronged by the crowd gathered around an elevated circular stage. The few hundred legacies gathered here today are separated into four sections, all wearing their House colors.

Blood red, for the House of Craving. It's the house of siphons—legacies like vampires, sirens, succubi and incubi, and a few others. They feed on blood, dreams, emotions, and so forth in exchange for their intimidating powers, including immortality.

Golden yellow, for the House of Shifters. There were once animal shifters of all kinds, but now only the apex predators remain. Wolves, bears, lions, tigers, sea serpents, griffins... Theirs is the House of primal instinct and territorial savagery.

Silvery blue, for the House of Elementals. The gods bless the descendants of this House with the ability to wield the four elements: fire, air, water, or earth. This House is far more devout in worshipping the gods, who handpick the elementals' abilities for them at birth.

And finally, emerald green for the House of Arcana. Full of magic-users—aka casters—of all origins. Fae, sorcerers, witches and wizards, mages…it's a mixed bag of various talents, but everyone here has magic in their very blood, which they can wield. It's the House I was sorted into.

I realize Kenzie has been trying to tell me something over the loud chatter of the audience when she finally taps my shoulder to get my attention. I take an instinctive step away even as I glance up at her. Like most shifters, she's on the tall side, but the heels just add to it.

"I'll see you up there later!" she says, face glowing with excitement as she points at the stage. "Good luck!"

She turns to disappear into the yellow group. Other shifters recognize her, and she's quickly swept up into the nervous excitement practically palpable in the air.

I slip into the House of Arcana section, surrounded by other casters who barely spare me a glance since I've made sure I'm easy to forget.

The crowd's chatter finally cuts off when the interim headmaster, Professor Gibbons, ascends the stairs to the stage, turning in a circle to greet everyone with a brilliant smile. The warlock's snow-white hair gleams in the morning sunlight as he casts a charm to carry his voice over the rapt onlookers.

"Welcome all to the Seeking! Whether you are here for the first time or part of an incomplete quintet hoping your missing matches will be revealed, I know everyone present has been eager for this day for a long time."

A resounding cheer goes up all around me.

"I'm sure we are all aware of why quintets are necessary. Still, it bears repeating. Two thousand years ago, our monstrous ancestors emerged from the hellish Nether realm and nearly ripped the world apart through war between the Houses. During that time, humans became little more than fodder for our feuding. They were treated like animals, fed upon, used, and slaughtered at the whim and desire of our kind."

That hits too close to home for me. I try and fail to unclench my grinding jaw.

"Finally, the gods could watch their beloved humans suffer no more," Professor Gibbons goes on. "In answer to humanity's prayers, the gods created the Legacy Curse. We were made to be incomplete without one another so that we would have no choice but to put aside our many differences and work as one. The leaders of the Four Houses were bound together as the Immortal Quintet and created the Divide to keep the Nether—and the dreadful Entity who rules it—from ever returning to this world. We are all safe because of the Immortal Quintet," he adds proudly.

The audience claps while I roll my eyes.

Safe. Such a subjective term.

"Unfortunately, the horrors of the Nether still seep into this world. The gods knew that dimension of darkness would forever seek to find a foothold in the land of the living, and so we descendants of monsters were appointed to hunt down and kill off these endless threats. Now we share a symbiotic purpose—and quintets bound together from the Four Houses are the foundation. Today, you will discover whether other members of your fated quintet are here."

Excited whispers fill the air as a woman dressed head to toe in white, including a shimmering veil obscuring her face, ascends the stairs. I swear she's glowing slightly, and it's not just from the blinding winter morning sunlight. Her movements are graceful and paced.

Professor Gibbons gestures to her since, apparently, she doesn't plan on speaking. "This is the high prophetess Pia of the Temple of Galene, goddess of light. She is here to divine the will of the gods for each of you, but first, she will seek out the keepers chosen by the gods to lead their quintets. If you are identified as a keeper, please come forward and wait for your individual divination of matches."

The prophetess makes an odd symbol with her hands, and it

sounds like she's muttering something under her breath. Maybe it's a prayer, but I wouldn't know since I gave up praying to the gods long ago. Everyone around me is holding their breath, straining to see the stage.

Then gasps ring out as legacies dispersed throughout the audience begin to glow. It's not a faint glow, either—they light up like fucking lightbulbs. One of the fae casters beside me is so bright I flinch away, only to bump into a witch accidentally. I vaguely recognize her from my Intro to Runes course. I think her name is Sheila.

"Watch it," she grumbles, squinting hard at me. "And you might want to get a move on before you're the last one in line."

Her meaning doesn't sink in until I glance down at my arms and realize I'm glowing, too.

Shit. That's not good.

How the fuck am I a keeper?

Maybe the gods just did this to mess with me. I don't know if they're omniscient, but if they are, they should know precisely why I refuse to be in a quintet—let alone *lead* one.

My moment of shock ends when Sheila nudges me forward. "You're seriously the last keeper in our House still standing around. Come on, get up there and represent."

I don't like all the eyes on me as I weave through the crowd, clenching and unclenching my gloved hands. But I'd stand out much more if I tried to resist this, and attention is the last thing I want. At this point, it's best just to see if some of my matches are here. If they are, I'm sure they'll take one look at me and be more than okay with me rejecting the quintet. They can appeal to the gods for a new keeper, and I'll be on my merry way.

The glow on my skin begins to fade as I approach the line of legacies waiting to go on stage one by one. Professor Gibbons is saying something but I've tuned it out, too busy stewing over this new inconvenience.

I'm so distracted with trying to keep my head down that I actually make a little, embarrassing yelp when a manicured hand shoots out and pulls me to the very back of the line.

"Oh my *gods,*" Kenzie gushes in a whisper. "Can you believe we're both keepers? What are the odds of that? This is amazing!"

I stare at her hand on my bare wrist until she lets go, offering an apologetic smile.

I must not be hiding my dread of going onstage very well because Kenzie grimaces. "Yeah, I'm nervous, too. So nervous I might puke. But in a good way—is puking from excitement good? Whatever. I'm excited for you, too, May. I hope you get matched up with some really great legacies. Doesn't everyone deserve their perfect matches?"

Her optimism gives me a headache, but I mean every word when I say, "Not everyone, but you do. Good luck."

I'm the last in line, but the queue moves quickly ahead of us. Finally, we near the stage, and I can see what's happening better. One by one, each newly identified keeper receives some sort of blessing from the prophetess. Then they stand in the center of the stage as any matches they have light up and make their way through the crowd, ascending the stairs. The headmaster announces each member by name, formally introducing the new quintet before excusing them.

A few quintets leave right away, probably to speak in private. That, or they're already eager to fuck each other's brains out. Not all quintets are romantic or polyamorous—some remain entirely platonic. But most quintets are made up of people who balance each other out, perfectly suited to work together as a group. That, combined with the typically high libido of their kind, tends to develop into sexual relationships sooner rather than later.

Finally, it's Kenzie's turn. She turns to give me a wide-eyed look before sashaying onto the stage. Pia, the prophetess, blesses her and steps back. For a moment, Kenzie scans the crowd, practically shimmying with excitement.

Then, one all-too-familiar vampire blurs onto the stage, and Kenzie wilts. I frown on her behalf because no fucking way is she supposed to be matched up with *Luka,* the vampire who bullied her for months before I got here. The one I hexed to make it impossible for him to have a boner.

A tall shifter guy and a dark-skinned elemental girl join them onstage. I only know the girl is from the House of Elementals based on her silvery-white dress, so I'm curious which element she can manipulate.

Professor Gibbons introduces Kenzie officially, along with her incomplete quintet. He adds that they'll likely be here for the next Seeking to find their missing piece, and then they're ushered off the stage. Poor Kenzie looks queasy about getting matched with Luka, and as they rejoin the crowd, I decide to find her as soon as this is over.

"And now for the last of this Seeking," Gibbons says, waving me forward impatiently.

Being the center of attention of hundreds of hopeful legacies practically salivating over the chance of joining a quintet is not pleasant. I decide to ignore the onlookers altogether, staring instead at Everbound Forest in the distance, well past the courtyard.

Time to get this over with.

Pia steps up behind me and rests her hands gently on the crown of my head. I wince momentarily before relaxing because, oddly enough, her touch doesn't bother me. Her voice is smooth and so soft that I'm sure only I can hear her.

"Maven, who has chosen the last name of Oakley."

I frown. No one knows that Oakley isn't my surname. I had to have a last name when coming to Everbound University, so I'd adopted Lillian's.

"Have no fear, my fearless one," Pia whispers, sounding like she's smiling behind that veil. "I know you far better than you might think. Perhaps better than you know yourself."

What a creepy thing to say. It almost makes me like her.

She says four words in a language I don't understand, but I feel them. Each word seems to wrap around me like a blanket, sinking into my chest to soothe the emptiness inside. It's the strangest sensation, this warmth. Like it was supposed to be there all along.

And then, one by one, three legacies light up in the crowd. Their Houses quickly part so they can make their way through, but I still can't see what they look like because of the multitude of people. There sure is a lot of whispering going on.

Three matches? This can't be happening.

But then a fourth one appears—literally just *appears*—directly in front of the stage before he saunters up the steps, his consuming gaze trained on me. His dark hair is messy, sweeping over his forehead except on one side where it's close-shaved, revealing that the mix of pale and dark swirling tattoos on his neck and arms also extend onto his scalp. His ears have multiple piercings, and a barbell piercing glints at the end of one of his eyebrows. His irises are a rich purple flecked with silver.

By the strong reactions of everyone watching, including the interim headmaster, I put two and two together and realize who this must be. After all, I've been hearing rumors about his whereabouts for two long weeks.

Crypt DeLune. An incubus better known as the Nightmare Prince.

He's the infamous illegitimate son of a member of the Immortal Quintet. Even without breaking his curse, he's made a name for himself. They say he's unhinged. A sociopath. He left the university five years ago without any matches. Now, I'm pretty sure every other unmatched legacy in the audience breathes a sigh of relief that he's no longer a possibility for them.

Crypt stops at my side without a word, but I can still feel his attention on me.

And if being matched to the Nightmare Prince wasn't enough of a problem, I recognize the next person to ascend the stairs. Chillingly beautiful, with white-blond hair and crisp, perfect features. An ice elemental model turned professor: Everett Frost, heir of the wealthiest family of legacies in existence.

The whispers are increasing, but Professor Frost doesn't look at me as he takes his place on the opposite side of the stage.

I'm so shell-shocked that it takes me a moment to realize my next match has stopped directly in front of me. I have to tip my head back to see the imposing shifter better, and I groan internally.

Baelfire Decimus's amber eyes gleam with nothing short of hunger as he flashes me a toothy smile. His dirty blond hair and tanned skin make him look like the epitome of a golden boy. I've never seen him this close-up since I've carefully avoided him and every other highly-ranked legacy at this school for the last two weeks.

We're not supposed to speak during the Seeking, but he whispers, "Finally found you."

Whatever that means.

When I give him no reaction, Baelfire just winks and moves to my other side. He stands close enough that I shuffle an inch away as subtly as possible.

The final legacy who joins us onstage has me barely refraining from cursing the gods out loud. Because I know him, too. How could I not? Even if we weren't in the same House, *everyone* knows Silas Crane. The other casters practically worship him. He was mentored by the revered and deadly Garnet Wizard, who practically raised him after the rest of the Cranes died within months of each other.

Now, Silas is the most cutthroat blood fae ever to attend Everbound University, and like all blood fae, he has dark curly hair, pale skin, pointed ears, and eyes red as blood. I quickly look away from his intense ruby irises as he moves to stand near Baelfire.

Fuck my life.

Why did my matches all have to be as high profile as possible? This is ridiculous. The gods must be laughing at me right now.

While the headmaster introduces us as a quintet and begins rattling off our names, I try to ignore the warmth humming through my veins at their proximity. I risk a glance to my right. Bael winks at me again while Silas's attention is firmly on whatever Headmaster Gibbons is saying. On my other side, Crypt still studies me. Professor Frost stares out at Everbound Forest just as I was earlier, as if he, too, would rather be anywhere else. Maybe he's embarrassed that he's been matched with a student, even though he can't be much older than I am.

It doesn't matter. I'm not staying matched with these legacies—or anyone else, for that matter.

They're probably all insulted that the gods would pick someone like me as their keeper. I'll use that to my advantage.

The moment we get somewhere private, I'll put us all out of our misery.

4

BAELFIRE

"...THE keeper of this very impressive duet is Maven Oakley of the House of Arcana," Gibbons drones.

Maven.

So that's my mate's name.

I catch her looking and can't help the smile that springs to my face just having this ounce of her attention. I wink, but once again, she turns away without an expression. It's fucking impossible to tell what this caster is thinking. I like that. She's a pretty little enigma.

My pretty little enigma.

For two weeks, I've been tortured with need, knowing my mate was nearby. I'd happened across a dead vampire in a hallway and planned on walking right past to report the body, but that's when I'd scented it.

Her fragrance. Subtle and cold, like a sweet midnight.

Of course, it had been mixed with the scent of blood. Probably the vampire's blood, but even just the idea of our mate bleeding had set my asshole inner dragon off something fierce.

I've been jacking off to just the memory of her scent for days, but no matter where I went or how much I changed up my schedule, hoping to track her down or run into her by chance, it never happened. She was always frustratingly just out of reach, almost like she knew precisely where not to be when I needed her.

But that all changes now.

My heart is pounding as I glance down at her again. I've never seen her around Everbound—never even heard of her—and now she's about to be the center of my world.

Maven.

My inner dragon growls possessively, and I smile in agreement. We won't be officially bound together until graduation, but that just gives me an entire semester to learn everything there is to know about my mysterious mate. She's hiding it well, but I'm sure she's psyched to have a rare dragon shifter all to herself.

I'm going to covet the fuck out of my mate. Keep her safe and *very* sated.

We'll be perfect together, even if the rest of our quintet is a clusterfuck. Which god thought it was a good idea to group me with Everett Frost and Crypt fucking DeLune? Silas is a force to be reckoned with and an asshole, but he's less of an asshole than the other two. Our families have run in the same elite circles since we were all little, so unfortunately, I've known all of them since we were practically in diapers.

Of the four of us, I'm bound to be Maven's favorite. They'll all be jealous motherfuckers.

I can't wait.

"And so this Seeking comes to a close," Professor Gibbons finally says. "As you all know, new quintets have time to move into matched student housing together if they so choose. Courses will resume tomorrow. To everyone who was not matched this year, may the gods grant you better luck next time."

Despite the many matches this year, there are still a lot of disappointed legacies as the audience disperses every which way.

Professor Gibbons motions for us to get off the makeshift stage, and instinctively, I take Maven's hand before any of the others can. Her hand is so tiny and cute compared to mine. I wonder why she's wearing leather gloves. Is she cold? She feels cold—but then everyone does since dragon shifters typically run at a toasty hundred and five degrees Fahrenheit.

I'm more than happy to warm Maven right the fuck up if she wants.

But immediately, she pulls her hand away, not meeting my curious look as she leaves the stage.

She must be nervous. I guess that's not surprising—I'd be overwhelmed if I were a sweet, quiet little wallflower being matched to such well-known legacies like us, too. Plus, I know I'm a big, scary motherfucker at first glance. Maybe she's intimidated by our size difference, but I'll show her just how gentle I can be as soon as we find somewhere private to get cozy.

Unless she likes it rough. Or kinky. Gods, I need to know if she has any kinks.

We all follow our new keeper off the stage as she makes a beeline through the crowd of disgruntled and curious stares. Once inside the castle, Maven veers toward the university's massive library. I stick close to her side, amused that she's pointedly avoided looking at any of us since leaving the Seeking. I try leaning down to capture her attention, but she keeps her eyes forward.

Aww. Who knew my mate would be so shy?

"The library is too public for formal introductions," Silas says on Maven's other side.

"By formal introductions, he means he wants to bone you," I stage-whisper.

Silas shoots me a dry look. "Unlike you, Decimus, I'm capable of thinking outside of my cock. We should find a private space because there are too many eyes and ears all over Everbound. Quintet rankings won't officially begin until next semester when the no-kill ban lifts, but even over the next two weeks, the competition will grow fierce, and they'll be looking for weaknesses in every quintet. Especially ours. I won't have others eavesdropping on us just because you love drawing attention."

"You have always been way too fucking paranoid," I helpfully inform him. "And I'm not some attention whore. People happen to *like* me, unlike you pricks."

"As mature as ever, I see," Everett drawls sarcastically from behind me.

I'm about to fire off a retort, but instead of stepping into the library, Maven suddenly turns into an extended nook that I didn't even know existed. Has this always been here? I can tell it's completely private when Silas immediately looks relieved.

Maven finally turns to face all of us. There's not an ounce of nervousness in her expression—in fact, she still has the perfect poker face. It's hard to tell much about her body under all the baggy shit she's wearing, but her features are pretty in an understated way. There's something hauntingly striking about her eyes, most of all.

I'm like a fucking crack addict, already sniffing the air to try to get another hit of her delicious scent now that we're not surrounded by people. But I wrinkle my nose at the overwhelming smell of aromatic plants. She's definitely been casting today, and so has Silas because they both smell strongly like burnt plants. It doesn't help that Everett's and Crypt's scents are also perfuming this alcove. Hers is impossible to pick out, which makes my dragon petulant.

"As far as moving in, I preemptively reserved one of the finest quintet accommodations in the northwest wing," Silas says, finally breaking the ice since Everett looks like he'd rather be anywhere else. The Nightmare Prince is studying our keeper just as intently as I am. "I'll have Maven's things moved in first—"

"No need," Maven cuts in with a surprisingly firm voice.

It's the first time I've heard her speak, and I'm intrigued. She doesn't *sound* like a shy wallflower. Have I been reading her wrong?

"Would you rather we all move into your little dorm room, cutie?" I ask, grinning. "Might be a tight squeeze, but I like the idea of close quarters with you. We can share your tiny bed. These other fuckers will have to sleep on the floor, though, because I want you in my arms every night. Might be an issue for Frost since he was born with a silver spoon stuck up his ass."

"Fuck off, dragon," Everett mutters.

"Move in together if you want. Where I stay doesn't matter because I'm rejecting the quintet so you can appeal to the gods for another keeper."

Maven speaks so casually, like she's just informing us that it'll rain later. That's why it takes my brain a second to catch up with why my inner dragon is suddenly losing his fucking mind.

But Silas is quicker to the draw as he holds up a hand to stop her words. *"Rejecting?"*

"Yes."

My mate is…rejecting me.

Unexpected pain blossoms in my chest, but I know why. It's because shifters like me start developing a bond with their mate right off the bat, and the idea of that being wrenched away so soon? It fucking *hurts.*

"Hang on. Let me get this straight. *You* are rejecting *us?"* I snarl without thinking, letting my emotions control my mouth as usual.

Immediately, I feel like a world-class asshole. It doesn't matter that I've never heard of her or that she's not one of the top-ranked students at Everbound—she's meant to be mine, and here I am, being a condescending dickhead.

Damn it, I probably just hurt her feelings. I never want to see her upset.

But Maven has no reaction aside from nodding once, matter-of-factly. "Yes."

I stare at her. Everett and Silas are staring, too. Meanwhile, Crypt slowly dons a creepy smirk like the psychotic fucker thinks this shit is amusing.

The pain of being rejected wells in my chest. I clench my fists to try calming the heat under my skin. I can't tell if I'm more perplexed, offended, concerned, or pissed—but my dragon is ready to claw his way out and throw a fucking bitch fit over this. Since I haven't gone hunting yet today, keeping him in check is more difficult than usual.

"You'd turn down a gift from the gods? Why?" Everett finally demands.

I scowl at him. Of course, the rich, pious elemental would be more testy about her slighting the gods than the fact that *she's fucking rejecting us.*

"Because we all know you guys deserve a better keeper. As Baelfire so sweetly insinuated, the four of you are completely out of my league."

I flinch. Damn. What a time to learn that my mate doesn't pull her punches. "Fuck, Maven, I didn't mean it like that."

"Except you did," Silas mutters. He turns to Maven. "You're making this decision rashly. There's no reason to reject this. We all want our curses broken, and we all want a quintet…no matter who else is in it."

His red glare flickers to Crypt, who only looks more amused. Those two must have more beef that I don't know about. But I don't care about that right now because Maven levels Silas with a bland expression.

"Wrong, wrong, and wrong. It's best if you four appeal for a new keeper because I won't be in this quintet. There's no point dragging this on, so I'll be on my way. Let's not cross paths again. Better luck next time."

And then my pretty little enigma just walks away, leaving the four of us to gawk after her in disbelief.

Better luck next time?

It takes me all of two seconds to decide that I reject her rejection. Maven is supposed to be my mate, and I'm meant to belong to her. Rejecting one's matches is unheard of, and legacies appealing to the gods for a new quintet member is extremely rare. Usually, that only happens years after a member of their established quintet has died, and the ones remaining can't take the empty hole left behind anymore.

She thinks I'll just drop her and hope the gods find someone as perfect for me as she's supposed to be? Yeah right. I'm not letting her go without getting the chance to know her. Not fucking happening.

"You fuckers can appeal to the gods all you want, but I'll refuse any other keeper," I grit, trying to ignore the throbbing pain in my chest from the rejection.

Everett gives me a disgusted look. "Appeal? I'd never question the will of the gods. Besides, there's no way she was serious about rejecting a quintet of our caliber. She's just playing hard to get, trying to get our attention."

"She has mine," Crypt speaks for the first time as he gazes in the direction Maven went.

And then the Nightmare Prince disappears. The air warps around him as he fades from sight, and then he's just gone.

I curse. "That motherfucker picked a bad time to bow out."

"He didn't. He just dropped into Limbo so he can roam and observe the mortal world from there, unseen," Silas says bitterly. He rubs his jaw in thought before shaking his head. "Everett has a point. It makes no sense for Maven to turn us down."

"Or maybe she just doesn't want you guys in the quintet," Everett mumbles. "I have to say, it's nice to see Bael has lost his charm. It's about time he got his big dragon head resized."

I give him a droll look. "Real fucking *mature,* Professor Snowflake. We all know if it were a competition between the four of us, Maven would pick me first."

Everett scoffs. "Over me? Good luck with that. I can give her anything she wants, give her influence in the top circles of the Four Houses, and keep her in the lap of safety and luxury for the rest of her life. I'll make sure she never has to fight at the frontlines of the Divide. Meanwhile, all you bring to the table is your ego, some scales, and a misguidedly proud family that can't mind their own damn business."

I go nose to nose with him, smug that he has to look up when I was once the youngest and smallest, back when we were all kids. Now I'm positive I can beat his frozen ass, and my bloodthirsty, newly spurned dragon is aching for any kind of violent outlet.

No one drags my family name in front of me without earning a few burns, bites, and broken bones.

"You really wanna do this here and now?" I growl.

The air plummets several degrees around us, making my breath plume as he sneers. "Why not? I've waited long enough."

Before either of us can move, a teeth-rattling wave of magic pulses through the air, knocking Everett and me back from each other. My nose singes with a smell like burning copper, the typical scent of blood fae magic. I glare at Silas, but he looks thoughtful. Scratch that—he has his *scheming* face on.

I used to hate that look when we were little, but now I raise a brow. "Well? Spit it out."

"A competition between the four of us isn't a bad idea. What if we make a wager?"

Everett makes a face. "A wager with a fae? No thanks. I'm still not over the time you needlessly tricked me into downing a glass of kraken ink."

"That wasn't needless. It was for science."

"I was seven years old, and it left me traumatized, blind, and sick as fuck for two months. It's a miracle I got my sight back. The healer said a legacy from a weaker bloodline would have died."

"And now I know not to mix kraken ink with my gin," Silas deadpans. "I say we each name our prize. We all want things from each other, either for our family or ourselves. Whoever Maven picks first will win the wager."

Name our prize? That's tempting. I narrow my eyes. "How big of a prize are we talking?"

"Land. Money. Rare ingredients," he adds, giving me a meaningful look.

That asshole still wants my dragon scales. I'm sure he'd ask for tons of them, and then I'd have to grow my armor back slowly and painfully. Dragon scales are scarce and sought-after ingredients since my family is the last branch of dragon shifters—and like most legacies, the inability to procreate is part of our curse.

Even in bound quintets, who can have offspring since their curses are broken, dragon shifters haven't managed to breed for several generations. None of my four older siblings have kids. I was considered a miracle child since my parents are older, even by shifter standards.

The lack of dragon shifter offspring is a sore subject in my family.

"I want land," I decide, looking at Everett. "Frost land. The Lyran mountain range, including the dormant volcano. It once belonged to my kind and I want it back."

"Oh, I'm sure you do," he replies coolly, leaning against the wall to pick lint off his lapel. "But I'm not interested in joining this wager."

He always was an angsty fucker. Anyone can see he's lying. Frosts love a good gamble. It's part of how they built their empire. Everett has always been incapable of turning down stuff like this. But when Silas and I stare at him, waiting for him to give in as he used to when we were younger, he shakes his head.

"Nope. Talk to the psychopath who just left. This is a bet I won't take."

"That sure you'll lose, huh? At least you recognize a contest you can't win."

He rolls his eyes at me as he leaves, probably to grade papers or whatever other shit he does working here at Everbound. I don't even know what he teaches, and I don't care.

"Think Crypt has left the university?" I ask Silas.

"I'm not that lucky."

"Then, since it's your idea, you can track down that freak and tell him about our little wager. I'm going to go hunt something so my dragon doesn't kill the first person to look at me wrong, and then I'm going to find my mate."

5

MAVEN

LESS THAN A SECOND after I knock, Luka opens the door, and his nose wrinkles.

"If it isn't the smug little hex-happy witch bitch."

"In the flesh. Is Kenzie here?" I peer behind him into the shared living space.

This is the quintet apartment that Kenzie painstakingly picked out and reserved last week in her hopeful excitement that she might get matched today. She dragged me here a few days ago to give me the grand tour. I see she took my advice to hang up all her erotic paintings in the living room. A bunch of boxes stacked next to a newly purchased couch is further proof of the others moving in.

"She's busy," Luka snaps.

I hear a faint moan of pleasure from behind the closed door of the main bedroom. At least Kenzie is already getting along just fine with the rest of her quintet. Looking back up at Luka, I barely hold back a smirk.

"Seems you've been left out of get-to-know-you nookie. Let me guess. Performance anxiety?"

He hisses and steps outside to face me, slamming the door behind him and glowering. If he had a decent personality, he would be passably handsome. Too bad he's a douchebag.

"That's it. Lift the damn hex."

"Not until Kenzie tells me to. She gets to decide when you've atoned for making her cry herself to sleep on more than one occasion."

Luka winces and rubs his face. "Look…I get it. I was a dick to her, all right? She drew my attention too much, and I overreacted. I never claimed I was Prince fucking Charming. It's just that she can be so… *Kenzie,* and I didn't want to deal with it. I didn't know *how* to deal with everything I felt around her. I thought it would be easier to just—"

"Do I look like your shrink?" I interrupt.

Luka opens his mouth to spew more words I'm not interested in, but then he looks behind me, nose flaring. I glance over my shoulder, but we're alone in this hallway.

"Thought I saw someone else in the hallway. Must've been a shadow," he mutters by way of explanation.

Then his sensitive vamp hearing must pick up more of the goodie-getting in the apartment because he groans and darts a desperate glance behind him. It's morbidly satisfying that he gets to hear just how stupid he is for how he's treated Kenzie.

"Okay. Look—what's your name again?" he grits, turning back to me.

"Hex-happy witch bitch has a nice ring to it. Why change it?"

Luka bares his teeth. "I'm not the patient type. It's Minerva or some shit, right? Listen, Minerva, you're going to lift this hex right the fuck now because–"

"Because you feel entitled to a woman now that you've been matched to her?" I cut him off, my voice turning sharp. "Or maybe you really do feel bad but need your dick to help you win her over since your personality isn't enough. Either way, I don't care, so drop it. I'm not removing the limp dick hex until Kenzie tells me to. Grovel to her, not me."

Luka finally loses his temper and snarls, fangs extending. Instinctively, my hand slips into one of my hidden pockets where another of my favorite blades awaits, even though I'm not sure Kenzie would appreciate me stabbing her new match. Maybe she'll understand if it's in self-defense.

But just as he steps forward the air wavers, and someone blurs into existence between us just as I hear a loud *snap*.

Luka screams and reels back from...the Nightmare Prince. Who promptly turns around and offers me the gleaming, bloodied fang he just snapped right out of the vampire's mouth.

"Fucking bastard!" Luka lisps, stumbling back into the apartment and locking the door behind him.

I study the fang in Crypt's hand, watching the residual blood and venom pooling at its sharp tip. Finally, Crypt arches a dark brow. He looks like a deadly, sultry dream, one corner of his mouth pulling up in a crooked grin.

"Don't you want it, darling?" His voice is accented, close to a rasp but somehow warmer.

Do I want that vampire's fang? Yes. I know Luka will regenerate a fang with no problem since siphons can regenerate at nearly the speed of a shifter. Still, I'm sure his expression would be priceless if he saw me walking around with his fang on a necklace.

But accepting this would make Crypt think I approve of him following me when I distinctly remember saying I didn't want to cross paths with him or the others again.

"Pass."

"Hmm. He should be punished more for daring to bare his fangs at you. Maybe I'll slip it under his pillow later like a backward, fucked-up tooth fairy. Possibly give him some night terrors for a few weeks. Would you like that?"

Very much. His offer is appealing, but he can't know that.

When I stare, waiting for him to get the hint and walk away, Crypt lifts the fang to his tongue and licks the venom from its tip, maintaining eye contact with me the entire time. Either it's a weird siphon flex I don't get, or he's trying to get a reaction out of me.

Even though my neck feels warm, I keep my face neutral. "I'm late for lunch. Have a nice trip leaving Everbound."

I walk away, but he strolls next to me, tucking Luka's fang into his pocket and studying our surroundings as if he's cataloging all the little ways the school has changed since he left five years ago.

"I'm staying."

"Then good luck finding another keeper here."

"Pass," he says, parroting me with a sly grin.

At that, I pause and regard him. I thought I spelled it out well, but maybe he didn't understand me earlier.

"I rejected the match, Crypt DeLune. We're not in a quintet together. We never will be."

"Darling, have you ever seen a raindrop fall upwards?"

I give him another unimpressed look. "If you're implying that we're as inevitable as the direction rain falls, prepare to be disappointed."

"Nothing about you disappoints me. You're brilliantly unexpected."

Can he hurry up and vanish back to wherever he came from earlier? "Is it true all siphons are unable to cross the threshold of an inhabited dwelling without explicit permission? It's not just vampires?" I check.

"Unless we're in Limbo, yes."

Right. I forgot that very strong incubi can freely pass between this level of existence and the unseen dream plane that overlaps this reality. That must have been where he popped out of earlier.

I can't have the Nightmare Prince wandering into my room when he's invisible—or worse, appearing in my dreams at night. Which means I need to track down a dreamcatcher to repel him. Maybe the university store has that.

Turning on my heel, I walk in the opposite direction. Crypt keeps up with me easily, giving me a languidly curious look.

"Changed your mind about lunch?"

I ignore him.

He smirks and I glimpse his sharp canines—not as sharp as vampire fangs, but sharper than a human's. It's a visual reminder that he's also descended from monsters.

"I'll fetch you food if you want. Tell me what you like. Anything at all, I'll bring it for you."

"No. Go eat lunch alone."

"As I'm sure you know, my kind doesn't get any true sustenance from mortal food. I feed on dreams. I wonder what yours taste like."

Probably like shit.

We pass another group of students in the hall and I tense when one of them calls out, "Maven! Congratulations on your quintet!"

"Yeah, you are *outrageously* lucky," another student grumbles, their tone implying that *me* being paired with my well-known matches is the outrageous thing.

They leave the hall without saying more to me, but that doesn't mean they won't talk about me later. What a pain in the ass. Usually, I can go anywhere without anyone sparing me a glance, but I'm sure plenty of students will add my name to the gossip mill, considering who my matches are. I wonder how long it will take for them to lose interest in me after my matches appeal for another keeper. Hopefully, I'll be long gone by then.

"You don't enjoy attention from strangers," Crypt surmises, studying me.

He can surmise whatever he wants. I don't care what he thinks of me. Besides, I'm sure he'll lose interest and stop tagging along if I don't acknowledge him for long enough.

Resuming my trek through Everbound, I round a corner and nearly crash into Baelfire.

Godsdamn it. These men are like a bad rash.

I try to step around him, but his hand finds my shoulder, gripping it gently to keep me close. Even with my shirt's buffer, the contact constricts my chest, and goosebumps ripple down my arms. I escape quickly from the contact, but Bael doesn't notice because he's busy glaring at Crypt.

"Is this DeLune bothering you, Mavie?"

Mavie? "Ew. Don't call me that."

"How about...Spooky Boo? Or just Boo, since you're my boo."

I roll my eyes. "You're both bothering me. I don't want to see either of you."

"As you wish," Crypt murmurs before dissipating like a mirage. He must be back in Limbo, watching and listening in from there.

Bael's gilded gaze drops to me and immediately warms. "Alone at last, more or less. Wanna grab a bite together? I'm ravenous. Food is entirely optional," he adds with a suggestive wink.

I stare at him. How blunt do I need to be for him to get the message? "Get lost."

"I just want to make sure my adorably spooky little mate has eaten."

That word sends a sensation pooling in my stomach that I can't name.

Mate.

Absolutely not. I can't be that to him—to *anyone.*

Before I can shut down that notion, Silas Crane also rounds the corner, slowing when he sees us. His attention skips down to me, and I swear his expression intensifies into something almost... possessive.

Which is insane. He doesn't even fucking know me. None of them do, and yet here they are. I keep my face impassive, but irritation prickles along my spine. It seems none of my matches took what I said earlier seriously.

"I was magically tracking the Nightmare Prince. That led me here," Silas explains, glaring at the hallway around us as if he suspects Crypt is nearby. "Maven, I'll craft a custom dreamcatcher for you. You deserve your privacy and believe me, Crypt doesn't know the meaning of the word."

Do I need a dreamcatcher? Yes. Am I a strong enough caster to make a functional one by myself? Not currently. But I can't accept anything from my matches, or they'll think I'm giving in.

"I already have one," I lie smoothly and step around them to escape. Over my shoulder, I call, "From now on, leave me alone. Your time is better spent asking for another keeper."

I hear them arguing quietly behind me until I turn and hurry up another set of stairs. But the tension doesn't leave me because I know I'm still being followed, unseen, by Crypt. His presence is a dark, alluring thing. Subtle enough to miss entirely if I wasn't hyper-aware of all of them in a way I'm choosing to ignore, just as I once again choose to ignore that Crypt is following me.

Reaching one of the on-campus university stores doesn't take me long. It's small and sells a laughable mashup of modern goods and shit only legacies need. There's a fridge stocked with sodas, energy drinks, and blood bags for the vampires in need of a quick fix. A lineup of nail polishes and cosmetics is on display beside a shelf stocked with heat and rut suppressants for shifters, jars of powdered unicorn horns, and other random potion ingredients.

While browsing the few aisles looking for what I need, Crypt's presence nearby finally vanishes. I smile smugly to myself. He must have finally decided to give up.

Along with purchasing a dreamcatcher that I hope is strong enough to keep the Nightmare Prince away, I buy a few essential ingredients to make another healing spell for my singed fingertips.

I'm not particularly gifted as a caster in the typical sense. I can manage minor, practical spells and potions, but most of my skills have nothing to do with day-to-day magic. Still, healing myself is necessary since I can't go to the university healers.

Thirty minutes later, I arrive at my dorm room and pause outside the door with a frown. Hanging on the handle is a delicate rope chain necklace with Luka's fang as its sole pendant. Directly beside it is a beautifully woven dreamcatcher, its feathers stained dark with what looks to be blood and sigils burned into the delicate web net. It's obviously the work of a skilled blood fae. And on the ground is a massive takeout box of Chinese food from a restaurant in Halfton, the nearest human town. It's still steaming.

Oh, my gods. They have no idea how to handle being rejected, do they?

If they don't respond to blunt rejection, how am I supposed to get out of this quintet? Grumbling to myself, I grab the unwanted gifts and slam the door shut behind me.

6

MAVEN

THAT EVENING, I've finished healing my fingertips and I'm watering my plants when Kenzie bursts into my dorm room with an excited squeal. She rushes towards me with her arms extended like she's coming in for a hug, but I block it by lifting the watering can.

"Wouldn't want to get you wet."

"Right—sorry, I'm just so excited I forgot the no-hugging rule." She wiggles her eyebrows and purrs, "But don't worry about getting me wet. I've been wet *all day* if you catch my meaning."

"Nice innuendo. I take it you like your quintet."

Kenzie clutches her heart and drops onto my bed, sighing at the ceiling. "Vivienne is the sexiest little angel in the world, and Dirk is almost as feral as I am in bed. And they're both so nice! We're going to be such a fantastic quintet once..."

She trails off, and her smile drops a little.

"Once that vampire stops being an asshole?" I guess.

"He hasn't been one today. Actually, he's politely given us our space today. He helped everyone else move into the apartment but said he wouldn't move in until I gave him the green light. There's all this awkward tension between us, and I can tell he keeps wanting to say something, but whatever it is, he keeps chickening out. I don't know how to feel about being matched to him. On the one paw, he clearly wants to make up for how he treated me before, but on the other paw…well, I don't get over things easily. Am I being petty?"

"No. You're protecting yourself."

"The gods wouldn't match me with someone who wouldn't be good to me, though," she muses, sitting up to braid her hair. "So maybe I should let go of the past and give him a real chance. But enough about me—girl. Can we *please* talk about your infamous, sexy, wealthy, ridiculously top-tier quintet? I'm so fucking excited for you! I bet you'll be in one of the highest-ranked quintets of all time!"

I look away. "They're not my quintet."

"What do you mean? Hang on…May, why are you still in this dorm? Aren't you going to move in with your guys?"

"They're not mine. I turned them down so they can find a better keeper."

Kenzie stares at me so long that I wonder if she heard me. Then she tips her head. "Wait. Why would you think you're not a good enough keeper for them? You're amazing. And if the gods made the match, then you know you five were all meant to be together. Nobody rejects their matches because it's fate."

As if the gods care about my fate. I shake my head and return to watering my plants.

"Trust me. Rejecting them was the right thing to do."

To my surprise, she throws a hand over her mouth to try muffling a loud laugh. "Gods. You actually *rejected* those legacies? I wish I were there to see the looks on their faces. How did they take it?"

I glare at the Chinese takeout in the trash can. The fang necklace is in one of my drawers, and I begrudgingly hung both dream-catchers up over the threshold of my dorm because as much as I don't want Silas's gift, I want Crypt getting into my room even less.

"They'll get over it," I mutter. Then an idea strikes me, and I face her. "Kenzie. You've dated a lot more than I have."

She grins. "As we've established, yes."

"I'm abysmally inexperienced in comparison."

"It's true, you're basically a monk," she agrees. "A virgin monk, I'm pretty sure. No offense."

I fight a morbid smile. "None taken. Tell me. What have your exes done in the past that made you dump them?"

Kenzie blows out a big breath slowly. "Oh, gods. Where to even begin? Honestly, there are so many reasons to dump someone. If they're boring, annoying, clingy, mean…oh, or if they're high-maintenance. That gets old fast."

Boring, annoying, clingy, mean…

I take mental notes, waiting for her to go on.

Kenzie scratches her nose as she thinks. "Cheating is obviously a huge deal breaker. I've never been cheated on, but I would drop them like a griffin turd if they betrayed me like that. I *did* have a boyfriend once who flirted with anything that had a pulse, which was irritating. He did it to make me jealous, but he learned fast that I don't play head games."

I watch as she stands, stretches, and meanders over to examine the magical orbs of light hovering over my plants. She shoots me a sheepish grin.

"I've only been dumped once, and they said it was because they hadn't realized just how high my body count is. Guess I intimidated them."

"It's not your fault they were insecure."

She laughs, but I'm keeping a mental list in my head. One I intend to write down and use to drive my so-called matches away. It will be far easier to break up the quintet if I can get them to hate me.

"It won't work, May."

I glance at Kenzie, waiting for her meaning. She smiles knowingly, looking both amused and sympathetic.

"I know what you're up to, but trying to make your quintet dislike you isn't going to work. You're too endearing."

Endearing? Me? I almost laugh out loud. She's too nice to everyone, but especially to me.

"You are the only person who's ever thought that about me," I inform her.

Kenzie shrugs. "You're a master of hiding your emotions, and you say as little as possible, but actions speak louder than words. I know the real you. It won't take long for your guys to see the real you, too, no matter how you try to hide it."

She's underestimating my acting skills. After all, no one here has questioned my backstory.

Changing the topic, I decide to come clean to her. "I ran into Luka earlier. One of my so-called matches snapped a fang out of his mouth."

She gawks at me. "No wonder poor Luka disappeared for so long today. Damn, your matches don't mess around." Then she wiggles her eyebrows again. "Sounds like they're protective."

"More like self-deluded. It won't last. Luka's fang is in my drawer if you want to parade it around in front of him."

She shuffles uncomfortably. "I don't want that. I know he was an ass to me, but as strange as it sounds…I don't hate him. I don't really know *how* I feel about him, but I don't want to hurt him. Maybe he and I can be friends, eventually."

Like I said, she's too nice to everyone.

Before I can say that she's far too forgiving of him, a sharp, sudden bloom of pain in my chest takes my breath away, making my vision blur. I grip one of the posts of my bed tightly, but otherwise, I carefully control any other outward sign of pain.

Gods, it hurts worse than usual.

"I need to work on a potion for class tomorrow before it gets too late," I lie quickly, trying to keep my voice even. "I'll catch up with you later."

"All right. But I want to hear all about your attempts to repel your quintet. Pretty sure this'll be *super* entertaining to watch," Kenzie teases before saying goodnight and leaving the room.

The moment the door shuts behind her, I crumble to my knees, clutching at my chest. Now that I'm not fighting it, the pain lances outward from my torso—almost like the center of my body is being sucked through the eye of a needle.

I know from experience that unless I speed along the process, I could be in for hours of agony before the message comes through. So, instead of waiting, I stumble to my closet, pulling out one of my many hidden vials of dark liquid.

Uncorking it, I down the disgusting mixture quickly, gagging on the taste. A familiar burn floods my system before everything fades to black as I slump to the floor. Then, I feel nothing but cold.

Telum.

That word reverberates through my mind along with a flurry of images, all one after the other. Twisted trees decorated with hanging bones. Shadows sliding over corpses. A sky cycling through day and night, fourteen times, while snow falls.

But the last images are the ones that burn into my mind.

Lillian being tortured. Her in a room with blood and gore, surrounded by dark smiles, screaming as she's slowly pulled to pieces. The screams of the others.

Telum…

The last echo dies out as a sudden, severe shock jolts me awake. I gasp and claw at my chest, trying to force the pain away. I'm lying on the ground in my room, head pounding while the cold gradually fades from my limbs. The vial I drank from is shattered on the ground beside me.

With a grimace, I try to pull myself up, but my body feels like it's made of wet cement. So, instead, I lay back down and scowl at the ceiling, thinking.

The winter solstice is fourteen days and nights away. That's what that image means. I have until the solstice to finish the first task.

And I certainly can't do that with four idiots breathing down my neck all the time.

With a renewed determination to drive away my supposedly *fated* matches, I force myself to move, to sit at my desk, and pull out a paper and pen. I jot down a game plan—my *Make Them Hate Me* list.

Once it's done, I reread it before nodding with satisfaction.

Tomorrow, if any of my rejected matches approach me, I'll use the first tactic on the list:

Bore them to tears.

7

SILAS

Before sunrise, I arrive at the apartment reserved for my quintet. The only one who slept here last night was Baelfire since Everett was nowhere to be found after the Seeking and Crypt was likely out devouring dreams all night.

Myself, I stayed in my old private dorm room. I have no plans to stay overnight with my quintet until after our curses are broken at graduation. Otherwise, my curse won't allow me to get a moment of rest around the others.

I set my hand against the apartment door, which I spelled to open only for my quintet members. When the door swings open, I raise a brow at the deer that Bael is skinning and cleaning in the large kitchen area to the left of the spacious entry.

"Delightful."

"Please," he huffs. "As if blood has ever bothered you. I haven't finished draining it if you wanna sip on a vein or something."

I don't bother explaining for the umpteenth time that blood fae only feed on blood from magical beings. Whether my kind should remain in the House of Arcana or whether we're more fit for the House of Craving has long been debated, given our similarities to vampires. But unlike other siphons, we don't *require* blood for our sustenance. It just makes our magic stronger.

Deer blood is useless. I know because I've tried it.

"You're up early."

He shrugs and snaps the dead animal's pelvis to remove more intestines. "Felt like getting an early start."

Sometimes, I envy the ability others have to tell lies since fae like myself cannot. And I know Baelfire is lying. His early morning hunt likely had to do with his curse.

I'm one of the few who know the specifics of his.

The draconic brute is shirtless, only wearing dark trousers. The rest of him is smeared in blood, dirt, dead leaves, and gods know what else. At least he's kept the apartment neat, keeping his mess in the kitchen.

"Clean this up before Maven arrives."

His eyes flash to me, and the hopeful excitement that lights his face is almost childlike. "She's coming? When?"

"I'll convince her to."

Mainly because the idea of my keeper staying in the tiny dorm room I identified as hers yesterday bothers me. It's not safe enough. Keepers are considered the ones in charge, but they are also fiercely protected by their quintet because they're the keystone, so to speak—the core of the group, without which the quintet would break and the curses would return. It makes keepers a target for other legacies hoping to climb the power rankings. Although the no-kill ban doesn't officially lift until next semester when quintets train together, Maven is still in danger—especially considering how highly ranked the rest of our group is.

This apartment is layered with all kinds of protective spells that would reassure me that my keeper isn't in any danger, and it's stocked with almost anything she might need for her comfort. Which is why I'll make sure she moves in sooner than later.

Baelfire grunts and returns to cleaning his kill. "I'm going to play hooky with Maven today. Take her out to Halfton for lunch and anything else she wants. My mate will accept me first, and after I spoil the fuck out of her in bed for a few days, I'll collect on that wager you proposed. If Everett hasn't joined the bet by then, I'll make sure to demand something that'll be a pain in your ass to pay up."

Cocky bastard.

I didn't make that wager lightly. Of course, it's crucial for us to make progress with our keeper, but I also need quite a few of Baelfire's dragon scales. He's known for years that I want to use them in experimental spells and potions.

What he doesn't know is *why* I want them. Certainly, they're a rare ingredient many spells call for, but I have two specific purposes in mind for his scales.

The first, I wouldn't dare breathe a word of to anyone I don't trust. And I only trust myself.

But the second purpose, I can't tell the dragon, or he'll think I've gone soft.

I watch as Baelfire accidentally jostles the table while sectioning the deer. My eye twitches. That, combined with the scent of the carcass, the smooth glide of that knife through the flesh, the dim lighting of a cold dawn, and that familiar creeping feeling sliding like chilled oil over my spine…

How easy it would be for that knife to wind up in your back, a voice like my father's whispers in my head.

My breathing quickens, and instinctively, my hand edges toward my pocket where my bleeding crystal is. I always carry it there in case I need to cast a powerful spell in the blink of an eye. I'm so accustomed to the slight ringing in my ears that I only realize Baelfire is trying to get my attention after the second time he's called my name.

The ringing fades. My eyes snap to his, and I'm not sure what he sees on my face, but he immediately sets the knife down and steps back, wiping his bloodied hands on his trousers.

"Whether we like it or not, we're in a quintet now. You know I wouldn't."

He means he wouldn't kill me.

Only Baelfire knows how my curse affects me, and that leaves a bitter taste in my mouth. Most people can't understand the severity of it, but he does because, in some ways, our curses are similar.

But just because he understands doesn't mean I can trust him.

He'll betray you. He'll turn Maven against you, too.

The other voices in my head agree. *If you don't get to him first, he'll rip you to shreds.*

I shake my head to dispel the suspicions crawling inside my skin like termites.

Baelfire scratches his chin, studying me. "On second thought, maybe I should show you some mercy and let you try to win Maven over first. Maybe being around her will make you less…you know."

Neurotic. Haunted. Incredibly fucking paranoid.

My curse is slowly driving me mad, making me expect foul intentions from perfect strangers. I see everything through suspicion-colored lenses. It's as if my nerves are always hardwired to everything, searching for the most minuscule way others might try to harm me. Some days, it's debilitating.

Baelfire may be right. Perhaps Maven will soothe the backstabbing demons in my head.

I'm going to find out. Though Maven is in my House, I'd never even noticed her existence until the Seeking, and I regret that heavily. It means I have no idea what to expect from her. She's a question mark to me, and I intend to know every tiny detail about her.

Her likes. Her hates. How strong she is. How well she'll be able to lead the four of us.

"Just clean it up when you're done," I mutter, leaving Baelfire alone in the apartment.

I'm halfway through Everbound on the way to Maven's dorm when the interim headmaster spots me in the hall and approaches, calling out my name. I try to ignore the lingering suspicions clinging to my skin. It casts everyone in a darker light, and I can't help eyeing Mr. Gibbons more than usual.

He's a brown nose, constantly checking in on me, expecting to impress me with preferential treatment. Everyone knows I became the Garnet Wizard's apprentice after the deaths of most of my family.

Since the mysteriously wealthy Garnet Wizard donates hefty sums to Everbound, Mr. Gibbons must see me as a cash cow to cozy up to.

I despise that he thinks I'd appreciate preferential treatment.

"Mr. Crane," he says with a smile, stopping before me. "I see you out and about by the break of dawn so often, long before any classes. A truly admirable quality. If only more of the other legacies were like you."

"If they were more like me, we'd all kill each other within a week."

He tries to laugh it off like I'm joking. Never mind the fact that I can't lie, even in jest.

"What a sense of humor you have. We might be descended from monsters, but we do have some decorum. You know the rules about killing. Of course, we must still allow the weak to be weeded out—but that's just how things have always been at Everbound. It's the way of legacies."

Annoyance prickles at me. The longer he gabs, the shorter the window of time I have to invite Maven to breakfast. "Is there a point to this discussion, Mr. Gibbons?"

"Indeed, I wanted to inquire about what emphasis you and your rather impressive quintet are leaning toward next semester. Everyone is curious to see what you'll choose, and I'd like to make sure you get first pick at classes."

Ah. He wants to know how to give me even *more* preferential treatment moving forward.

I should have anticipated this.

Until First Placement, students will go about their regular classes from this semester as they get to know their matches. But starting next semester, new quintets will study and train together, whether their group is complete or not. Our individual rankings will change into quintet rankings, with cutthroat competition to establish the most powerful. After graduation, those rankings carry over into where we will be assigned for active combat.

Most legacies are assigned to guard and patrol the Divide, which is a large demarcated border extending all along the eastern border of North America and most of South America. It's where the Nether is kept at bay, frozen through the efforts of legacies so it will spread no further into the mortal realm. We're responsible for hunting down anything that escapes.

But not all quintets are stationed there. We get our assignments from the Immortal Quintet, who might instead send us into private security positions, roles inside the legacy government, protecting the temples of the gods, or even allow us to live in the high society of legacies—a spoiled, pampered lot who rarely get their hands dirty with real work.

Everett's family falls into the last category. It's why he was bragging about his ability to give Maven a life of security and protection. I don't mind that idea. I'd prefer to have my keeper far from danger. Especially because I'm positive she isn't competitively ranked here at Everbound, so she's likely not skilled with magic.

"So, which emphasis are you and your matches leaning towards?" Gibbons asks, cutting into my thoughts. "Defense and combat? Holy guard? Covert operations? Or perhaps a less common emphasis, like administration or human relations? We need more valuable quintets to help the rapport between humans and our kind, after all, since it's taken a nosedive for the last twenty or so years. They're such squeamish, mistrustful creatures—meaning no offense to your keeper's family, of course."

That captures my attention. "Maven is from a human family?"

He blinks. "Why, yes—you didn't know? She came to Everbound a mere two weeks ago as a newly manifested atypical caster. Not from a magical bloodline at all. You know how magic sometimes pops up within humans with no prompting, entirely of the will of the gods. I thought she would have told you that by now...but then, she is rather a tight-lipped little thing."

I consider this new information. Atypical casters aren't affected by the Legacy Curse, so they don't have the same burning desire to find their quintet to finally feel complete and break their curse as the rest of us. Is that why Maven talked about rejecting us? Does she find the idea of binding her heart to four monster descendants terrifying?

It just adds to my many questions, and I regard Gibbons. Perhaps his brown-nosing isn't so problematic after all.

"Tell me more about Maven's family."

He strokes his white beard nervously. "Well, now…when it comes to her family, I'm afraid all I know is that they passed away while she was a child. She has no emergency contacts to speak of."

She's an orphan like me.

Not bothering with more small talk, I leave the interim headmaster to go to her dormitory. I don't want to miss the chance to talk to her before classes begin.

When I finally arrive in the hallway where her dorm is, Maven is just leaving her room. She spares me an impassive glance before walking past as if I'm not studying her.

I can hardly help it. She has such a unique type of beauty—subtle yet complex. Today, her dark hair is swept into a braid over one shoulder. She's again dressed in ill-fitting clothes several sizes too big for her, and I note that she's wearing the same pair of leather gloves she wore yesterday.

Interesting. Is she germophobic?

I quickly catch up to her. "I trust the dreamcatcher came in handy."

No reply.

"Someone left you a necklace. Was it one of us, or is it from an outsider woefully mistaken in thinking you're on the market?"

Just the idea of someone outside our quintet sniffing around Maven, taking up her time, eyeing my keeper…my jaw clenches.

"I've never been on the market," she drawls.

I drop the subject as we walk through the vaulted stone hallways. "I'll treat you to breakfast."

"Not hungry."

"Lunch, then. Later on between your classes."

"No."

She's stubbornly not looking at me. I'm unaccustomed to trying to pique someone's interest since too much of my time is spent avoiding people who won't leave me alone. I also haven't had a strong interest in women over the years, outside of brief instances of sexual relief. After all, having a close relationship with someone just opens the door to more ways they can betray you.

Paranoia makes a poor bed companion.

But if she's so intent on ignoring me, I may as well test her resolve.

"How did your family die?"

Maven slows to face me, expression unreadable. We're close to Everbound's largest courtyard, which houses a massive greenhouse. I can smell the sunlight and soil from here.

"Slowly and painfully, or so I was told. How did yours die?"

She doesn't bat an eye, but her voice has an edge. She wants no sympathy, and something in my chest melts slightly. I understand that part of her. I hate sympathy, and I especially hate when it's offered for my family's demise.

"Most of them killed each other," I quietly confess. "Including my parents."

In front of me. When I was thirteen.

There's a faint flicker of something in Maven's eyes, perhaps even empathy, before she turns to enter the empty greenhouse. I follow, determined to make more progress.

"Do you always come to the greenhouse first thing in the morning?"

"I am a botany aficionado."

I study her. If she's telling the truth, why haven't I seen her in the greenhouse more often? I'm here frequently since I have a plot of thriving plants in one corner. An affinity for nature is the one thing I look back on with fond memories passed down from my family.

Is Maven the same way?

I gesture at a nearby cluster of white-petaled flowers. "What do you suppose this is?"

I already know what it is, but it's not an outright lie to feign ignorance. I'm testing her.

When she speaks, her voice is flat and monotonous. "Death camas.

Also known as meadow death camas, which is a part of the Melanthiaceae family. The leaves, bulbs, and flowers are all poisonous, but that poison is far more potent when the plant has been dried. Not usually fatal to consume in small amounts, but it can cause severe illness."

Then her eyes sweep to me, and she looks unimpressed. "It looks remarkably like wild garlic blooms to the untrained eye. I'm sure that's the answer you were testing against."

Impressive…and perceptive.

Curious, I point out another plant. Not only can Maven identify the plant, but she knows an array of facts about it as well as the potions it's commonly used in. Without my prompting, she moves on to another, and another…and another. Her voice is a measured drawl. Most people would find it dry and uninteresting. Incredibly dull, even.

But I'm captivated.

By Maven's intelligence, her calculated movements, even the way the dappled morning light dances across her skin when she walks under a trellis in bloom. For someone who's supposedly so quiet all the time, she's articulate to a point.

Whenever she's not looking, I find my attention skimming over the frumpy clothes completely obscuring her body, curiosity building in me. Obviously, I want to know what she looks like naked, but more importantly…why does she dress like this? For comfort, or is she self-conscious?

She glances over her shoulder. "I must be boring you."

A smile tempts the corners of my lips up. It's a foreign expression on my face. "On the contrary. Go on. I intend to listen to you commentate on the entire greenhouse."

Maven turns away to run her gloved hand softly over the ferns. I've never been jealous of plants before, but my attention suddenly can't seem to budge from her gloves.

I want to feel her bare hands on me. All over.

"I see. Tell me what topics do bore you."

"Very little," I admit, struggling to pull myself out of that arousing train of thought. "Even knowledge of the driest of subjects can be a useful weapon when least expected."

Maven turns to study me with her first hint of genuine curiosity. I'm standing nearer to her than I have to date, and this close, I discover her dark irises are truly a mysterious blend of dark shades —brown, gray, deep blue, shadowy green.

And…she doesn't look away from me.

Most people find my full attention and blood-red irises too intense, but she doesn't flinch or try to fill the quiet with small talk. She's steady. Immovable. Stubborn.

Beautiful.

"So there's no chance of me boring you to tears," she summarizes.

"Is that what makes you want to reject the quintet? You worry we'll lose interest in you?"

Immediately, her voice steels. "I don't just *want* to reject it. I did."

"There must be a reason. Is it because you come from a human background, and quintets seem strange? Or is something else scaring you away? Perhaps we intimidate you."

Maven snorts and brushes past me without making the slightest bit of contact despite the close quarters. Still, my pulse jumps, and my mouth goes dry. The dark, morbidly sensual thought surfaces, and my mouth waters as I suddenly wonder what the magic in Maven's blood would taste like.

What *she* tastes like.

"I don't owe anyone an explanation. Go find another keeper, Silas Crane."

I make no move as she leaves the greenhouse, but the longer I stand here, the more it sinks in.

My paranoia was silent the entire time we were alone.

No thoughts of her trying to kill me, no jumping at shadows, no hearing voices.

"Intriguing," I murmur to myself.

But not half as intriguing as my keeper is. She must have a reason for resisting the bond. I intend to find out exactly what she's keeping from us.

8

MAVEN

THAT WAS A BUST.

Internally chastising myself for trying to bore my most studious match with *plant facts* of all things, I make my way through a crowded corridor toward my first class of the day. I rarely take this route since I prefer passing as few students as possible, but I quickly realize just how terrible an idea it was to take it *today* of all days, right after the Seeking.

Everyone knows who I am now.

That's painfully obvious with the amount of stares tracking my every move. I can hear whispering, and a few people even wave and try to say hello. Others size me up. And since glowering at them or using choice words would be seen as a challenge and drum up more legacy-power-struggle drama, I decide to take the easy way out and stare at my feet as I walk, pretending none of it is happening.

Just a couple more weeks until the winter solstice. If I don't fulfill my mission by then, I'm leaving Everbound anyway.

Stepping into my Introduction to Runes class, I climb the stone steps to the right of the amphitheater-style seating to get to my spot in the back, where I'm sure people will leave me alone. But when I arrive at the section of long desks and benches, I pause at the sight of the annoyingly chipper dragon shifter waiting for me.

Baelfire's smile is dazzling. "There's my Boo."

"I'm not your anything. You're in my seat."

He points at his face and winks. "I've got a better one right here for you."

Fucking dragon.

When I just stare silently at him, carefully avoiding letting my emotions seep onto my face, he scoots over slightly to make room for me on the bench.

"I've never been to a casting class before, but I'm excited to see what you've got hidden up those adorably oversized sleeves."

I want to huff that he has his own classes, but noticing all the PDA-infused groups getting settled in the classroom—many of which are not in the House of Arcana—I remember Kenzie mentioning over a week ago how matches typically go to their keeper's classes for the two weeks after the Seeking. The school allows it because they place such extreme importance on quintets.

Inconvenient, but whatever. I'm nothing if not adaptable.

I sit on the edge of the bench, as far away from him as possible, while Professor Crowley starts class. The rest of the legacies present quiet down, but there is still a stomach-churning amount of soft arm caresses and cheek kisses. Gods, just looking at it all makes my skin itch. I try to focus on the lesson.

But I quickly learn that dragons make terrible desk mates.

First of all, Baelfire is such an enormous mass of brawn and heat that he encroaches on my space without meaning to. He's keeping his hands to himself but not his eyes. I can practically feel his gaze memorizing my profile as I look straight forward, purposefully ignoring him.

"I didn't sleep worth shit last night," he says suddenly.

Ignore.

"So, to pass the time, I made two very long lists."

Ignore.

To show him just how little I care that he's made me the center of all his attention, I pull a notebook from thin air—a useful little enchanted book that anyone can buy at the university store. I open it and start skimming my notes.

He adjusts on his side of the desk to face me slightly more. "The first was a long-ass list of questions I have about you. Promise me you'll answer at least five of them."

"Not happening."

"Come on," he pouts. Pouting is childish and unattractive, yet somehow, he pulls it off. He even makes it flirtatious as he leans over to catch my eye. "Little questions. Questions that don't even matter, like your favorite flavor of ice cream or the three movies you'd take with you to a deserted island. I just want to get to know you, even the insignificant shit you think I'll forget. I won't pry or ask uncomfortable questions—cross my heart that now only beats for you."

"Are all the Decimuses this annoying?"

"The word you're looking for is *charming*. And nope. I'm one of a kind, and now I'm all yours."

Could he be any more aggravating? I can feel his body warmth so close to mine, and I edge away, trying to focus back on my notes.

"I'm in class."

"Yeah, but it doesn't even look like you casters will be using magic today. Every legacy knows the shit this guy is covering."

He jerks a thumb at the front of the room, where Professor Crowley points to five illustrations on the massive chalkboard as he summarizes the five planes of existence.

"At the top is Paradise," he orates. "Home of the gods. Mortals aren't admitted there, even after death. Below that is where we are now. Earth, also known as the Mortal Realm. The middle layer, which is easily forgotten much of the time, is Limbo—the plane of existence where only strong incubi can navigate while conscious, although every living thing's subconscious dallies there when they're fast asleep."

At the reminder of Limbo, I abruptly wonder if Silas and Baelfire aren't the only matches who've bothered me today. Is Crypt here somewhere, unseen but watching me?

Yes. I can't describe how I can tell he's nearby, but I suddenly know with certainty that he is. It's a subconscious feeling I didn't notice until this moment.

Gods, I really need to shake these guys.

"Come on," Baelfire presses quietly. "Just five questions. You can pass any you don't like."

"Shh."

The professor goes on. "As you all know, beneath Limbo is the Nether, the parasitic layer of existence that we legacies are in charge of keeping at bay to keep it from getting a foothold in the Mortal Realm. It's a disturbing, lifeless void filled with the Undead, shadows, monsters, and other unpleasantries, to put it lightly."

He taps the board. "And finally, below the Nether is the Beyond. It's where we all go after death, sent off to be sorted into our respective afterlives by Sachar, the judge and ruler of that unscalable realm. Souls don't come back from the Beyond—not even the gods, according to my favorite theologian, Forner. Forner wrote extensively on the death of the goddess Reniah during the Great Wars when humans and legacies…"

The lesson continues, but I'm focused on the illustrations. Most legacies here grew up hearing about the five planes of existence. I heard about them, too, though my education growing up was different from my peers.

Finishing my notes, I glance at an empty row to my right and down a few steps.

It *looks* empty, anyway. But when I narrow my eyes in suspicion, the Nightmare Prince flickers into view for barely a fraction of a second. He's sitting on the desk, looking half amused as he takes a drag from an odd-looking cigarette. And just before he disappears back into Limbo, he blows me a godsdamned kiss, leaving nothing but smoke behind.

It happens so fast that when Baelfire glances over to see what I'm glowering at, he misses Crypt altogether.

"Someone bothering you, baby?"

"You are. There. That's one question answered. You have four left."

He grins, looking pleased at my answer instead of frustrated as I'd hoped he would be. "What kind of caster are you?"

I pretend he never spoke, turning back to the front of the classroom.

Bael leans an elbow on the desk and rests his chin on his fist. "That's fine. Didn't expect you to answer that one anyway, Miss Mysterious. How about this instead: favorite ice cream flavor?"

"Pass."

"Seriously? Why? It's just ice cream. Okay, how about…favorite flower?"

That's harmless enough. "Dead snapdragons."

He frowns. "Why dead?"

"Because when they shrivel up, they resemble tiny human skulls."

It's surprisingly difficult to keep from laughing at the expression that crosses his face—a mix of taken aback, confusion, amusement, and something like concern.

"Okay then. As far as flowers go, that's pretty damn metal." Then he shakes his head at me, his smile warming so it feels far hotter in this room in the blink of an eye. "I fucking love that my mate is secretly a little on the kooky side."

More than a little.

Still, his casually dropping the *l* and *m* words together extinguishes any bit of mirth I felt a moment ago. I turn back to my notes with icy composure. "I am not your mate."

"Keep telling yourself that. So. My next question is…"

I don't hear the rest of the words coming out of his mouth because my hearing short-circuits when Baelfire absentmindedly reaches up to adjust some of my hair, tucking it behind my ear. The brush of his warm knuckle against my temple has my spine going ramrod straight. I lean away from him as my lungs clench, unable to keep the sharpness out of my voice.

"No touching."

Baelfire freezes before pulling his hand back. His brows draw together as he studies me, confusion and alarm warring in his molten gaze. "Shit, I didn't know that was…I'm sorry."

He's silent, frowning at the desk in front of us as I listen to the end of Professor Crowley's lecture. Class ends, and the other legacies start to file out. Some of them get Baelfire's attention with waves or hellos. And from the way he interacts with them, shaking off whatever was bothering him to smile and make effortless conversation with everyone else, I can tell Kenzie was right about him having what she calls "rizz." It's obvious he's naturally a social butterfly.

But I notice that whenever the other students so much as glance in my direction, Bael steps in front of me slightly. It's a barely noticeable gesture, but he's making it crystal clear that they don't get to talk to me unless I want it. Which means that I don't have to have a single conversation with my peers who have been whispering about me since yesterday's Seeking.

I admit it's convenient to have this massive dragon shifter shield to keep me from all the idiotic small talk.

That doesn't mean he's not an overly persistent pain in the ass.

I'm the last to leave, with Baelfire strolling beside me. And I'm almost certain Crypt is, too. Maybe I should just wear a dreamcatcher as a necklace all the fucking time to keep him away. If only there were an easy repellant for all my no-longer-matches.

"Wanna go to Halfton for lunch after your next class?" he asks.

"Not with you."

"Ouch. Careful with my heart, Boo. It's far more fragile than I am," he laments theatrically.

I roll my eyes. "You're now down to three questions."

"Noted. So why the no touching rule?"

I'm not about to open that can of worms, now or ever. Instead of answering, I pause in the hallway to frown at him as I recall something he said earlier. "What was the other?"

"Hmm?"

"Earlier, you said you made two long lists. One was questions. What was the other?" Normally, curiosity doesn't faze me, but it irks me that he never expounded on that.

Baelfire's grin turns wicked, and he bites his lower lip. "All the ways I plan on worshipping you in bed. It took up too many pages, and I got sidetracked a couple of times jacking off just thinking about it all."

Oh.

Gods. He's such an oversharing idiot. That's not a mental image I want in my head...mostly because it is impossible to think of anything else now. A small part of me wants to see this list. Call me morbidly curious, not to mention a glutton for punishment, because it's not as if any of the scenarios he wrote down will ever play out.

Ignoring the oddly fluttery sensation in my gut, I resume the trek to the eating hall. Baelfire keeps up easily. Of course, he does. His legs dwarf mine because he's fucking giant.

I descend a staircase and walk into Everbound's massive dining hall. It's an impressive display, with large tables and seating for hundreds, a cafeteria, several small chain restaurants operating along one half of the long room, and a vaulted ceiling made of arched glass high above. The other wall is a series of tall arched windows that give a fantastic view of the wintry woods in the distance.

It's not crowded right now, which makes it easier for Silas Crane to spot us the moment we walk in. His scarlet eyes hold mine from across the room, but he motions at Baelfire.

"He wants us to sit by him," Baelfire mumbles. "Selfish dick. It's my time with you. He had this morning."

As with the first time I met my matches, I pick up on a slight edge between them as Baelfire and Silas have a silent conversation I don't understand. Though whatever tension is between them seems mild compared to how obviously Silas disdained Crypt—or the way Everett and Baelfire made jabs at each other.

Fine by me. If they're not friends, that makes breaking up our quintet easier.

Silas gestures for me to come to him. He picked out a good table, away from the bulk of other legacies chatting as they chow down. If

I'm honest, it's my favorite place to sit in the dining hall. But instead of going to him, I turn and walk to a table in the opposite corner.

Bael follows with a quiet laugh. "You're so damn cute."

"No. I'm not."

"You're like an adorable little raincloud. I get the feeling you'd be cuddly, too, if you just gave me a chance and lifted the no-touching rule."

I sit at the table and fix him with a look. "If you try to cuddle me, I'll hex you so that you shit thunder for a month."

It's a bluff. Casting the limp dick hex on Luka was already barely inside my magical powerhouse since I'm running low on my ability to cast at the moment. I'll have to remedy that soon.

Bael sits directly beside me and winks. "We'll get there, Boo."

It doesn't take long for Silas to come to us, sitting across from me and studying me as intensely as he did when we were in the greenhouse. It's seriously inconvenient how gorgeous all my matches are, but all in their own way. Silas? His dark curly hair is mussed, and something about his shifting red irises makes him look ill at ease, but he emanates dangerous intelligence. Like he knows every possible way someone might try him at any given moment, and he's already calculated what weaknesses to take advantage of.

"How was your class, Maven?"

"You need to leash your dragon. He won't stop following me around."

Baelfire makes a sound of indignation. "*Leash?* Fuck that. Leashes are for dogs. I'm a damn dragon."

I ignore him. "Between the Decimus and the DeLune, I get the impression you three don't know how to handle rejection. That's going to have to change."

Silas frowns slightly, ignoring the latter part. "You mean, you can sense Crypt nearby?"

"Wouldn't be surprised if he's been tailing us all day, that creep," Baelfire grunts.

I glance over my shoulder. Sure enough, the air ripples to reveal the Nightmare Prince leaning against the nearest wall. His lips curl up into a pleased smirk as if he's flattered that I can sense his presence.

"What a keen keeper I have," he murmurs.

I've had enough of this. Looking at them each in turn, I spell it out. "I. Am. Not. Your. Keeper. So fuck off."

Crypt and Silas both look mildly amused, and Baelfire openly grins. "I *love* hearing you swear with that pretty little mouth."

Oh, my *gods*, these assholes are exhausting. Why can't a bitch just ditch her god-selected soulmates and move on? I can't complete my mission with them constantly hanging around, and my time is going to start running out. The winter solstice is less than two weeks away.

And I can't let them figure out my secret, or they'll kill me themselves.

Fine. I'll have to use the strongest tactic on the *Make Them Hate Me* list. Skipping right past *annoying, clingy, mean,* and a bunch of others I'd written, I settle on *play head games.*

But first, I need to pick a candidate they all hate. Discreetly, I glance around the dining hall to see if there's anyone here I could stomach cozying up to for a week or two.

My attention is arrested by the strikingly handsome elemental sitting several tables away with a group of professors. He's in academic attire, but he makes the others look bad since he may as well just have walked straight out of a modeling shoot. All women and several guys within a hundred-foot radius of him are openly drooling, including one of the faculty members sitting across from him with stars in her eyes.

Merciless jawline. Icy white hair. Glacial eyes that sweep over to me before looking away just as quickly.

Everett Frost.

That's not a bad idea.

Silas notices where I'm looking, and although he speaks matter-of-factly, his voice has an edge. "He should be getting to know you too."

Baelfire looks equally annoyed at the sight of the professor. "Nah, she's better off not dealing with that frozen prick until she has no other choice."

Bingo.

This strategy should have been obvious from the beginning. Maybe I can sink this ship from the inside. They're already on thin ice with each other. Let's see what jealousy can do for me.

"Actually, I *would* like to get to know the professor better. He's exactly my type."

Three sets of eyes swing to me.

"*Frost?*" Baelfire scowls. "You're twisting my tail. There's no way that pampered icicle is your type. How would you even know when you haven't said a word to him? He's the biggest dickhead of all of us."

"A gorgeous dickhead," I muse. "He used to be a model, right?"

Baelfire scowls, but Crypt snorts. I can't tell what he thinks is more amusing, what I said or this whole situation. Whatever his thoughts on it, he ripples and disappears once again, and after a second, I don't sense him nearby anymore.

Silas looks skeptical. I'm ready to get this jealousy show on the road, so I leave the table and cross the room. It's true what Baelfire said—I haven't spoken to Professor Frost outside of that initial rejection. He's been the only one to leave me alone like I asked, which has been a relief.

But for the sake of turning them all against each other? I couldn't have asked for a better scenario than cozying up to a man of ice who is indifferent to my existence.

9

MAVEN

As soon as Professor Frost sees me approaching his table, he stands. I'm not sure what to make of that. Either he's being overly respectful in an old-fashioned manner, even though he can't be more than five years older than I am, or he's about to run.

I'd prefer the latter.

But when I'm close enough, he turns and walks to the nearest serving area without a word. And since I can feel the weight of Baelfire's and Silas's stares on my back, I pretend this is exactly what I expected as I follow the ice elemental. I wait beside him as he politely tells the girl behind the counter what to put on the plate. She keeps getting distracted and messing up the order because she's gawking at him so hard.

Finally, Professor Frost clears his throat. "Need something, Oakley?"

"I have a proposal for you."

That clearly isn't what he expected, and he turns to raise a brow. He does pull off the frigid, aloof asshole look. He looks like a deep winter morning personified. "I can't say I'm interested."

Thank the gods. He won't make this complicated.

"I'm not interested in you either, Professor Frost," I reassure him.

His expression ices over as he lifts one shoulder in a jerky motion. "Good. I'm glad that's been so clearly established."

The legacy behind the counter overheard, and now she's openly glaring at me. "Hey. Are you going to order something? If not, get lost. No one wants a snobby bitch who doesn't appreciate what she has holding back the line."

The professor's attention returns to her as he pays for the food, but I'm distracted by my breath coming in plumes in front of my face out of nowhere. Did someone open a window?

He leads me to a separate, smaller table, sitting and scooting the tray toward me. "So. Your proposal?"

I sit, glancing at the tray full of steaming sauce, meat, and cheese with a side of toasted bread. It must be a dish I'm unfamiliar with. That happens a lot since I grew up eating the same bland foods every day.

"Aren't you hungry?" I ask.

"I already ate."

"Then why get all this food?"

"Because you didn't eat," he says like I'm the slowest person alive.

I haven't eaten all day, but I'm still not accepting anything from them, so I scoot the tray to the middle of the table and fold my gloved hands in my lap. "I want to pretend we have a thing for each other."

He blinks rapidly before understanding crosses his features. "You want to make them jealous."

"Yes."

"Because you want them to want you even more."

An unfeminine snort escapes me before I can stop it. I clear my throat and compose myself again. "Sure. Why not?"

Professor Frost glances over his shoulder to the table where Baelfire and Silas don't even try to pretend they're not watching us. They're also clearly in the middle of an argument.

"But if it's not to make them jealous, then why?" he asks.

"Let's say it's for shits and giggles."

He rubs the back of his neck. "This is a bad idea."

"Can't be. It's mine."

His brows go up, and then he scoffs. "You're not what I expected, Oakley. At all. And that's both a very good and a very bad thing."

I don't have time to puzzle out whether that's an insult or a compliment. "Here's my proposal, Professor Frost. We—"

"Call me Everett," he cuts in coolly. "Everyone does."

"Fine. We pretend we like each other, Everett. We have *mild* PDA in front of the others. Otherwise, I promise to leave you alone if you do the same for me. And when you four finally get a new keeper, I'll be cheering along with everyone else."

He looks away. "I'd rather not have that."

"Fine. Then I'll be booing and throwing rotten tomatoes," I deadpan.

The professor meets my eye, and for a fraction of a second, a strong emotion I can't identify flickers over his face. It's gone just as quickly, though, replaced by cool indifference as he shakes his head. "I'll think about this proposal and get back to you."

"I'd prefer a yes or no now." I'm already losing time trying to get them to leave me alone.

He mutters something under his breath about needing to visit a temple and stands from the table. "Later. And if you want to convince those arrogant assholes we're falling for each other, you should eat the food I got you. It'll make me look like a gentleman and make them feel guilty for talking your ear off instead of taking care of you."

"If we want them to think we're falling for each other," I counter, "Then you should pat my head or smile or something before you go. You look as if this was a highly unpleasant conversation."

He hesitates for several beats before leaning toward me, and I catch the barest hint of a soft, fresh mint scent clinging to him. I expect him to pat my head as I suggested, so my soul almost leaves my body when his lips brush ever so lightly against my forehead.

They're cool to the touch as if he was just out in the wintry wonderland and hasn't had time to warm up.

Then he leaves quickly.

It takes me a moment to unfreeze from my spot, and I just barely resist reaching up to scrub the place where his lips touched my skin. Baelfire is at my table in the next second, dipping down to try to read my expression with furrowed brows.

"Did he ask for permission to touch you, or do I need to hunt him down and beat the frozen shit out of him?"

Acting perfectly unfazed, I shrug. "He's the only one who doesn't need to ask for permission. Out of all of you idiots, he's my favorite. Excuse me."

I make my way out of the dining hall, taking the quickest route that will spit me out into one of the main hallways of the eastern wing of Everbound. Baelfire doesn't follow me yet—he's telling Silas what I just said, and I can hear them arguing in hushed tones. Hopefully, that means they'll be at each other's throats soon.

Ignoring some of the legacies who are openly sizing me up as I leave the dining hall, I turn the first corner I come across. This massive corridor is empty except for three girls walking in my direction. I swap to the other side of the hall to get out of their way—but they swap, too, looking right at me as they approach.

I recognize two of them as the high-ranked legacies Kenzie warned me to avoid on my first day here—the redhead's name is Sierra, and the tall, dark-skinned girl with the nose ring is Harlow.

I'm unfamiliar with the angry girl in the middle, but she would be stunning if she weren't wearing such a nasty expression. Her dark skin and eyes are a stark contrast to the silvery-white streaks running through her black hair. If I had to make an educated guess, I'd say she's another highly-ranked, overly competitive legacy who Kenzie would warn me not to get on the radar of.

They stop directly in front of me, all leering.

Guess I'm on their radar.

"So you're Maven Oakley?" Angry Girl snaps, looking over me with hatred practically glowing in her eyes. "I can't believe he was matched to *this*."

I open my mouth, ready to tell them I don't even care which of my matches she's referring to because they're not *my* matches anymore since I rejected them. But I pause, realizing this is an opportunity that shouldn't be wasted. I'm trying to play head games to get those guys to hate me, and here are three pissed-off, jealous girls.

All I need to do is piss them off even more.

Child's play.

I tip my head. "Problem, ladies?"

Sierra scoffs. "Yeah. *You're* the problem. Take a look at yourself. Gods, you just got matched with the hottest fucking legacies in existence, and you're still dressing like *that?*"

"I didn't know my worth as a keeper was determined by my wardrobe."

Angry Girl pipes up, glowering at me. "No, it's determined by how useful you are—and you're *not*. We did some digging, and we know what you are. I can't believe that four of the most powerful legacies in the world got matched with a weak, germaphobic little asscaster."

Germaphobic?

Oh. She must think that because of the gloves.

"You're nowhere near their caliber—and you'll just get yourself killed trying to pretend otherwise," Angry Girl emphasizes as if she wouldn't gleefully kill me herself this second but for the danger of getting caught by the faculty, who would cut her ranking down as punishment. "Legacies like you are destined for administrative support and shit like that—far away from anything remotely dangerous. Far away from your quintet since everyone knows they're destined for great things. Far greater than *you*."

Sierra lifts her chin. "And forget about having anything but a platonic work relationship with them. Think you have what it takes to hold their interest? You're wrong. And you can take my word for it because I fucked Baelfire *and* Silas Crane this semester. I know what they're into, and you're not it."

There's a weird clench in my throat that I actively choose to ignore. Meanwhile, Harlow glances at the redhead, resentment flashing across her face. Clearly, they have a catfight on the horizon.

But I'm over this conversation. It's time to wrap it up, bait them, and move on.

Sierra is the easiest target.

"And you think *you* are what they're into?" I look her in the eye.

She sneers and steps forward, getting far too into my personal bubble but I hold my ground.

"Yeah. I am. Because they might've been matched to you, but you will never be enough for them. You'll always be the asscasting little bitch they have no choice but to come home to—they might even fuck you once or twice out of pity. But make no mistake, they're not yours. Virile legacies like them will always crave someone who can satisfy them—someone like *me*. Now that they're facing the bleak prospect of *you* for the rest of their lives, I could have any of them with a bat of my eye."

An emotion I've never experienced before wells in my gut, but I push it out of mind and lift my chin.

"Prove it. Steal them from me."

For a moment, I think she's debating attacking me right here in this hall, but Angry Girl cuts in with, "We will," and marches past me, fuming. The other two follow after Sierra spits on one of my black boots.

A real charmer, that one.

I take a deep breath and try to relax my gloved hands, which I realize clenched up without my notice. There. If this situation were a chess game, I've just sent three pawns to stir up trouble with the quintet. That should do some damage.

For a moment, I consider how each of my so-called quintet members would react to someone like her trying to seduce them. I barely know them, but I've seen a small snapshot of their personalities, and I've heard plenty of rumors, some of which I'm now sure are true.

Silas is intense. Merciless. He hooks up with girls sometimes, but they say he'd just as easily slit their throat if he thought they posed a threat to him. Still, he might go for her.

Everett won't. Everyone knows Professor Frost ignores women

completely, especially university students. He equally ignores the advances of men, ruling out any whispers about him being gay. He's basically an icy, rich, off-limits sex icon educator who would probably freeze Sierra without a second of remorse if she bothered him.

Crypt is...Crypt. I doubt anyone knows what the Nightmare Prince's sex life is like, but he's far from predictable. He strikes me as someone who acts purely on impulse, meaning seduction will probably be effective where he's concerned.

And Baelfire has a reputation for having a sky-high sex drive, even compared to others in his House. He's hot-blooded, which makes sense. Shifters are said to experience emotions far stronger than others. When they're sad, they're inconsolable. When they're angry, they're murderous.

And when they're a horny, cocksure dragon who has been sexually frustrated by a mate who rejected him…

It all comes down to animal instincts.

He's the most likely to sleep with her.

I try to smile smugly to myself since that was precisely my goal here. After all, the sooner they fuck up, the easier it will be to destroy any hope of our quintet getting along. I should be thrilled.

But strangely enough, my breathing feels tight as I continue down the hall. Emotions threaten to surface, but all it takes is repeating my mantra and remembering *why* I'm here.

"I am nothing but deadly calm," I whisper to myself. "I feel nothing."

As if the universe decides now is the perfect time to mock me, I freeze in place when I definitely feel *something*. Familiar pain blooms in the center of my chest, and I stumble to lean against the wall with a ragged gasp. The edges of my vision blur.

Fuck. I can *not* be found like this.

I already know Silas, Bael, and possibly Crypt might find me any moment since they've been following me all day. I'm too far from my room to make it in time, so I duck into the nearest women's bathroom, trying desperately to pull air into my failing lungs.

The pain is spreading like wildfire now, agony like cold needles prying every vein open on the way down my torso and arms. I barely manage to make it into a bathroom stall and lock it before my world caves in on itself. I'm so far gone that I don't feel my head smack the stone floor, but I know it's hard enough to split me open somewhere.

That'll leave a fun, bloody mess for later.

10

CRYPT

OBSESSION IS FASCINATING.

I've never felt anything similar, but there's no mistaking it. Every moment without her in my sight makes my bones ache. She's in every thought, every pulse of my blood, and all my sick and twisted fantasies, which have had no end ever since I found her to star in them.

After feeling nothing for so long, this fixation is suffocating.

Addicting.

I'd forgotten how heady emotions can be.

So when I return to the eating hall from an unavoidable errand, still unseen in Limbo, and find not even a trace of Maven Oakley's aura remaining here for me to follow, I'm taken aback by the slew of unmoored panic that floods my system. I don't realize I've unleashed mania on the nearest students until I notice a couple of shifters are trying to rip each other's throats out while their friends hold them back.

As entertaining as it would be to watch, I kick off the ground and leave the eating hall, intent on finding Maven.

Being in Limbo is similar to laying in a pool looking up through the water's surface. Most of the time, I can hear and see the waking world, but it can sometimes be muffled and distorted. Here, I am unfettered by gravity, with free rein to drift and roam wherever I please, through walls or the thickest metal safes. Barring anywhere protected by a dreamcatcher, of course.

Most incubi can't stay in Limbo for longer than a handful of hours at a time, but my relationship with this unstable subconscious realm is *unique*. I spend most of my time here out of necessity, and to date, it hasn't driven me to madness.

More madness, rather.

After far too long of drifting through classroom walls and castle halls, gritting my teeth at the absolute lack of Maven anywhere, I realize I'm a fool. All I need to do is track down the auras of the others, and they'll lead me to Maven. After all, they wouldn't be so thickheaded as to leave our precious keeper without any protection.

It's easy enough to track Crane down. He's always had a singularly *crimson* aura, but when I follow his trail, he's in the interim headmaster's office, reading through a file with a frown. The interim headmaster happily gabs at him even though it's clear the blood fae is only interested in whatever the papers in his hands say.

If it's anything relevant—meaning about Maven—then I'll hear about it at some juncture. I'm far more concerned about getting her back in my sights.

I come across Frost's soft blue aura as I drift through a nearby hall, but I don't bother following it. Whatever crock of shit she's trying to sell about him being her *favorite*, it's not like she'd be spending time with that reticent sap.

Finally, I find myself in the hallway leading to Maven's dorm room after following Decimus's obnoxiously bright aura. He's standing outside her door, clearly debating knocking. She must be there, ignoring him in all her adorably stubborn glory.

I let my feet settle on the ground, attention pinned on the door as I wait for her to come out.

A few minutes pass before we both snap to attention when someone else walks into the hallway. But my eagerness to see Maven's face turns to ash when it's just a redhead whose attention is laser-focused on Decimus. Her aura is a sickly piss yellow.

"Well, hello, Baelfire," she purrs, sashaying up to the agitated dragon. "Lucky me, running into you here."

Her intentions toward him couldn't be more obvious from where I'm standing, but I find myself curious to see how my quintet member will respond when he thinks no one is watching. I'm always intrigued when people show their true colors—and although I've sometimes observed Decimus, Crane, and Frost over the years without their knowing, I've rarely cared much about the outcome of their choices.

But now, their choices affect Maven. Anything that affects her interests me.

"Hey, Sierra," he grunts but doesn't look away from Maven's door.

"Gods, what a wild past couple of days, huh? I can't believe the Seeking is already over. Feels like we were talking about it while laying in your bed just yesterday," she says in a sultry tone, eye fucking Decimus and moving closer. "Hard to believe that was three weeks ago. I haven't seen you much since then. In fact, I'm starting to feel used and neglected in this relationship."

At first, I'm sure Decimus will showcase his typical charm and smooth things over with her. But his inner dragon must be in a particularly shitty mood today because instead, he shoots her a warning look.

"The hell are you talking about? We hooked up once, and you fucked my friend Grayson the morning after, right after you set my room on fire and claimed it was from me getting *overly passionate*. And from what I've heard, you've been getting plenty of attention from unmatched legacies. So cut the manipulation shit and scram."

I grin to myself at the way her jaw drops in outrage. She looks both insulted and out of her depth. If Decimus wasn't insufferably egotistical most of the time, he might have earned a smidge of my respect with how efficiently he called her out.

Sierra recovers and brushes off his words, stepping even closer to him. "It's true, we were never exclusive, but that's because we wanted to see what would happen at the Seeking. And now that we know…"

She lifts onto her tiptoes, throws her arms around his neck, and plasters her mouth over his.

A ferocious snarl rips out of Decimus as he shoves her away, his lips curled in disgust and fury.

"What the fuck do you think you're doing?"

She stammers, trying to save face as she reaches up to trace her fingers over his shoulders. "You seem pent up. Let me help."

"I'm mated," he snarls, batting her hands away. "Get lost."

It's a big deal for a shifter to declare himself mated. I applaud him in Limbo.

Sierra's eyes widen before she throws her head back in a laugh. "Yeah, right. You don't have a mating mark. Besides, there's no way you're actually mated to that frumpy, pathetic b—"

Before she can finish signing her death warrant with those words, I materialize and step forward, lowering my face to her level so she can see just how much she does not want to fuck with either of us right now.

"Choose your next words very carefully. Insulting our girl will end with your body found in a ditch." Then I smile thinly. "Or parts of it, at least."

The color drains from her face, and she makes a choking sound before scrambling out of the hall without another word to either of us. It's always entertaining to me how strongly people react based only on what they know of one's reputation.

Though I suppose in my case, my reputation is fairly accurate.

Decimus swears at me. "How long have you been following me, you creepy fuck?"

"Don't flatter yourself. I'm only here for her."

He scowls but turns back to Maven's door, calling through it. "Boo? My dragon is seriously about to break this damn door down to see if you're here or not. This is your last warning. Speak now or forever hold your peace."

Wait. Does he not know whether she's here?

Is our keeper missing?

I want to pass through her wall and check for myself, but the dreamcatchers would rip me apart. I can feel their burn even from where I'm standing. Damn that blood fae and his insistence that Maven keep her privacy.

Fuck privacy. I need to know where she is.

Which is why I reach out and touch Decimus's arm to send a jolt of my power through him. If he were asleep, it would flood him with all manner of disturbing parasomnia that would send him spiraling into mind-melting madness, trapping him in an inescapable nightmare. But for the waking, it's merely akin to an overdose of adrenaline.

It has the exact outcome I hoped for, with him unleashing a draconic snarl and smashing his shoulder through Maven's thick mahogany door.

Whatever protective magic wards she left on it apparently weren't very strong, which sours my mood further. I dislike the idea that anyone could've burst in on her as we just did. While Decimus is gripping his head, trying to clear out the lingering haze of mindless violence, I peek past him into the room.

My darling obsession isn't here.

Damn them all to hell.

The shifter whirls on me, teeth bared, and pupils shifted to a dragon's narrow slits as his rage boils up and he starts to lose control. He's always been terrible at controlling his inner beast.

"I'll fucking *kill* you, Crypt. If you ever use that shit on me again—"

"Where is she?" I cut in, utterly uninterested in hearing his slew of threats.

His attention snaps back to the problem at hand, and he growls again, breaking open the rest of her door to go inside and check more thoroughly. I'm left waiting in the hall, glaring at the edge of a dreamcatcher I can see just through the doorway. Certainly handmade by Crane. It reeks of blood magic.

When Decimus reemerges, he looks even less in control. "Go look for her in Limbo. *Now*."

I go toe to toe with him, only vaguely aware that my building anger is affecting the space around us. My light markings begin to glow, and he stiffens when our clothes and hair begin wafting as if gravity is glitching—a sign that I'm close to ripping a hole in Limbo. He's seen it once, and from the way he bites his tongue, he clearly doesn't want to experience that again.

"Tell me what to do one more time, dragon, and you'll wake up with a mind so twisted, you'll pray the gods put you out of your misery. I already searched for her aura and found nothing."

His fury swaps abruptly to something like panic. "Where the fuck would she have gone?"

Before I can strangle Decimus for letting the one and only person I have ever felt anything for out of his sight, we both hear the sound of footsteps echoing up the stairs at the end of this corridor. But just as before, it's not Maven approaching. It's her shifter friend with wild blond curls—the one with the fluffy pink aura like candy floss.

She spots us, and her eyes go wide. "Oh, shit. Did you guys just…break that door down?"

"Kenzie." Decimus sounds slightly relieved as he sidesteps me to address her. "Please tell me you know where Maven is."

The lioness shifter hesitates, looking between us as her brow furrows. "Actually, I came looking for her, too. I wanted an update on, you know…" She gestures at us vaguely and then shrugs. "If she's not in her room, she might be at the eastern library or one of the greenhouses. And I know she sometimes sneaks out to Everbound Forest when she thinks I'm not paying attention."

"Alone?" I grit.

The nearby forest is off-limits to humans, warded heavily by magic, and regularly stocked with dangerous creatures of all kinds—including shadow fiends that the Legacy Council sends here from the Divide. They are for real-world practice during combat classes, but plenty of students have been found ripped to shreds or never found at all after coming across fiends.

Kenzie shuffles, not meeting my eyes as she swallows hard. It's a typical reaction. Most people, even legacies, are frightened when my markings start to glow. On instinct, they know it's a bad sign without knowing why.

Instead of facing me, she glances back at Decimus with an apologetic wince. "I'm not sure. Have you guys tried calling her?"

"Fuck. I haven't even gotten her number yet," he huffs.

She cracks the tiniest smile. "Well, that doesn't surprise me. She's so fucking weird about phones and technology—not to mention she probably doesn't want you guys blowing up her phone whenever she needs space…" She trails off and looks pointedly at the door. "Speaking of which, she'll legitimately be pissed off if she sees this. Did you guys snoop through her stuff?"

Would that I could. Just as I've never felt obsession before, I've never experienced burning curiosity like this. But ever since seeing my darling standing on the Seeking stage, her dark eyes boring into mine without even a hint of flinching…

Not to mention her aura.

I've never seen an aura like hers. What I told her was no lie. I'm dying to know what her dreams taste like.

"My dragon is ready to hunt Maven down and barbecue anyone in his path. Do you really think I'm about to stop and rummage through her panty drawer?" Decimus scoffs. Then he pauses, clearly considering the idea as he glances back into her room. "On second thought, do you know where she keeps her panties?"

Kenzie laughs and shoos him away from the door, wisely refraining from doing the same thing to me. "Okay, look. I know newly matched legacies are all protective when it comes to their keepers, but you can both calm your tits because I'm sure Maven is perfectly fine."

"Are you?" I challenge, allowing my lips to curl up in a dangerous smile. "Because my keeper is undoubtedly the top target of countless legacies at this school who won't wait for the kill ban to lift before making attempts on her life to try to raise their chances of ranking above our quintet."

This shouldn't be news to anyone. It's common sense that highly competitive legacies will try to wreck other quintets by targeting quintet leaders. But Decimus clearly hadn't put together how much danger Maven is in because he goes stock still and shuts his eyes, breathing in and out at a measured pace. He used to do the same thing when we were younger in an attempt to remain in control of the dragon lurking under his skin.

The blood drains from Kenzie's face, and she wrings her hands. "Shit. You're right. Um…okay, when was the last time you saw her?"

"Forty minutes ago. At lunch." Decimus begins pacing.

"Oh! That's not that long. You made it sound like she's been missing for hours. Maybe you guys are overreacting—" Kenzie cuts off when she makes eye contact with me again and gulps, taking a step back at whatever she sees on my face. "Er, n—nope. Totally proportionate reaction. I completely agree. All right, I'm going to go look for her, too, so just…don't break down any more doors. Okay?"

No promises.

The longer I go without knowing whether my dark little obsession is safe, the more unhinged I feel myself becoming. Without waiting for another word from either of them, I step back into Limbo and kick off into the air, intent on scouring all of Everbound Forest for traces of Maven.

11

MAVEN

I DON'T KNOW how much time passes before I'm brutally wrenched back to the cold bathroom floor, choking back a sob. The side of my face is sticky with cold blood. So is the hair plastered against my cheek.

Trying to keep my groan to a minimum in case someone else is in this bathroom, I sit up and grimace at the amount of dark blood pooled around me. That's certainly enough to kill a normal person. When I reach up, my head is tender—but the wound is gone.

I suppose that's the one perk to my *condition*.

Unfortunately, my face, hair, and clothes are all stained with blood. If I pass any vampires on the way back to my dorm, they'll think I'm advertising a free snack. I glance around the stall helplessly, but there's not much I could use for cleanup. No ingredients for a cleaning spell. And to be honest, I'm shit at those, anyway.

Well. I suppose there's one way I could spin this.

Pulling my cell phone from one of the hidden pockets in my baggy sweatshirt, I wrestle with the damn thing until I manage to shoot a text to Kenzie.

> Help. Period came early. I look like I lost a fight with my uterus.

She responds immediately.

> OMG I was worried sick. Uteruses are such bitches. Where are you? I gotchu.

For the first time ever, I thank the universe for modern technology. Then I quickly send her which bathroom I'm in before cleaning up as much blood as possible. No one else is in the bathroom, so I slink out of my stall to wash up—but it's still all over my clothes. I use up all of the paper towel dispenser rolls, mopping up the mess.

Luckily, by the time Kenzie sweeps into the bathroom in a glittering purple halter top and a miniskirt that shows of her long legs, I've made it look like this was all just a horrible period.

"Poor thing, are you okay? What happened to your pretty olive tones? You look so damn pale! No offense. Do you need painkillers? I brought extra clothes and pads and shit, but I should've thought of painkillers!" She smacks her forehead.

"You're enough of a lifesaver as it is," I insist, thanking her for the big purse she hands me that's full of some of my most oversized, comfy clothes and anything else I could need. Of course, I can't tell her that my pallor is because I just lost a *lot* of blood.

By the time I've changed and reemerged, looking no worse for wear, Kenzie is chattering as she sits on the bathroom counter, picking off her manicure and swinging her long legs.

"—and so I made a list of pros and cons for all of my quintet's emphasis options. I mean, *I* would love to do something like covert operations or even the holy guard just because it would keep us away from the Divide, but we'd still be decently ranked in those careers—but I know Dirk would love to be stationed at a more challenging active combat location. Vivienne is okay with anything as long as we don't have to wake up too early, wherever we end up."

She pauses her chatter to look me over and smiles. "Ta-da! You look good as new. You're still way paler than I've ever seen you, though. Do you have skin like mine that goes pale in the wintertime? Maybe after graduation next semester, we should all take a trip somewhere warm! Get some sun. I'm thinking Bermuda. I'd *love* a beach vacation with my matches. Speaking of matches…your guys were *freaking out* when they couldn't find you."

I pause in stuffing my blood-soaked clothes into the bag and frown at her. "Firstly, they're not my guys. Secondly, did they bother you?"

"They didn't threaten me, if that's what you mean. Although the Nightmare Prince looked like he was debating ripping my head off a few times." She does a full-body shudder and shakes her head. "Gods. I still cannot believe you're going to have your heart bound to his. I mean, a lot of people say that legacy doesn't even have a heart."

A sharp laugh escapes me before I can help it, but I quickly clear my throat. "It's a moot point because I'm not getting bound to any of them, remember?"

She quirks a brow. "Oh, yeah? How many of them have you fucked so far? And be honest! I'm dying for deets. As possessive as your matches are, you've got to be having some *hot* sex."

"No dice."

Kenzie boos loudly, hopping off the counter and stretching to pop her spine. "Okay, fine, you gloomy, stubborn monk. But still, I wanna hear about everything." Then she frowns and throws a glance at the door. "Although…not sure now is the right time for a catchup sesh. I'm pretty sure Baelfire is about to burn this place to the ground, and if the rest of your quintet is as worked up looking for you, I doubt the "ladies only" sign will keep them out of here."

A couple of weeks ago, I never would have thought I'd say this, but now I face Kenzie and sling the bag over my shoulder. "How about a girl's night out in Halfton? I could use a break from my not-a-quintet."

Kenzie's brow jumps up. "Uh…they were really worried about you, Maven. And it's true that you're a target, so shouldn't you at least reassure them that you're okay so they don't needlessly worry? They'll probably be pissed if you just ghost them."

"Even better."

Understanding dawns on her face, and she blows out a big

breath. "Damn. You're, like...*really* trying to get rid of your quintet, huh?"

"Yes." As soon as fucking possible.

She snorts. "Then this is going to be even more entertaining to watch than I imagined because there's no way a bunch of scary, possessive alpha-type legacies will let their keeper go."

They'll have to.

"Enough boy talk. Halfton or no?"

Kenzie mulls it over for another second, throwing another hesitant look at the door.

I want to go to Halfton tonight not only to get rid of my matches but also to take my mind off the lingering ache in my chest from my most recent *episode*. Plus, if I'm candid with myself, I've grown accustomed to hanging out with Kenzie. I may have even...*missed* her over the last couple of days since the Seeking.

I'm not above bribery, so I add, "Dinner is on me."

"You drive a hard bargain, May," she grins, grabbing my velvet-gloved hand. She's a true diamond for bringing me another pair of gloves. "Sure! Let's go. I'll let my matches know I'll be back later. But forget about dinner—let's stop at the Witch's Brew while we're there. I want to say hi to Jackie."

Leaving Everbound University without running into any of my matches is relatively simple since the castle is a veritable maze complete with servants' entrances and exits from hundreds of years ago. According to my History of Monsterkind professor, Everbound Castle was built as a stronghold not long after humans began colonizing New England. They'd fled Europe to escape the bloody warfare of the monsters overrunning that continent and tried to establish a humans-only society here in America...which didn't go according to plan since the monsters followed.

But after the gods put the Legacy Curse in place and forced legacies to protect humans from the Nether, the castle was abandoned until the Immortal Quintet turned it into the mandatory finishing school for anything that goes bump in the night.

Leaving through one of the servants' exits, we make our way

down the path that leads to a small parking area, where Kenzie's old baby blue Mustang is parked.

She once told me it was a gift from her first sugar daddy. Apparently, she's had a few of those.

Halfton is a thirty-minute drive away. It's a nosy small town, the kind that could either be the setting of a saccharine holiday movie about two awkward humans falling in love or a horrifying murder mystery novel. It has two or three ma and pa restaurants, a handful of bars, five stop lights, one mall Kenzie calls the Pit of Fashion Despair, and one adorable little coffee house called the Witch's Brew whose owner, Jackie, is married to a legacy.

Jackie is one of the few humans in Halfton who enjoys their proximity to Everbound University. From what I've observed, the others are either lukewarm or downright annoyed about it, as if it hasn't been here for a few centuries longer than they've been alive.

When we step into the coffee house, Jackie looks up and smiles from where she's carefully aligning cake pops in a display case. "Come on in, you two! Kenzie, I just pulled a batch of those pumpkin spice cookies you love out of the oven."

I don't know how Jackie remembers specific names since plenty of legacies come to the Witch's Brew so often. She rounds the counter, and I watch as she settles her hands on her *very* pregnant belly.

"Yikes. You haven't popped yet?"

Kenzie shoots me a wide-eyed *shut up* look, but Jackie just laughs.

"Nope. This is what I get for marrying a sexy-ass wolf shifter. You know his kind is big on the whole breeding kink thing, right? Sometimes, we get a *little* carried away. Goodness. Last time, it was twins. This time, it's triplets. But I couldn't be more excited," she sighs happily.

Twins *and* triplets?

I think my womb just flinched a little.

Meanwhile, Kenzie oohs and aahs and asks what names they're considering as we each get a cup of hot chocolate and a pumpkin spice cookie. Jackie gets a call and excuses herself, leaving us alone in our favorite corner booth.

Well, it's *Kenzie's* favorite booth. She's been coming here far longer than I have since I've only been to Halfton a handful of times since arriving two weeks ago.

"It's sad that so many people consider legacy-human relationships taboo," Kenzie sighs. "I think they're so freaking adorable. Anyway, spill. I want to hear all about your schemes."

There's not much to tell, but I give her a quick recap about failing to bore Silas and my gambit to make them all turn on each other by making them jealous of Everett. I leave out the bit about the three girls confronting me since she doesn't need to know I'm officially on their radar.

When I finish, she nods thoughtfully, eyes straying to the storefront window behind me. "And you think that playing head games will make them start to hate you?"

"Yes."

"Pfft. Somehow, I seriously doubt that. Just accept it, May—they're obsessed with you."

I set down my mug. "No. They're obsessed with the idea of me. They want a keeper to break their curses. Who I actually am is of little interest to them."

Not to mention, if they knew the truth about me, they might kill me.

She smiles evilly and finally pulls her gaze away from the window to wag her brows at me. "Little interest, huh? Well, I'm pretty sure they actually want *you*, or else they wouldn't have stalked you all the way here."

I stare at Kenzie in confusion for a moment before she flicks a look over my shoulder. Sure enough, behind me and through the glass of the bakery windows, I spot Silas striding through the town square, looking absolutely lethal—not to mention out of place in such a human environment, with his blood-red eyes and sinfully sharp good looks. Humans around here are accustomed to seeing legacies, but they all dart out of his path like he's a shark among fish.

Even through the glass, I can hear the roar of a dragon in the distance. Which means Baelfire isn't far behind.

Hopefully, they're pissed enough that they'll finally understand they don't want me.

I'm so distracted with frowning out the window that when Kenzie shrieks, I jolt in surprise, turning quickly to find—

The Nightmare Prince is barely an inch away from my face, seated directly beside me. I've never been this close to him before, and I swallow, trying to ignore the alluring scent of leather and something intoxicatingly sweet, like a plant I can't identify.

"Sorry," Kenzie says quickly, grimacing. "He just popped out of nowhere. Scared me into spilling my hot chocolate everywhere. I'll be right back...plus it seems like you might need to have a little chat with your quintet," she adds sheepishly, shooting me an apologetic smile as she hurries away to slip into the bathroom.

Crypt studies me, and I try to ignore his gaze lingering on my lips and the way it makes my thighs clench without my permission.

"Where were you?"

His voice is a harsh rasp, surprisingly...emotional? That can't be right.

"Odd that you don't know since you're stalking me from Limbo."

But thank the fucking gods that he didn't witness my little incident earlier. I need to avoid him witnessing anything like that at all costs.

"Answer me, darling."

The bell jingles. I glance over, expecting Silas, but I'm surprised to see Baelfire striding into the Witch's Brew along with him. The shifter sure caught up fast, and he barely spares the rest of the bakery a passing glance before locking eyes with me and visibly relaxing.

As they approach, I can't escape Silas's intent ruby gaze. He scans me a little too possessively—and then he abruptly halts in place just as he reaches the table. He inhales deeply before swearing viciously.

"I'll ask this only once. Why the hell do you smell like blood?"

The other two tense, and Baelfire also tests the air and snarls.

Thanks to his obnoxiously sizable muscular frame, he barely fits into Kenzie's side of the booth, and then he demands, "Are you hurt? Where? And more importantly, who am I turning to fucking ashes tonight?"

Gods. They're acting like I'm made out of glass. How laughable.

But I'm not about to correct them. It's better that they think I'm weak and helpless. They won't want to hang on to a weak keeper, and the more people underestimate me, the more opportunities I'll have to do what I came here for.

So, I take the easy way out and lie without blinking. "Menstruation hardly warrants such extreme reactions."

Silas frowns, skepticism coloring his tone. "I didn't scent your period at lunch."

Ew. Blood fae are so fucking weird. "Aunt Flow popped in as an unpleasant visitor shortly thereafter."

Crypt vanishes from my other side without a word. I take it he isn't the type to ever say where he's going or coming from. Some of the tension slips away from Baelfire's shoulders, and finally, his mouth pulls into a crooked grin.

"I hear heat helps with cramping. So does sex. I'm more than happy to help."

I roll my eyes. "How noble of you."

"We just want to help you, Boo. That's it. Until you ask nicely for more," he adds, easily slipping back into his flirtatious charm now that he's not worked up over my safety.

Silas pulls a chair up to the end of the booth and looks over me carefully as if he's searching for any sign that I'm lying about not getting hurt. I guess fae always have to wonder if other people are lying since they don't have that ability.

His attention lingers on my hair, where it was matted with blood earlier, and I don't miss the way his tongue rolls over his lower lip—just once, slowly.

Right. *Blood* fae.

But before he can call me out, Kenzie returns from the bathroom and slides in beside me, flicking her gaze between the two intimidatingly strong legacies. Even though she's modestly ranked among the grad students at Everbound, she's known Baelfire for a while—but it's evident by the way she gawks at Silas that she doesn't know how to make small talk with the Garnet Wizard's apprentice.

Baelfire seems to catch on to her hesitation and snags a broken piece of cookie from my plate, popping it into his mouth. "Don't let us interrupt your girl talk. Just had to check on my mate after she went MIA."

That does the trick.

"Oh my gods! You already call her your *mate?* That is so fucking cute," Kenzie croons, ignoring the daggers I'm hurling at her with my eyes.

"She *is* cute, isn't she? I keep telling her that myself," Bael teases, tossing me a smug grin. Then he perks up. "Hey. You're her friend. You probably know her favorite ice cream flavor, right? She wouldn't tell me what it is."

Kenzie tips her head. "Shit, maybe I'm a bad friend because I have no idea. What is it, May?"

I've never had ice cream.

But if I tell them that, they'll have follow-up questions. More questions about my past means more lies. And it's far easier to maintain a false identity with as few flourishes as possible.

I'm just here for my mission. Keeping things simple is best.

"Vanilla."

"There, see? That wasn't so hard," Baelfire grins triumphantly down at me. One of his hands lifts to adjust the hair that's fallen over my temple, but he checks himself at the last moment and pulls it back. "All right. What else does she like?"

This time, when I give her a meaningful look, Kenzie rolls her eyes and chooses to back me up. "You'll have to figure it out yourself, guys. I'm not a snitch." She lowers her voice to a stage whisper. "But a little birdie *did* tell me that she likes a certain sexy, rich, ex-model professor."

Helping to stir the pot? Not bad.

I fight a smile when Baelfire's amusement immediately drops

away, and Silas glares out the window. They say nothing, but I can take a wild guess as to what they're thinking. Legacies aren't human, but they have the same emotions. As much as legacies tote this idea of perfect groups who complete each other, there's no way that jealousy simply ceases to exist among quintets.

If I focus all my attention on Everett, it's just a matter of time before they all snap.

And the sooner they give up on me, the sooner I can focus on fulfilling my oath.

12

SILAS

I'M UNWELL.

That must be the only explanation because as I sit in my private dorm room preparing components of a tracking spell for my keeper, I can think of nothing else but the scent of her blood from earlier.

She lied to us. I'm sure of it. That scent was all over her, lingering in her hair, taunting me as she brushed off any concern about her safety.

But something happened to make her bleed.

Setting down a vial of banshee tears, I rub my face. Blood fae are not vampires. We aren't blessed with immortality or an array of heightened senses—except for the ability to perceive magic. We smell it, sense it, and crave the taste of it, which can only be found in magical bloodlines. Blood powers our magic, whether we drink it or infuse it into our spells. It's what makes us the most powerful class of the fae.

I've never actively *craved* the scent of someone's blood before.

But Maven's…

My mouth waters and I suddenly feel feverish. My damn erection won't go down.

Trying to refocus, I flip through the blood-stained grimoire on the table in front of me, my knee bouncing restlessly. The silence of my dorm stretches on, broken only by the grating ticking of the grandfather clock in the corner.

Tick. Tock. Tick. Tock.

My breathing feels wrong. Too shallow. I straighten to try to inhale fully, but that's when my eyes snag on the dark curtains covering my window. The way they're bunched sends my pulse pounding behind my eyes. The ringing in my ears muffles every other sound as I get to my feet, clutching my bleeding crystal in my hand so hard that it pierces my palm as I move toward the curtain.

Anyone could be in here. Watching. Laying in wait, the voices in my head whisper.

Logically, I know my dorm is the most secure place in Everbound. I went to exhausting lengths to ensure that before I enrolled. Thanks to my magic wards, no one but myself can be admitted into this room.

But right now, I'm not thinking straight. My curse hums in my veins, turning the air thick as sludge and stringing my muscles like a thread. My heart pounds painfully against my ribs.

Not safe, the voices chant. *Not safe. Not safe. Not safe—*

Finally, I rip the curtain down and glower at the nothingness left behind. No one lays in wait with a knife intended for my back. Still, I scan the rest of the room, pushing my fingers through my hair and trying to steady my rapid breathing.

It's getting worse. The end of next semester, when my quintet will be bound together to break our curses…it won't come fast enough. I wonder which is worse, losing your sanity without knowing or being fully aware as you slip away piece by piece, as I am now.

The sound of dripping draws my attention to my hand, and I finally loosen my hold on the crystal so it stops drawing my blood. After a shuddering breath, I make a split decision and tuck the crystal back into my pocket before leaving my dorm room.

It's late. Past midnight. The "student curfew" at Everbound is eleven o'clock, but not a soul here pays attention to it, not even the instructors. Still, the dim hall I walk is empty as I eye my surroundings, hands still trembling in my pockets.

It's just a shadow, Si, my mother's voice echoes, but this time, it's a memory, not a voice in my head. *That's what they'll tell you. They think it's silly to be afraid of the dark. But you and I both know that darkness is danger. After all, it's easier to kill when they don't see it coming.*

My father's voice is firm. *That's why we never turn out the lights in this house. We don't want to find out what our curse will drive us to do to each other in the dark.*

"There you are," Everett's voice cuts in, startling me.

I don't realize I've moved until he inhales sharply. I have him pinned to the wall by the neck, my bloodied crystal poised above his carotid artery, pressing into his skin enough that he doesn't even dare to swallow. Or rather, he can't because I've cut off his oxygen. To his credit, he doesn't overreact or struggle.

When Baelfire speaks, I realize he's standing just beside us. "Silas. Relax."

They just turned the corner and took me by surprise. Odd that they were looking for me together since they've been on terrible terms for years.

Not odd. They're both waiting for the right moment to rip your heart out.

Everett makes a slight sound in his throat when my unsteady grip finally causes the crystal to prick his neck. When it does, frost blooms across his skin, traveling to coat my hand and seal his injury before it even has the chance to bleed. A small flurry starts in the hallway, a subtle warning that he's not as calm as he's acting.

"I don't think Maven wants you choking the life out of her so-called *favorite*. Even if I do understand the sentiment behind it," Bael grumbles.

Maven.

Right. I was coming to find her.

Gradually regaining control, I drop Everett and step back, warming my frozen hand in my pocket as Baelfire raises a brow.

"Judge all you like. Your curse comes with a balm to bear it easier. Mine has no such thing."

Everett inhales several gulps of air and brushes himself off, shooting me a nasty look. "Dick."

"You know better than to take me by surprise."

Bael grunts in agreement but gestures at me. "We were going to finalize our wagers, but you look like shit. Maybe you need to take a beat."

He shouldn't say things like that out here in the open. Someone might overhear that I'm vulnerable. Instead of pointing that out, I lead them to a hallway that branches off the nearby library. I know voices don't carry here, and this hall is often forgotten. Pricking my finger to lay a cloaking spell, I turn to face the two of them.

But I don't let go of the crystal. If ever they were looking for a time to get me alone and finish me off, this would be it. They know I'm off balance right now, but that doesn't make me less dangerous in a fight. Quite the opposite.

"I'm joining the wager," Everett finally says.

Baelfire rolls his eyes. "No shit. I figured you would since my mate has taken an inexplicable liking to you. What'd you even say to her earlier, at lunch?"

"Wouldn't you like to know? Anyway, it seems she's already picked me first."

I shake my head. "Not officially. This competition needs a clearer finishing line."

"Fine. We'll say whoever fucks her first wins."

Baelfire's snarl is fierce. "I swear on all six gods, if you try to pressure Maven into sleeping with you, I'm going to fucking—"

"Ever the hypocrite," I interrupt. "You've been panting after her like a bitch in heat. If anyone is going to push her limits before she's ready, it will be you. And if that happens, you'll be answering to me."

Bael's eyes connect with mine, and the feral edge of violence in them makes it clear he's just as ready for a fight as I am right now. Perhaps he needs to go hunting again.

"I'd sooner cut off my dragon's wings than upset Maven. We should be more concerned about Crypt crossing her lines about physical touch before we even know why she has them there. Who's to say he won't manipulate her dreams to make her do shit that she'll wake up horrified about?"

As if on cue, the Nightmare Prince appears beside us. Everett flinches back as the room chills, and I swear viciously—*this* is precisely why I need to break my curse. Usually, my magic would be far more potent, and I would have known he was within my magic wards, even in Limbo.

"Fucking *creep*," Bael balls his hands into fists.

The incubus casually boosts himself up to sit on a large decorative antique console table, which I'm fairly sure is older than his immortal father. He yawns.

"You didn't expect me to miss our little pow-wow, did you? If it concerns Maven, it concerns me."

"Yeah, right," Everett scoffs, adjusting his tie. "Not a single thing has ever concerned you. You're incapable of feeling anything remotely like an emotion, which is exactly why you're a well-documented psychopath."

"That has been my lot in life," Crypt agrees breezily. "It's been quite boring. Until now. Our little keeper is far from boring. Just look what she's done already, bringing us together to speak like civilized monsters in the dark of the night. One would almost think our past slights were all water under the bridge," he smirks at me.

Past slights.

An insultingly mild term for what he did to my family.

"Whatever you say, freak. Moving on to final bets," Bael folds his arms, glancing between us. "Frost, I still want that land. And from Silas, I'll take a custom spell of my choosing whenever I ask for it. Crypt, I'd want you to make a godsdamned blood oath to stay the fuck out of my head for the rest of my life."

Blood oaths are utterly powerful—said to transcend lifetimes and even the five planes of existence. Virtually unbreakable, it would ensure even a deviant like Crypt would have to abide by the magical contract.

"There you go, flattering yourself again," Crypt muses. "There's nothing interesting in your subconscious anyway. Silas's is far more entertaining."

My fists clench. I'm perfectly aware that he's just needling me. He's never been in my subconscious. But everyone present knows that his just suggesting the idea is going to have me paranoid out of my mind for weeks.

Everett leans against the wall, tucking his hands in his pockets. "I haven't decided what prizes I'll claim, but expect them to take a toll."

I nod. "I still want the scales. And from the Frost estate, I'll want free rein to browse your family's ledgers and past records."

Everett scowls at this, which doesn't surprise me. Thanks to the Decimus family, the Frosts have been exposed for many illegal activities over the years.

I turn my glare to Crypt. If my nerves were chalkboard, he'd be the jagged nails scraping across every square inch of it.

He grins. "Go on. We all know I have nothing of value."

"If I win, I get to enter your subconscious."

Baelfire whistles low. For once, the arrogant amusement on the Nightmare Prince's face drops away. The other two look between us, as curious as I am if this will drive Crypt to showcase his least enjoyable character trait—unpredictability. It's impossible to tell when he'll snap, going from zero to a hundred in the blink of an eye, but we've all seen it at one time or another.

Which is why I want to see inside his head. For incubi, letting someone else into their subconscious is incredibly rare, usually only done with a spouse or their chosen muse. Someone they trust completely.

But if I can figure out what makes him tick, perhaps I won't end up losing my temper and killing him after we're all bonded and capable of telepathic communication. Particularly powerful quintets can experience one another's thoughts, feelings, desires, and so on. Unless I find a new way to deal with Crypt in his subconscious, I'll end up killing him if I have to share any amount of headspace with him.

I'd like to spare Maven that unpleasantry.

Instead of responding to the severity of my wager, Crypt looks out the window of this moonlit hallway as he pulls out a cigarette and a lighter, the brief flash of flame fading before he takes a long drag and exhales a puff of smoke. The sickly sweet scent of it tells me it isn't a regular cigarette—and I frown when I can't identify what it is he's smoking. I know every type of tobacco, herb, and plant under the sun, so what could it be?

"Odd that Maven arrived so late in the semester, isn't it?"

Quite the topic change.

"Maven is an atypical caster," I explain, having read her sparse file of student records earlier. "She manifested magic from a fully human bloodline less than a month ago."

Everett's pale gaze flickers to me. "You're saying Maven came from a human family?"

"Yes. Why?"

He shuffles uncomfortably. "It's nothing."

"Just spit it out, Snowflake," Baelfire huffs.

"Fuck off, dragon," Everett mutters, just as irritated by the nickname as he was when we were children. "Fine. There's a rumor going around the faculty here that the legacy-human peace treaty is in peril. Supposedly, a political movement among humans advocating for war with our kind has been gaining momentum. They view legacies as monster spawn that should be eradicated or sent back to the Nether. They seem to think that all the Nether wants is to get our kind back."

"There's always some tension between legacies and humans," I acknowledge.

"Well, it's gotten worse. To the point that all staff members and professors have been asked to look for anything suspicious among atypical casters or any other students who might sympathize with that political movement and cause trouble at Everbound."

"Define *suspicious*."

"Vague backgrounds. Antisocial behaviors. Inexplicable disappearances, open rejection of legacy traditions or culture, advocating for human ideologies among other grad students, open contempt for the Legacy Council or Immortal Quintet, and anything else out of place," Everett summarizes.

For a moment, that sinks in for all of us, and then Crypt hums thoughtfully.

"Come to think of it, Maven's background is something of a question."

Bael growls. "She's not a fucking sympathizer."

Crypt shrugs. "I wouldn't care if she was."

"You wouldn't care if Maven was a fanatic who thinks our kind is better off dead?" Everett asks, incredulous.

Instead of answering, the Nightmare Prince tips his head as if listening to something nearby. His intricate markings—which I can't ever remember him not having, even as children—begin to glow softly. It sets off my paranoia again, wondering if I've missed someone approaching.

But after a second, he hops off the table, steps on the butt of his cigarette to put it out on the marble floor, and announces, "Our reputations have drawn too much attention to our keeper. Some imbecile two floors away is dreaming about besting our quintet by getting his hands on Maven. I'm starving, and his psyche will make the perfect snack if I don't break his neck first."

For once, none of us has a single protest, and he drops into Limbo in the next second.

"Who even cares if the humans are getting antsy?" Bael huffs, getting back to the matter at hand. "They're mortals. We're legacies. I'm pretty sure we'd trump them if war broke out, which I doubt will happen anytime soon. So even if Maven *is* a sympathizer, which she isn't, there's no harm, no foul."

I don't reply, distracted as I consider whether Maven could really be part of the anti-legacy movement. Admittedly, she does fit some of the criteria for suspicious behavior.

"I've worked among humans more than the rest of you," Everett says, shaking his head. "Don't make the mistake of thinking they're harmless. They far outnumber legacies, and they're more resilient than our kind gives them credit for. They pose a real threat if things get worse."

"I'm more concerned about how little we know about our keeper than her political views," I decide. "Something is keeping her from accepting the quintet as a gift from the gods. I want to find out what that something is."

"And *I* want to know what's made her so damn wary of physical touch," Baelfire adds.

That catches my attention. "What do you mean?"

"The gloves. That little frown she makes whenever anyone gets too close—and I mean *anyone*, because I watched her with Kenzie earlier, and even her closest friend sitting too close made Maven uncomfortable. Don't tell me neither of you have noticed that our keeper avoids physical touch like it's the plague," he grits, looking between us.

I hadn't. But all the reasons my brain supplies for why she might be touch-averse make my fists clench.

"She didn't seem wary of me earlier," Everett drawls.

Baelfire scowls. "Yeah, well, enjoy her while you can, Snowflake. Because I'm going to charm my mate's socks—and hopefully panties—right off."

The professor rolls his eyes. "My competition is an egotistical manwhore of a dragon, a psychotic dream demon, and a pointy-eared bookworm with trust issues. Something tells me I'll be just fine."

They continue bickering, but I've had enough of this. I leave them and make my way to Maven's dorm room several halls over. But when my eyes lock onto her destroyed door, a wave of panic and paranoia capsizes any rational thought in my head.

It's just like earlier when Baelfire finally told me she was missing.

She's dead, a voice whispers in my head.

They got her. They destroyed her, and they're coming for you next.

You lost your keeper. You're stuck with us, another voice triumphs.

Nausea curdling my stomach, I rush to the opening, ready to step through the door and find Maven—

But I promptly step on a box of chocolates.

I scowl and pick up the crushed box. Someone must have left this out here for her.

"Just because there's no door doesn't excuse you from knocking."

Blinking, I realize Maven is watching me through the doorway with her poker face intact. She has a bag slung over her shoulder and shoes on, standing like she was just about to exit before I so gracefully squashed this gift that was clearly meant for her.

The sight of her melts the tension away from my temples and chest. The ringing is gone. The shadows are empty. I breathe again. Unfortunately, my godsdamned erection returns with a vengeance—even though she doesn't smell like blood anymore.

She must have showered.

Gods above, the thought of Maven in the shower is *not* helping with the painful pressure against the fly of my pants.

I clear my throat. "I was just..."

"Stalking me. At night."

"Yes," I admit with a sigh, unable to tell anything but the truth. But then I notice she's dressed in day clothes, about to leave her room well after midnight. That's...odd.

Some might even say suspicious.

"Were you going somewhere?"

"Not that it's your business, but yes."

"Where?" I pry anyway.

An anti-legacy sympathizer meeting, perhaps? voices whisper in the back of my mind.

She doesn't miss a beat, holding my eye contact with exasperation staining her voice. "In case you didn't notice, my door is in splinters because the assholes I rejected think they're entitled to break into my personal space when they don't know my whereabouts. You try sleeping in a dorm with a gaping hole for all passers-by's viewing pleasure."

The idea of sleeping where anyone could peek in sets off my paranoia—but the idea of them being able to watch Maven while she's in a vulnerable sleeping state?

Unacceptable.

"You'll sleep in our quintet apartment tonight."

"Hard pass."

She steps out around me, making her way down the hall, but I keep up easily. "*Pass?* Where else would you stay so late?"

"Kenzie offered a spare room in her apartment."

My keeper staying with another quintet? I don't care how much she trusts her shifter friend. The others might slit her throat in her sleep to get a head start on the quintet rankings next semester.

That thought has me reaching out to grip her arm before I can think better. "Absolutely fucking not."

Maven halts and faces me slowly, something flaring in her eyes that I haven't seen before. Something intoxicatingly dark and…unexpectedly dangerous. It's as if some level of her facade has slipped, and she's rearing her true personality for the first time.

When she looks pointedly at my hand on her sleeve, I slowly remove it. Baelfire was right. Touch is a trigger for her and yet another thing I need to understand.

"Let's get something straight, Crane. I give exactly zero fucks if you don't like where I rest my head. Whatever interrogation you have in mind to try to understand my motives for rejecting all of you, it will wait. This has been a shit day, and I'm exhausted."

She's not at all the reserved wallflower we all initially took her for.

But although her tone is savage and her glare could kill, something in my chest softens as I study her. I can tell she truly is tired. That's not a lie. I can't stand that she has no place to stay tonight because of those bastards' reactions to her earlier absence. I'll take care of her door myself.

She's right. It's late, and I should leave her be because the longer I stand here with her, the more I don't want to watch her walk away. I'm just procrastinating leaving her presence because I don't want to be sucked back into the void of paranoia that I've been existing in without her.

"Forgive me," I murmur. "Sleep well."

Maven walks away, leaving me with a budding feeling that I have no idea how to handle.

13

MAVEN

HEAVY, slow heartbeats echo in my ears until I jolt awake soaked in a cold sweat, shaking from the residual monsters clawing at my mind. When my magical alarm spell dissipates, I roll out of Kenzie's spare bed and catch myself on the floor in a plank position, inhaling deeply before dropping into my usual reps.

Push-ups, crunches, burpees, squats, lunges, tricep dips, mountain climbers…

The list goes on.

Repeat, repeat, repeat.

Finally, when the sun is just coming up outside, and my core and limbs are on fire, I drag myself to her quintet apartment's sizable shared bathroom, grateful for the icy-cold blast of water overhead that washes away all traces of the horrors that haunt my nights. A brutal workout routine first thing in the morning is the only thing I know to calm myself down after my nightmares. It helps that it's the same routine I grew up on.

Toweling off, I toss on more of my oversized clothes and return to the guest room, glancing at my phone charging on the nightstand.

Last night, I snuck out to a seedy bar in Halfton to track down the number of a supernatural black market dealer. I need to obtain nightshade root powder—a spell ingredient that is highly monitored by the Legacy Council due to it being a potent ingredient used in so many outlawed dark magic spells. All my digging and careful listening last night got me an encrypted number to call.

I'm just glad Silas didn't insist on escorting me to Kenzie's apartment, and it's a good thing Crypt must've been busy eating dreams all night. I didn't sense him the entire time.

But how the hell am I going to get away from my not-a-quintet long enough to call this black market dealer today? Not to mention, I can't allow them to witness me have an episode like the one I had yesterday. It's already a miracle that no one else, not even Kenzie, has witnessed that.

The sooner I break up the quintet and get them to appeal for a different keeper, the sooner I can complete my mission without so many eyes following me all the time. So today, to make them jealous, I'll have to flirt with a modelesque professor who also happens to be one of the wealthiest legacies alive.

Boo hoo, poor little me.

A muffled sound nearby makes me tense. I frown and listen harder.

"Yes, yes, yes…" a breathy voice chants. Someone grunts, and I hear something get knocked over before more panting ensues in the nearby room. Someone else moans.

Sounds like Kenzie's quintet is waking up, which is my cue to leave. I didn't mind crashing one night with them, but it's a good thing I've already sent a maintenance request to Everbound's dormitory management to get my door replaced as soon as fucking possible.

I tuck my phone in my back pocket, sliding on gloves from my overnight bag as I step out the door.

I'm not even surprised to see Baelfire waiting for me. You'd think that after I've given him nothing but brush-offs and purposefully let him spiral yesterday not knowing where I was, he would lose the enthusiasm—but no. Instead, his entire face lights up, gold eyes glittering as he falls into step next to me.

"You still owe me three questions, you know. I'm cashing in on them today."

"Before or after you apologize for destroying my door?"

He grins not at all apologetically. "Crypt's more to blame for that than I am. So. Three questions. Ready?"

Stop being so fucking persistent. I'm tempted to find you charming.

But I can't say that, so instead, I tell him, "Make them bland. They'll suit me better."

"Please. You're the furthest thing from bland, my sexy little Boo."

My neck feels unusually warm. Which is terrible timing because we've just passed into a large corridor full of legacies who keep sneaking glances at us. Bael is used to being high-profile, but I'm looking forward to being done with the shifting eyes and whispers that carry my name.

"Just ask your damn questions before we get to my combat course."

"All right. What was your family like?"

"Dead."

He winces. "I meant before they…you know."

"I don't remember. I was a baby when they passed." Which is a mild term for what happened to my parents, or so I've been told.

His voice is softer than I've ever heard it. "That's really shitty that you didn't even get to know them. Who raised you, then?"

I hesitate momentarily before deciding it's probably better to get this over with. "I was adopted by a strict man who wanted a family but never got the chance until he found me."

"Was he a good father to you, at least?"

Gods. I don't even know where to start with that question.

"There's far worse out there. He did his best. And now you're out of questions."

We're approaching the door that will let out to the training grounds. He slows and drops his voice to a whisper.

"Wait—one more. And please, please, *please* answer this one. Because I know it's invasive, intimate, and borderline rude to ask, but my inner dragon has been hell to put up with for the last couple of weeks since I first scented you, and I just need to know."

"Know what?"

Baelfire stops, prompting me to pause, too. He leans close until his lips nearly brush my ear. The heat from his body wraps around me, along with a pleasant musky scent like singed cedar wood.

"Are you a virgin?"

Why does his voice have to be so gravelly and sensual? Its raw hunger sends warmth tingling over my skin, settling low in my belly. Instinctively, I press my legs together in an attempt to keep Bael from scenting what he just did with his heightened shifter senses, but when I hear his soft groan, I know he can smell the arousal I'm trying to hide.

"Damn it, Maven, it'll be so embarrassing to walk out there with this raging boner," he rasps.

It's difficult to steady my voice. "Then go attend one of your classes."

"No. I want an answer. Do I get to be the first to worship and spoil the fuck out of your sweet pussy? Or do I get to put anyone who tried to please you in the past to absolute shame? I won't touch you until you tell me to, but I want to know how to fantasize about fucking you when I jack myself raw later. Gentle and sweet for a virgin or rough and hard for my mate?"

Oh gods.

I was not prepared for dirty talk first thing in the morning.

My pulse is pounding, and against everything I know I should say or do to push away Baelfire—because he is *absolutely* overstepping with this question—I dare to look up into the scorching intensity of his full, hungry focus. He's leaning down, so our faces are too close together. If I lifted on my tiptoes, our lips would brush. I'd be kissing someone for the first time in five years.

I'm supposed to be nothing but deadly calm. I'm supposed to feel nothing.

Because gods, if I let myself feel *this*, just for a moment…

Stop wanting him. You can't do this to them.

"Aren't you going to answer him, darling?" Crypt asks, materializing right beside us.

I'm ashamed to say I gasp and startle away, but at least Baelfire's string of obscenities mostly drowns it out as he whirls on the Nightmare Prince with a murderous expression.

"Get your own damn time with Maven," he snaps, muttering something about a cockblock.

"All my time is Maven time," Crypt says jovially, offering me a hand. I notice the tattoos circling his wrist curl inward to splay across his palm, a display of swirling symbols and stars that twist around each of his fingers, as well. "Did you enjoy the chocolates, darling?"

It takes a moment to register that he must have left the ones Silas stepped on. Did he do that because of the whole fake period thing? That's...

Whatever. At least he broke me out of what was almost a huge mistake. Composing myself, I brush past him and ignore Baelfire's protests as they both catch up with me. Unfortunately, I run into *another* one of my matches before I can even step outside.

Silas straightens from where he was leaning against the wall by the vaulted exit. His scarlet irises brush over every inch of me before hardening into a sharp, warning glare as he glances over my shoulder at the others.

"If they're bothering you, tell me. I'll cast a restraining curse to force them to keep their distance."

"Please try," Crypt says. I don't bother glancing over my shoulder to see his expression since I'm sure he'll have that same dark smirk that seems to get under Silas's skin.

I walk right past Silas, too.

Trailed by three legacies who couldn't define rejection if they had a dictionary shoved up their asses, I make my way to the back of a large cluster of legacies. The air is brisk today, flurries falling from the white sky in halfhearted gusts of wind that rustle the barren branches of nearby trees. We're in the farthest reaches of the training grounds today, at the edge of Everbound Forest, so it comes as no surprise when Coach Gallagher, the combat instructor, announces that today we'll be training in the woods.

"Think capture the flag, only today you will each have a flag for someone else to take. The normal restrictions and limits apply—no severe maiming. And don't forget that the no-killing policy is still in effect! Legacies caught killing will be punished accordingly, but minor broken bones, cuts, burns, and such is fair play."

I almost snort out loud. The no-kill ban at Everbound is always weak, but during combat training, most people ignore it completely. It's not like any of the homicidal monster spawn attending will get expelled from this very mandatory finishing school. Everyone here craves violence and competition. I wouldn't be surprised to see a corpse or two after the training exercises, especially now that everyone will be trying to weaken newly formed quintets.

"You'll all be sectioned into specific quarters of the forest to begin courtesy of a faculty member's spell, which is already set up, and the magic wards around the perimeter of Everbound Forest will keep you in there until the time is up. Keep an eye out since a pride of manticores was transferred into the woods from New Zealand a couple of days ago, and this is their hunting season. Whoever returns with the most flags will be awarded 20 points."

Legacies murmur to each other because that's a significant number of points—enough to move someone up the rankings a couple of spots. Everbound University doesn't use a standard grading scale. Instead, it's all about placing near the top of the class because that gives you and your quintet higher priority in choosing a career after graduation and the mandatory active assignment all legacies have. Quintet rankings don't start until next semester, but individual student ranks are factored into their groups.

The coach is still talking, but Bael leans toward me to whisper, "You can have my flag in exchange for the kiss I almost got back there."

"The only thing you almost got was busted dragon eggs."

He throws his head back to laugh heartily. I hate that his laughter is so contagious because keeping a straight face around them is already getting hard enough.

Silas is observing the forest to our right as if he's already planning the best strategy. "Take my flag for free."

They really must think I need all the help I can get. I'm not about to tell them how wrong they are since I *want* them to underestimate me, but it's a challenge to keep from rolling my eyes.

Crypt notices my expression. "Our keeper prefers to earn her own stripes. Isn't that right?"

It's annoying that he thinks he can read me. It's also annoying that he's right this time.

To distract myself, I sneak a peek at the other students here. I still don't know the names of most legacies in my classes since I've only been here for two weeks, and I rarely talk to anyone besides Kenzie, but the first person I make eye contact with several yards away is none other than Sierra. The redhead who said she would steal my quintet away. For whatever reason, she appears even more pissed off today, her savage glare flipping from me to the guys surrounding me and back. When she notices me looking, she sneers and flips me off.

What a treat she is. Guess I'll be seeing her in the woods.

Right beside Sierra is a new quintet, fully formed with five legacies from the Four Houses. They, too, have a female vampire keeper with four males. But the stark difference between their quintet's dynamic and mine is obvious as I watch a guy holding each of her hands, one pressed behind her whispering something in her ear that makes her laugh, and the fourth grinning at them all like a lovesick idiot.

They're all beautiful—seriously, they could be the metaphorical poster child for bound quintets. The guy on the right kisses the vampire, and the one on her left immediately turns her head to steal her lips for himself. They touch each other so eagerly and freely.

What would that be like?

I look away quickly. That's not for me. I need to stay focused.

"You all right, Boo?" Bael asks, bending to try and catch my eye. "I have a couple of friends in the quintet you were staring at. If you want me to introduce you to their keeper, you two might hit it off, and then you'd make a few more friends—"

"I don't do friends." That's another one of my mottos, one I won't budge on.

Silas tips his head, lips twitching. "Then what is Kenzie?"

"A close acquaintance."

"And another thing," Coach Gallagher adds, speaking over everyone. "I know you're all getting nice and cozy with your new matches since the PDA here is fucking insane, but the quintet rankings don't start until next semester. So I'm fine with all you additions who tagged along today, but this is an *individual* training exercise. As such, quintets will be magically separated at the start of combat."

A chorus of complaints goes up from the others here. But I'm so relieved, I could almost get over my haphephobic tendencies to kiss Coach Gallagher.

Hmm. Maybe I should just to see if *that* messes with their heads. I mentally add it to my list of possible ways to get my matches to leave me alone.

"And remember that *top weight classes* of shifters are prohibited from shifting in the woods for this challenge. I'm looking at you, Decimus. We don't want you burning down half the damn forest since there are a fair amount of rare creatures living in there."

Bael shrugs it off, shooting me a toothy grin. "Dragons are at the top of the food chain, so I'm used to imposed limits. They like us at the Divide to burn up all the fiends, but I'm a little big for other legacies to take on in practice. But don't you worry your spooky little mind. I'll find you quickly."

"Do yourself a favor and don't."

"Gotta keep my mate safe. And warm," he adds, frowning as he realizes I'm not wearing a coat over my baggy sweatshirt. "Want my shirt for an extra layer? As a bonus, you'd get to see me half naked—and don't even pretend like you don't want that. Feel free to touch as much as you want."

Oh, my gods. There's no point even trying to with this guy, is there? I need to start being an absolute bitch starting now if I want to have any chance of sparing all of us of this quintet.

I open my mouth to say something scalding, but Silas beats me to it.

"Feel free to go fuck yourself, dragon," he mutters. He reaches into his pocket—probably for his bleeding crystal. All blood fae have them. "A warming spell will last longer. Hold still, Maven."

I look at him sharply, taking a step away. "Don't."

His jaw clenches, and he's clearly about to argue, but the coach instructs all the legacies to line up outside the woods to prepare for the whistle.

"I doubt the separating magic will affect me in Limbo," Crypt muses as he stands beside me, studying the darkness of the woods ahead. "The faculty were rarely so thorough with their spells during my time here. So I'll see you on the other side, my darling."

"Stay with her," Silas agrees. "Plenty of legacies here want to weaken our quintet—"

"We're not a quintet," I mutter, but he talks over me like that's a non-issue.

"—and Maven will be their first target if they find her. Kill first, act sorry about it later."

Baelfire pops his neck on both sides, and Crypt slips back into Limbo without argument.

Apparently, they also think the no-kill ban is a joke. Good to see we're on the same page with that one thing, at the very least.

Glancing to my right, I see an incomplete quintet look away from me quickly, whispering low to one another. Other legacies openly glare at us. It's clear no one is thrilled about going into this training with the Nightmare Prince, Silas Crane, and a Decimus.

They assume we'll work as a team. They see me as the weak one here, so it's easy to deduce that Silas is right. I'll probably get more real combat than I usually do in this class because instead of ignoring me, people are going to actively try to kill me.

That puts a small smile on my face as I turn back to the woods.

The whistle blows. I step past the border, and magic whisks me away.

14

MAVEN

Transportation magic is a bitch.

For a moment, I feel like I'm being pulled in eighteen different directions at once while the world twists in on itself, and then all at once, I stumble to my feet in a section of barren forest floor just as a flag appears in my left hand.

Righting myself, I glance down at the fabric marked with the Everbound University symbol—the colors and signs of the Four Houses with a golden heart in the center, uniting them all. Tucking it into my pocket, I eye my surroundings.

Flurries filter down through the barren canopy above, swirling softly past gray and white tree trunks marred with long scratches from otherworldly creatures. Though the sky is pale far above, the wintry wood surrounding me is wreathed in mist and shadows, hiding any dangers or other legacies lurking nearby. Whenever a breeze passes through the twisted treetops, it turns into spine-chilling whispers, like dozens of ghosts hissing to beware. A few dozen yards away, Everbound River rushes past its rocky banks, white with ice and forbidding rapids.

Utterly beautiful.

I don't sense Crypt's dark, chilling presence nearby, and I assume he would have appeared by now if the magic hadn't affected him. Which means I'm really on my own as I wait for danger to find me.

Just the way I like it.

Climbing up into one of the twisted trees takes only a minute, and then I watch the ground below at my leisure, enjoying the sinister ambiance and the chilly, fresh air. The white noise of the river is soothing.

And as I sit and wait, I mull over my options.

Using Everett to turn the guys against each other is a good plan, one I still intend to use. Acting like a bitch might annoy them a bit, but I'm guessing that I'll have to do some significant damage for them to reject me completely like I need them to.

Which makes me wonder…

What are their curses?

If I can exploit whatever weaknesses they have, they'll be pissed. And once they're disgusted by me and move on, I'll be able to do what I need to do.

It's not a pity party when I say they'll be better off without me. It's just a fact.

A branch snaps several yards away, barely audible over the river. It draws my attention to a legacy creeping through the woods. Not just any legacy, though. It's Sierra. She's sticking close to the trees, on high alert.

I still don't know which House Sierra is in, but watching her tiptoe around makes me roll my eyes. Poor thing has no idea how to check her surroundings. She'd already be toast if I were a competitive legacy who wanted to up my ranks and took this flag-collecting exercise seriously.

Deciding to get this over with, I slip down from the tree, allowing my feet to thud loudly against the forest floor. She doesn't turn around. So, to give her another nudge, I fake a sneeze.

That makes her whirl to face me.

There you go. Good job. You get a gold star.

"You," she jeers.

"Me," I agree.

She whips her hair back and takes a defensive stance, looking at me like I'm a pile of manticore shit. "Bet you're feeling pretty good about yourself, huh? Thinking your men will show up in time to rescue you from me? Give that shit up because it's not going to happen. I hope you enjoyed them while you had the chance, bitch, because you're not walking out of here."

I roll my eyes. "Make your move, Miss Steal Your Men."

"Shut the fuck up," she snaps, marching towards me. "You're so pathetic. I could kill you with my bare hands. And that's just what I'm going to do."

She's going for hand-to-hand combat. My favorite.

Her pace is lacking, but the moment her fist flies, I deflect it against my forearm just as I turn, hooking the crook of my elbow with hers and using her momentum to send her spinning away. She stumbles, scowls, and turns again, this time launching toward me with her total body weight, arms reaching for me.

It's easy to catch her wrists, cross them, and pull until her face connects with my bent knee. A sharp *crack* fills the air. She shrieks in pain and rears back, broken nose streaming blood like a faucet.

"You *fucking bitch!*" she snarls, scrambling to her feet and baring her teeth.

For a moment, I wonder if she'll give up on hand-to-hand and shift into something or pull some other surprise attack. Instead, she starts *monologuing* again. Seriously. She just can't seem to help herself.

"No magic? It must be weak as shit! Asscasters like you aren't even real legacies—just fragile little mortals. You probably came here thinking you could fit in with us monsters, but you deserve to be with the rest of the weak, pathetic little humans at the bottom of the food chain. Where they *belong*."

Of all the things she could've said, it had to be the one thing that genuinely gets under my skin.

Still, I make no expression. Keeping a poker face is second nature since it was drilled into me from such a young age. Instead of a resting bitch face, I have a resting blank face.

"Words are cheap. Take your shot."

She circles me while wiping blood off her face. "Wonder what it would take to get your robotic plain-ass face to show some emotion. Gods, I can't even imagine all the awkwardness I'm sparing your matches. Especially Baelfire. Take it from me; he *loves* to watch a girl's expression when he's railing them," she smirks. "We skipped a couple of days of class to stay in bed a few weeks ago, but that dragon is *insatiable.* And the hickeys he left all over me? Gods, that was so hot."

She really doesn't know when to stop talking. To my surprise, her words are starting to make my skin itch. Which is annoying since there's a good chance she's just lying to get me riled up.

"You talk too much," I enunciate clearly, warning in my voice.

She doesn't get the hint as she circles closer, hands flexing at her sides. "I'm doing them a favor by getting rid of you. This way, they don't have to fuck an emotionless, fake-ass legacy for the rest of their lives. It'd be like fucking a corpse! And you? You're better off dead anyway. Not one person will mourn you when you're gone."

It's just as unexpected for me as it is for her when I find myself straddling her back, having rounded a kick to the back of her knees so she'd fall flat on her face. She wasn't prepared for my speed, but when she shouts in anger and tries to reach back for me, I grip her forearm, plant my foot on her upper back, and yank.

Her shoulder dislocates with an audible pop. It's a beautiful sound.

"You're wrong about three things. Let's count them together, shall we?"

When I break the radius bone in her forearm, her scream splits through the forest.

"One. I don't want anyone to rescue me. Ever."

She struggles underneath me, twisting her other arm back frantically, but I snag that one, too, breaking her wrist and pinning it behind her in one smooth movement. She chokes on pain and fights harder beneath me, but it's futile.

"Two. Humans are not weak, and they can be just as monstrous as legacies."

I move my foot from her upper back and land a kick to the side of one of her knees at precisely the right angle, moving the bone out of place and fracturing her patella.

Snap.

Satisfied with her scream tapering off into hysteria as she writhes, I finally let her go, wiping my gloved hands on my shirt. She rolls over, sobbing when she can't move her arms right to get up, and her knee bone slips to the side under her skin. With her in this state, it's easy to lean down and snag the flag hanging out of her pocket.

For a moment, killing her is a real temptation. If I don't, she'll come for me again. She'll end up telling others that I'm not the weakling I've been pretending to be. I could also use the buzz of a kill.

But I learned from a young age what taking a life means. As annoying as Sierra is, she's just a jealous legacy who has no idea who she's been pissing off. She doesn't deserve death...yet.

"And three," I sigh, looking out at the misty trees. "There is one person who will mourn me. She's a real softie and would probably tell me to make nice with you. So, in her honor, you get to pick. Either get the fuck up, walk it off, and never speak to me again...or try me one more time so I can put you out of your jealous misery."

She gives up on her attempts to get up, glaring at me with a beet-red face as she hisses, "I can't get up and just *walk it off*. You fucked up my knee!"

"Be grateful I left one intact. Either limp out of here or pray someone comes looking for you before a manticore has you for dinner."

I start to walk away, ignoring her curse-filled shrieks behind me. Turning my back on her turns out to be a small mistake, since she finally manages to lurch up to a semi-sitting position. Just as I glance over my shoulder, she flops one of her arms towards me, crying out from the pain of the broken arm as she finally shows what House she's in.

Elemental. Fire.

Shit.

The blazing inferno that encompasses me is powerful enough that even though I dive away in record time, it still catches on my pants. I scramble to pat them out, but elemental fire isn't like normal flames. It's similar to Greek fire, quickly spreading.

Along with the flare of panic flooding me is exasperation. This bitch just *had* to wait until the last moment to surprise me with this. Why couldn't she have whipped this attack out sooner? I never would have engaged with her if I'd known this was her element.

Taking off in a dead run, I don't give myself time to hesitate before plunging into the nearby raging river.

Immediately, the fire singing my skin is snuffed out—but the subzero temperature of the water shocks my body into near paralysis. The rapids are far stronger than I'd anticipated, and I feel myself getting swept downstream and sucked further down, the cold and pressure making it nearly impossible to hold my breath.

Dying right now would be so inconvenient.

Just as water finally fills my mouth and nose, the swirling river calms enough that I can kick hard, breaking the icy surface with a raw, painful gasp. I'm so distracted with treading water that I barely register the shouts ringing out—until someone dives into the water beside me.

Strong arms encase me, and within seconds, I'm pulled onto the rocky shore. Someone is trying to cradle me, but that is *absolutely* not fucking happening, so I scramble away, blinking up in surprise…

At three legacies who look utterly pissed to find me in a river.

Silas is the one who pulled me out, and he looks ridiculously good sopping wet, with water droplets clinging to his dark curls and his red eyes a beautiful contrast against our wintry backdrop. He reaches for me again, brows pulled down in a severe frown, but I wave him off as I cough up the rest of the water.

Baelfire is agitated. "Fuck. Just breathe, Maven. There you go. Just—"

He cuts off in a choking sound when I finally get to my feet, and when I hear Silas swear on a harsh exhale, I realize all of their stares have gone from furious to ravenous because...

I'm pretty much naked.

My dripping clothes are in tatters, my pants practically gone, and the little left of my baggy sweatshirt barely holding together. The massive burn holes in it expose most of my body, even though my black sports bra and panties are intact. Although I know the sports bra is covering the center of my chest where *it* is, I still instinctively lift my arms to cover that area.

The one part of me that hints at what I truly am.

"Fuck me," Bael groans, voice hoarse. He reaches down to grip his erection in his pants, looking pained.

I've worn anything and everything to disguise my figure since the day I got to Everbound. I made sure everyone thought of me as a frumpy, forgettable wallflower. And now this. The gods really do have a wicked sense of humor.

The one upside is that I didn't carry any special weapons into training today, so I didn't lose any of them in the river. Unfortunately, anything else hidden in my pockets is now gone.

When I meet Crypt's silver-flecked purple gaze in a silent glare, he swallows harshly and shoves Baelfire toward me. "Stroke off later. She's freezing."

Bael doesn't miss a beat, stripping out of his shirt to offer it to me.

Holy shit.

He's even more jacked than I expected. A glorious expanse of muscle upon muscle, all under smooth golden-tan skin. The ridges of his abs and the sharp V cut of his pelvis momentarily distracts me from the fact that I'm in a similar state of undress.

What would it feel like to touch all of that? That body pressed against mine...

I kick myself internally. I already know it will be revolting.

Now is not the time to start second-guessing that aspect of my life.

Before they can notice where my attention has lingered, I grab his shirt, careful to avoid touching him, and tug it over my head quickly.

It's so big on me that the hem brushes my mid-thigh. It smells like him, that same singed cedar scent I caught earlier.

"Shit, I'm so sorry. I was just…you're just so fucking pretty that I—"

He's interrupted when Silas swears, gently but firmly grabbing my bare wrist and lifting it to show the faint burns along my arm. Immediately, I wrench my arm away, jaw clenching.

"Hold still," he grits, pulling out his bleeding crystal.

He's going to try to heal me. Everyone knows Silas Crane is among the most powerful blood fae alive, so a healing spell would be nothing to him, merely a prick of the finger and a drop of his potent blood. But the last thing I need is someone trying to heal me with blood magic.

"No," I warn.

Silas's glare is heated. "I will not tolerate you being hurt. Ever. Now, don't move."

He tries to step closer, and I let my poker face fall away so he can see how pissed I'll be if he tries to use magic on me right now. "Fuck off."

When he moves toward me again, obviously more focused on my scant injuries than the threat of my wrath, Crypt grips his shoulder and warns coldly, "She said no, Crane."

Silas whirls with a snarl, breaking the incubus's hold on him, and for a moment, I wonder if they'll go for each other's throats. Then Crypt turns his back on the fae, a clear insult, and looks down at my bare hands.

"Your gloves are gone."

No shit. "They burned off."

He hums nonchalantly, but I notice that all of the pale markings in his skin glow faintly purple before fading. Something in his violet irises reminds me that this is my most unpredictable match. The one they call a psychopath.

"Out of pure curiosity, and not at all because I'm about to feed them their own spleen…who did this to you, darling?"

That captures Silas and Bael's attention, too, and now three high-profile legacies are hanging on my next words, like hunting hounds salivating before a chase.

"Just forget this happened," I tell them before trudging away from the river.

It really is cold out here, sopping wet like this. I wrap Bael's shirt tighter around myself, whipping almost frozen hair out of my face.

They don't let me go that easy. Baelfire is suddenly on my right, instinctively reaching for me and then pulling his hand back with a harsh swear. "Damn it, Boo, your feet are going to freeze into solid blocks of ice. At least let me carry you."

I'm prepared to ignore him completely, but suddenly, I can't think about anything except what Sierra said. Baelfire and her in bed. The hickeys. Him fucking her, watching her face.

Maybe she was lying, but just picturing all of it sends an entirely foreign emotion roaring to the surface, scalding my skin worse than fire ever could, and I do possibly the stupidest thing I have ever done.

I plant my back foot, turn, and punch a dragon shifter in the face.

Hard.

Baelfire reels back from the force, gripping his jaw as he freezes with shock. Silas blinks between us at an equal level of surprise. Meanwhile, a vicious smile curls one side of Crypt's mouth up.

I shake out my hand, pretending like it doesn't throb. It will definitely bruise, but if I draw any attention to it, they'll just be even more impossible to shake right now.

And I have to get away from them quickly. Because I just slipped up. I lost my cool, and I can't let it happen again. My emotions are dangerously close to the surface when I shouldn't be letting myself feel anything at all.

I am nothing but deadly calm. I can't want them.

"For the last time, you all need to *fuck off.*"

My voice isn't as steady as I'd like, but at least my glare keeps them from coming any closer. And as if the universe has finally decided to give me a break, the echo of a shrill whistle sounds far in the distance, signaling the end of combat training.

I march away.

15

BAELFIRE

I RUB my jaw in bewildered disbelief. I'm one tough son of a bitch, but that punch was no joke. Maven walks away without a single glance back at the three of us, but there's no way she can't feel how hard we're staring after her.

Can she blame us? She looks so godsdamned *fuckable* in my shirt, the hem riding up slightly around the backs of her beautiful, toned thighs. I can't rip my eyes away from her delicious ass and the sway of her hips.

Mine, my inner dragon growls with need.

Hell yes, she is.

"Maven just…touched me," I finally manage, coming back from my shock as a grin splits my face.

"Yes, in precisely the only way any of us ever want to," Silas mutters. Then he turns and glowers at me. "What did you do to piss her off like that?"

I start to tell him I did nothing, but then I hesitate, frowning. *Did* I do something to upset Maven? Just the idea of mistreating my mate in some unknown way has my stomach sinking, the growl of my inner dragon causing me to bare my own teeth.

I leave them behind quickly, using my shifter speed to catch up with Maven. She's already stepping out of the woods when I reach her side, fingers itching to pull her close. She looks cold, and I'm always warm.

Before I can say a word to her, my heightened sense of hearing picks up on Sierra Hill saying Maven's name under her breath, mixed in with a string of vicious cursing. She's sitting on the grass outside the edge of Everbound Forest, looking like shit and grimacing as another legacy pops her arm back into place. She turns to glare as Maven passes by, but when she spots me, her face turns even redder than it already was.

"Bael," she whines, blinking away tears. "Come help me?"

Fuck that.

Her family has been friends with mine for years, so I've had a front-row seat to Sierra's manipulative personality and extreme temper tantrums for a while. I hooked up with her once when I was bored and regretted it heavily when she set my room on fire while I was still sleeping. Good thing I'm fireproof, but none of my shit was. She's toxic as hell.

I'm tempted to scare her straight so she keeps Maven's pretty name out of her mouth, but it's a waste of my time when I need to make sure my mate is okay.

Ignoring her to keep up with Maven, I follow her through a concealed servants' entrance that puts us in an empty, narrow hallway skirting one of the wings lit dimly by fae lights. I'm so distracted by my inner dragon's sharp need to comfort our mate that I reach for Maven's hand to gently turn her to me.

"Boo? What—"

She stops and wrenches her hand away, breaking my hold on her. Although her face is still eerily composed, the flash in her dark eyes as she glares at me has heat curling up my spine.

"Why are you so touch-averse?" I demand. "Why—"

The words die on my lips as a possible reason crosses my mind. Why else would she hate touching people unless something happened in her past? What if she was…

Stark horror mingles with fury, and I suddenly can't breathe. My dragon reacts by nearly taking over, and I have to stop and cover my face with both hands, fighting the searing burn spreading in my veins.

"Maven. Tell me it's not what I think it is," I manage in a strained voice.

"What?"

She sounds exasperated, but my brain has latched onto this possible reason, running wild with it, filling my head with unwanted images and—oh my *gods*. I'm going to be sick. My skin tightens, my eyes shift, and fire burns in my gut.

"Baelfire?"

"You don't want people to touch you. Is it because someone…*did* touch you? In the past? Did they—"

Fuck. I can't do this. I'm going to shift any second, my temper running out of bounds and burning me alive. I strain for control because shifting too close to someone else is dangerous for them, and I'd sooner die than hurt Maven.

"Just tell me who I need to kill."

A couple of seconds pass where I'm in hell before she speaks.

"You're jumping to conclusions. I wasn't sexually assaulted."

Thank all six gods.

The pressure in my chest loosens as relief courses through me. I'm pretty sure I would have burned everything in sight down if I found out anything like that happened to Maven.

Sometimes, I hate how intensely we shifters feel every emotion. It's an open invitation to my inner monster, especially on days when I haven't killed something to appease my curse.

After a couple more breaths, I rub my face and clear my throat before regarding her. She's watching me with her typical poker face in place—and it's a damn good poker face, but I know she's not truly emotionless. She's just an expert at hiding how she feels. She didn't ditch me just now when I was about to lose my shit…so that must mean *something*, right?

"Okay, but I'm pretty sure you don't wear gloves all the time because you're scared of cooties. So what is it, then?"

"Hmm. It's odd. I distinctly remember punching you in the face and telling you to fuck off, yet here you are."

She folds her arms, but when she does, the fabric of my shirt she's wearing bunches and shifts, and my eyes again drop to her mouthwatering thighs. Yet the hunger pulsing through my veins takes a spot on the back burner when I spot a couple more light burns on her legs.

All shifters have an overwhelming urge to care for their mates, but dragons have it twice as bad because of our naturally obsessive tendencies. I have an instinctual need to covet, and now that I have a mate? All I want is to take care of Maven in every possible way.

"You should have let Silas heal you," I huff, the sight of her beautiful skin in that condition driving me to take another step toward her.

She takes a step back.

I sigh. "Why were you pissed at me, Boo? Did I do something wrong?"

"Hard to say. Right and wrong are subjective."

"Why did you punch me?"

She tries to step around me but I cut her off. Lucky me, there's not a lot of space in this narrow old servants' hall, so she doesn't have room to get by my much bigger frame unless she presses against me. Honestly, I'm hoping she'll try so I can finally feel her.

"Move."

"Was it because I asked if you're a virgin?" I guess.

Maven sighs. "I said *move*."

"I won't leave you alone until I know what's upsetting my mate. For once, I just want a straight answer. Tell me everything you're feeling."

"For the last time, we are not ma—" She surprises me by huffing in the most adorable way, half growling with exasperation before narrowing her eyes at me. "You mean it? You'll leave me alone if I tell you all I'm feeling?"

"Pinky promise."

I can't look away from the anger in her dark eyes as she glowers at me. "Fine. I feel frustrated. I feel desperate. I feel like breaking rules. I just fucking *feel*."

"And that's a bad thing?" I shake my head, baffled by my little Boo.

I suddenly wonder if I'm hallucinating when her gaze drops to my bare upper half and *heats*. She moves closer until we're less than an inch apart. Every part of me aches to reach out for her, especially when her eyes trail slowly back up my frame, lingering on my lips.

I catch a hint of her mouthwatering scent—that soft, floral night-time aroma that instantly makes me harder than godsdamn steel. I inhale sharply, trying to get another hit of her delicious fragrance… and I realize there's a note of arousal.

Fuck.

My mate is turned on right now.

"You have no idea how bad," she whispers.

Only it sounds a hell of a lot like *you have no idea how bad I want you*.

Lust crashes through me, along with a need to please my mate so fierce that it's dizzying.

"Use me," I growl. "You said you're frustrated, so use me. And before you argue," I cut in just as she opens her pretty little mouth. "I can smell that you're wet right now. Don't deny it."

My cock feels like it's trying to bust straight through the zipper of my pants. I don't hide how turned on I am when I reach down to finally adjust my throbbing erection, and heat licks down my spine when Maven's eyes follow the movement.

"However you want, wherever you want. Just use me. I'll be your free-use fuck toy, totally at your service," I add with a grin.

I meant it teasingly, but her eyes flash, and the scent of her arousal grows stronger. It's almost enough to bring me to my knees.

"*Gods*, Maven," I whisper. "Be honest. You like the idea of me totally at your service, don't you? Is that what you want? Fuck, baby, you can do anything you want to me. I'll be good. Just say the words."

My mate shocks the ever-loving hell out of me when she hesitates and then whispers, "I have one rule."

I can barely think through how excited I am—and godsdamn it, if I'm this keyed up from so little, what would it be like to get completely lost in her?

"*Anything,*" I promise.

"I can touch you, but you are not to touch me."

My heart thunders in my chest, mouth dry as I nod in agreement.

Something in Maven's demeanor shifts, like a layer peeling away and leaving her almost…vulnerable. Uncertainty radiates from her as she reaches out her hand slowly, and I exhale hard when her bare fingertips graze up the center of my chest, drifting until she places her palm flat over my heart. I'm surprised it's not echoing in this narrow passage because it sure feels like it's trying to slam its way out of my chest.

Shit, I think I might explode.

I watch her micro-expressions closely, and it's like the second she can feel my heartbeat, a tiny bit of her wariness fades—but I can tell this is still difficult for her. I want to know why, but I'm already pushing her boundaries, and asking more questions will drive her away.

She swallows and meets my eye. "How far is the quintet apartment?"

Oh, my gods. She wants a bed.

"Follow me," I manage.

Less than five minutes later, after taking all the back passageways I could think of to get her to our shared apartment without anyone seeing my mate looking so godsdamned edible, I shut the front door behind us, my mouth watering as her sweet scent perfumes the space we'll share together.

Maven pauses, eyeing the luxurious apartment. "This is excessive."

"Silas has spoiled-ass tastes. He's almost as bad as Everett with that shit," I shrug. "But anything you want to be changed before you move in, I'll absolutely—"

"I'm not moving in. And if you say one more word about it, I'll leave."

I clamp my mouth shut, even though I'm tempted to smile when she wrinkles her nose slightly at the massive home theater room as we pass it on the way down a hallway. Seemingly without intending to, she steps into the central room at the end of the hall, the biggest and most opulent. When she sees the overly massive bed in the center of the bedroom, she arches a brow.

"Is this where your egos sleep?"

"Your bed," I correct with a smirk. "Big enough for all of us so we don't have to fight to the death for who gets you each night."

I *know* I didn't just imagine her squeezing her thighs together. But she turns to me with that same semi-vulnerable, curious heat in her eyes.

"Lay down, and no matter what, keep your hands behind your head."

I'm so eager to do anything she wants that I rip my pants as I yank them off before getting comfortable on the bed, lacing my fingers behind my neck. Pride and desire wash over me when her eyes widen slightly, latching onto the tremendous bulge in my underwear.

"I—" She clears her throat. "I didn't tell you to get naked."

"You'll never have to tell me to get naked around you, Boo. I'll look for any excuse because I love how you can't stop looking at me," I tease.

I'm trying to lighten the mood because I can see her at war with herself in her head. She takes a step back, then forward, clenching and unclenching her hands—but the scent of her arousal is slowly filling the space, and she isn't looking away from my body, so whatever she's fighting in her head, I know it's not on my account. It still makes my dragon twitchy, impatient for her touch, yet far more anxious to know what's made her so wary of this.

If anyone is going to push her limits before she's ready, it will be you, Silas's voice pushes through the cloud of hunger in my head.

I sit up immediately, ignoring the growl of my inner dragon. "Maven…if you've changed your mind and this is too much for you, I'm not going to pressure you—"

"As if you could. This is about me, not you. Lay back down."

I obey, and finally, she sits on the bed beside me, tipping her head as she studies all of me. She reaches out and gingerly trails her fingers over my arm. I shut my eyes and bask in every second as her soft touch traces over my muscles, up my neck, and down to my abs. Heat gathers under my skin wherever her exploration lingers.

When she hums softly and brushes her palm against the cock straining in my underwear, desire bolts down my spine, and my hips lurch, eyes flying open as I gasp.

"Oh shit."

Maven's eyes darken as she repeatedly traces the outline of my erection through the thin fabric. By the time she stops, I'm panting, fingers flexed behind my neck.

I've never been teased like this. I've always taken charge in bed—and hell, I still want to pin Maven down, bury myself to the hilt in her, and leave love bites all over her body so people know she's fucking *mine*, but this?

I want this even more.

When she suddenly frees my leaking cock from its confines, and her hand skims the length of it, fire pumps through my veins. It only worsens when I see her mouth part slightly at the size of me. Like I said, I'm a big motherfucker—everywhere.

"That's…" She trails off.

"It'll fit, baby," I promise hoarsely. "I'll make it fit. You'll love every godsdamned inch of me."

That snaps her out of her small daze, and she gives me a droll look. "I am not fucking you, Baelfire. Now or ever."

My inner dragon writhes at those words. "Maven—"

"But I like seeing you so hard for me," she adds, her voice turning liquid. "Good boy."

Good boy.

Those words sink in and holy. Fucking. Gods.

"More," I growl, muscles clenching and rippling wherever her featherlight touch brushes next. It's sweet, tantalizing torture. "Say more like that."

Her pretty little mouth quirks up in a deliciously evil smile, and she leans over, close enough that damp tendrils of her hair frame my face, and I stop breathing altogether, world screeching to a stop as I pray to all six gods that she's going to kiss me.

But instead, she whispers, "You want my praise?"

Her fingers skim the head of my cock. I grit my teeth as my hips jerk up of their own accord again, desperation and need taking the reins until all I can think about is getting more from her. More of anything, but *especially* her calling me a good boy.

"Gods, I need it. Please," I pant.

"Good answer. But my praise is earned."

Everything about her voice is smooth and deceptively gentle, yet there's that same powerful undertone in it that I'm realizing is always there. My mate is exceptional at hiding her emotions, but her mask is nowhere to be found as she smirks down at me, dark eyes glittering.

She's the one calling the shots, and it's addictive.

I am so fucked.

I jerk again, swearing harshly as Maven's little hand finally—godsdamned *finally*—curls around my hardness, swiping through the precum that's been leaking out since we started this heavenly torture. Her fingers can't reach all the way around, but I clench my teeth at the agonizingly perfect pleasure as she pumps it once, so slowly it hurts. Then twice.

"Such a good dragon, keeping your hands where I told you," she muses.

"Maven. Gods, Maven," I chant, arms straining behind my head.

Her arousal is permeating the air, driving me absolutely *feral*. Fantasies I've never had before pop into my head, all centered around this intoxicating dynamic. Me on my knees for Maven, head buried between her thighs so I can get high off her scent. Tasting her when she lets me. Her praise when I beg the way she likes. Her disciplining me when she sees fit before letting me worship every inch of her body.

I want to hear that I please her. I burn with the need to touch her.

But no. I promised I wouldn't, and I have to make this last longer.

Her third stroke is rough enough that she presses hard against my aching balls. I gasp again, all my muscles straining against the intense need to come settled low in my spine.

Maven's beautiful, excited eyes capture mine, and I swear nothing in the world will ever be the same for me again. Now that my mate has looked at me this way, I'll never be the same.

"Now be a good little pet and come for me," she whispers, stroking me hard.

Pet? Oh, holy *fuck.*

Her words destroy any chance I have of making this last, and my vision whites out as the most powerful orgasm I've ever had has me shouting with release. Needing an anchor to hold onto as the pleasure wipes me out, my arms whip out and seal around her, gripping my mate tightly to me as the ecstasy takes me, along with a psychological high unlike anything I've ever experienced.

Fuck, fuck, fuck.

When I finally start to come down, I'm dizzy, but that doesn't keep my still-hard erection from twitching again, eager for more of my mate. Moaning, I bury my face in Maven's cool hair, letting her scent envelop me. This is bliss.

"Gods, Maven. That...I can't even...that was—"

One moment, I'm so delirious with pleasure that I can't speak right, but the next, I freeze when I realize Maven is tensed, dead silent, and trembling.

Because I broke my promise.

I'm hugging her to me.

Immediately, I let her go and sit up. "Oh, gods. *Gods*. I'm so sorry. I didn't mean to—"

Without letting me see her face, she shoves away from me, rolls off the bed, and bolts from the room, slamming the door shut behind her before I can even get to my feet. All that euphoria I was feeling quickly transforms into bile crawling up my throat.

Damn it. Damn it, damn it, *damn it.*

It was instinctive. I didn't mean to touch her without permission—but I did, and now I feel like my chest is caving in. My mate just unearthed the biggest fucking praise kink and gave me the best orgasm of my life, and in return, I crossed her lines. I screwed up.

I have to make this right.

16

MAVEN

THIS IS what I get for punching and subsequently fooling around with a dragon shifter.

I slam my dorm door behind me and rapidly back away from it, my chest still rising and falling from running all the way here. Very few people saw me bolt through the halls in my limited state of dress. Seeing that someone already replaced my door was a massive relief because I'm not in a good state to deal with no privacy right now. I'm so shaken that I trip backward over the edge of my bed, landing on my back and clenching my teeth at the ceiling.

Stupid Maven. Stupid, stupid, stupid.

I can still hear the echo of Baelfire's gasps. The soft moans and harsh swears. His glorious muscles bunching, all of him reacting to my slightest touch. The way he looked at me, a mixture of hot, pure need and begging.

And when he lost control after I called him my pet...

Driven by a mind of their own, my fingers skim down the front of Baelfire's shirt, slipping into the front of my charred panties. I can't help the sound that escapes when my fingers slide against my wet clit.

Of course, it's wet. I'm completely soaked.

Meanwhile, the rest of my body is so fucking confused.

When Baelfire's strong arms trapped me against his solid, blazingly warm body, I felt all the familiar horror—the unbearable sensation of someone else's skin on mine, the tightening of my throat, and the complete inability to breathe or even think straight.

But there was also…something else. Tingling warmth. An electrical flush spread over my skin that created mayhem throughout my body.

I can't tell if I need to puke or come.

Never in my life have I been so aroused, and despite what Kenzie thinks, it's not because I'm a virgin. Squeezing my eyes shut, I allow my fingers to tease my wet pussy, circling the upper corner beside my clit the way I've always enjoyed. I moan at the feeling—it's been a very long time since I touched myself.

Maybe that's why *they* pop into my head.

The way Silas's dark hair curls around his forehead and the nape of his neck. The strain in Baelfire's arms as I turned him into a panting mess. Crypt's deliciously twisted smile and intent stare. Even Everett's strikingly pale blue eyes and how his lips felt on my forehead.

What would his cool skin feel like against my flushed body?

Unbidden, I slip a finger into myself, crying out softly and throwing my other arm over my face to block out the light as my back arches off the bed. From the darkness, the image surfaces of them surrounding me, devouring me with their eyes as ravenously as they did by the river, their voices whispering against my skin. They're relentless.

Giving into them would be so easy.

And in this moment, swept away by the pleasure I'm crafting for myself, the idea of bringing all my gorgeous monsters to their knees to worship me is a dark, irresistible siren. I bite my lower lip hard as I moan, fingers circling my clit quickly and need making my chest ache. The orgasm approaches and then recedes again and again until I can't think straight. I desperately need that release.

I could stop fighting them. *Make them mine.*

No.

Fuck, no.

With a vicious swear, I rip my hand away, feeling the building pleasure slip away as frustratingly unsatisfying as always. *This* is why I haven't touched myself in forever. I forgot just how pissed off it makes me when I can't ever seem to push myself over the edge. It leaves me overheated, slick, and extremely unhappy.

I can't let myself fantasize about them. And they are not *my* gorgeous monsters. I need to get a grip and stay focused, or this will end terribly for me.

More terribly than it already will, anyway.

One cold shower and a slew of swear words about how stupid I've been later, I dress in new clothes and pull on new gloves quickly, ignoring their sting against my still-sensitive burns. As always, I slip some small but useful weapons into hidden pockets. I can't help glaring at Baelfire's shirt, crumpled on the floor by the desk, mocking me for losing my self-control earlier.

My potion crafting class doesn't start until after lunch, and at the moment, I'm *finally* alone. This would be the perfect time to call the supernatural black market dealer…if it wasn't for the fact that I lost my cell phone at some point during combat training. I memorized his encrypted number, but I need to track down a phone.

Someone knocks at the door. There's a high chance it's Baelfire, Silas, or Crypt out there, and I can't afford to let my emotions slip into play any more than I already have today. Taking a deep breath to compose myself, I run through my plan in my head.

Mess with their heads. Use their curses against them. Make them all hate me.

I open the door, prepared to be a bitch, and blink in surprise at the interim headmaster holding a tablet in front of me. Mr. Gibbons' bushy brows jump up in recognition.

"Ah, Miss Oakley! I see you're still alive."

"Disappointed? Me too."

Not understanding my sense of humor, he once again looks scandalized. "Of course not! It's always wonderful to see atypical casters make the cut. I'm only here to verify whether you're alive because…

well, there's been a rather tragic death at Everbound that is under investigation."

He marks something on his tablet, and I realize it must be a student record of some kind.

"What makes it tragic?" I ask.

He frowns, scratching his neck uncomfortably. "Well, obviously, death is always tragic...."

"Hardly. But as I understand it, legacies rarely get more than a letter sent home to their families if they die here. What would warrant an investigation?"

Mr. Gibbons seems reluctant to say anything. "We faculty are supposed to keep this under wraps, but several students stumbled across the scene and took pictures, which are now going about the school, so I suppose there's no point hiding it. I might as well inform you that a rather gruesome group of pyres was put on display in one of the castle courtyards, set aflame and advertising anti-legacy ideology. We haven't identified the burned remains yet, so we're doing a sweep to see which students might be missing."

Burning pyres? How deliciously morbid.

I barely keep from smiling, but it must slip through a little because the interim headmaster looks disturbed as he regards me. "Miss Oakley, do you know anything about who did this?"

"What makes you think I would?"

He scratches his neck again, harder now, like a nervous twitch. "Well, after all, you're a...never mind. If you learn of any missing students, report it to one of the faculty offices or an instructor immediately."

It doesn't take a genius to deduce that he suspects me of having a hand in this purely because of my atypical background. Curious.

Mr. Gibbons turns to leave, but I stop him by asking, "Will this little incident bring Headmaster Hearst back to Everbound?"

"Well...that's hard to guess at. We'll finish the investigation and report to the Legacy Council. They'll decide what to do, but if we don't find the culprit, the Immortal Quintet certainly will."

He retreats, disappearing down the hall while I snort at his faith in the Immortal Quintet. But my amusement quickly vanishes as Kenzie crosses my mind. I haven't heard from her all day. What if she was one of the corpses on fire in the courtyard?

Alarm courses through me, and I step outside my dorm, ready to look for her.

"Your friend's all right, darling," Crypt murmurs, appearing before me in the hall like a mirage has melted away.

He surprises me so much that my hand immediately goes into one of my hidden pockets where a knife is hidden, but to my credit, I don't squeal, scowl, or make any expression. "Exactly how long have you been standing out here?"

His purple eyes grow devious. "Long enough. I almost made a mess in my pants hearing your delicious little sounds through that door. But you sounded unsatisfied at the end. Care to remove those damned dreamcatchers and invite me in so I can give you what you need?"

The asshole must have either incredible hearing or he had his ear pressed literally right up against the door like a stalker. Mortification threatens to rise into my cheeks, but I choose to ignore it. After all, legacies are incredibly uninhibited when it comes to sex. As if he hasn't heard shit like that before.

"Kenzie is all right?" I demand, bringing us back to the topic at hand.

"Fit as a fiddle and trading sappy nonsense with her quintet in one of their classes."

The Nightmare Prince is known to care about nothing and no one. What could have motivated him to check on Kenzie's safety?

Crypt sees my skepticism and smirks. "I agree with what you told the balding interim headmaster. Death is hardly tragic, and one less shifter wouldn't bother me in the least. But if someone hurt you by hurting your friend, I would bring you their head on a platter within the hour."

I relax slightly, turning to lock my door and realizing this new one doesn't have one.

"No lock needed. Silas had this installed first thing this morning and it will only open to you, from what I understand. I've never seen so many magic wards placed on the same door," Crypt muses. "He boosted the dreamcatchers in there with more of his blood as well. Paranoid bastard."

That is just...annoyingly thoughtful.

I'm not used to people doing things for me. I don't even know how to react to it.

Deciding to move on quickly, I side-eye Crypt. If Kenzie is all right, then it's time to make a call that would land me firmly in the hot seat with the Legacy Council if anyone else here finds out about it.

"Do you have a phone?"

He tips his head thoughtfully and disappears, air warping and leaving nothing behind. I hesitate only a second before shrugging it off and heading toward the eastern exit, planning on getting a new phone from Halfton during lunchtime to make this call. But before I can reach the steps, he reappears with someone else's cell phone that he clearly just stole, holding it out to me with a grin.

I glance at it. "It's locked. Needs a code."

He huffs and disappears again. Several more moments later, I hear a shrill scream from somewhere nearby, and then Crypt appears in front of me with a now-unlocked iPhone and...blood splattered on his hand.

"They resisted," he explains casually, placing the phone in my gloved hand. "So I popped one of their eyeballs."

That triggers a grin to spread before I can help it. "Very efficient."

Crypt goes stock still, fixating on my mouth. I realize this is probably the first time I've slipped up and actually smiled around him. I wipe the expression away quickly, feigning boredom as I try my best to navigate to the phone section of the newfangled device.

Then the Nightmare Prince tenses and my attention skips down to where several of his markings light up in a soft purple light. He's dressed in a ripped T-shirt, jeans, and a leather jacket that all start to drift slightly with his hair as if he's underwater. It looks like he's listening to something far away, with his head tipped, and then he grumbles something I can't make out and disappears back into Limbo. I no longer feel his presence a second later.

Interesting. Something to do with Limbo?

I've never considered what he does when he's there. Of all the layers of existence, I've only studied three extensively, and Limbo certainly wasn't one of them. I have no idea what the Nightmare Prince does with his time.

I remind myself that I don't care—because right now is the perfect window to call the black market dealer.

Silas laid a lot of protection on my door, but if Crypt could overhear my *moment* earlier, I can't risk someone else coming along and listening through the wards to my conversation. So I leave Everbound Castle using a virtually unused ancient hallway not far from my dorm and slip away from the university grounds into the forest.

As I near my favorite spot in Everbound Forest, I take a deep breath and dial the number.

It only rings once before he answers.

"I don't get unknown calls," the voice rasps. "So how the fuck did ya get this number? And if this is Kevin, I'm gonna hunt you down, rip your head off, and—"

"Boring. Pick a different threat."

A long pause. "Ex-fucking-*scuse* me?"

"Ripping heads off is outdated. Try something else. Testicles, maybe. Whoever Kevin is, he probably values those over his head anyway," I muse, side-stepping what looks to be a legacy's skeleton on the ground. Probably someone who didn't survive a combat class. "As for where I got your number, there are a few loose-jawed drunks who frequent the Twisted Tavern in Halfton. You might want to snuff them out for tossing your number around so freely."

There's another long moment before I can hear a smile in his rough voice. "Fuck me with a pitchfork, I thought you were a myth. *Telum*. That's what they call you, right?"

I've always hated that nickname, so I decide to move on. "Are you still in Pennsylvania?"

"Infernal hells, you're really her." He sounds baffled before he cackles on the other end, apparently not as ready to move on from introductions as I am. "You're real! And—no. Don't tell me…you're at Everbound University? Ha! Devils and dicks, I can't even believe it. This is too damn funny."

"Hysterical," I agree flatly, stepping through the trees into the clearing I set out for. It has a small semi-frozen pond and plenty of silence, except for right now when he won't shut up. "I need nightshade root powder."

That finally gets through to him, and he stops laughing. "Tall order for someone I just barely met. Look, I don't make deals without really gettin' to know who I'm dealing with first, kid."

I let my voice steel into a calm tone I've rarely had to use throughout my life. "We just established that you know exactly who I am. And I know exactly who you are, Melchom."

He makes a choking sound. Probably because for a demon like him, someone else knowing your true name is both taboo and humiliating. If I was interested in getting mixed up in demonology, discovering his name would be the first step in gaining power over him.

"How the flaming shitballs did you—okay. Relax. Look, I'll get the nightshade root powder, but it'll cost you a helluva lot."

"Name your price."

Melchom chuckles, but it still sounds a bit strained. "I don't want money, but seeing as how you are who you are, maybe you'd be interested in a trade? A gram of nightshade root powder for, oh, I don't know, say…a still-beating heart."

A gram of nightshade root powder will be just enough for what I need to do.

"Whose heart?"

"Does it matter?" he laughs. "If the rumors are true, this should be a cakewalk for you."

I pause, glaring out at the frozen pond. Along with a few other types of uncommon monsters like changelings and banshees, demons are one of the monsters that were never allowed in the mortal realm in any legal capacity. Demons are hunted constantly and are nasty to everyone, but tend to be especially cruel toward legacies…and innocents, whose fear they prey on.

I don't kill innocents. But he can't know that. No one can know that, despite how fucked up I am, I still have that one rule.

"Give me a name," I press.

He exhales long and slow, the sound of someone smoking. "So eager. Seriously, I can't believe I'm actually talking to *the telum.* Whatcha look like, anyway? You as sexy as you sound? Maybe I should up my price a bit..."

"Shall we revisit my ripping-off-testicles suggestion?"

"Yeesh. Fine. I enjoy a little pain as much as the next demon, but that's a bit too kinky even for me. The guy whose still-beating heart I want? His name is Orson Lykoudis."

That name sounds familiar, somehow. I try to put a finger on it but then shrug it off. Whoever it is, I'll do my research and decide whether or not he's worth killing to get this ingredient. If he's an upstanding guy, I won't lay a finger on him.

If he's not, then more fun for me.

"Deal. I'll have it to you within a week as long as you hold up your end of the deal."

"Great. I'll meet you in Pennsylvania. Can't wait to see what you look like. Maybe we should call it a date. My girlfriend'll be out of town, anyway."

I sigh. "Melchom."

He hisses. "Fucking devils. *Stop using my name.* What?"

"Try to cheat me in any way, and I'll add your horns to my collection."

Demon horns are notoriously tricky to obtain. They can't respawn without them, and cutting off a demon's horns causes severe mental breakdowns, psychosis, and hallucinations for weeks. Extremely unpleasant, to say the least. But to make a point, I'll do it if I have to.

"You're an unhinged little shit, aren't you?" he mutters. "No worries. I don't stiff my customers, and I ain't gonna let anyone know about *you,* of all people. Just bring the heart. I'll call you when—"

"No. I'll call you."

Hanging up, I drop the stranger's phone to the ground, crush it under my boot, and then toss the remains into the pond's center, where there is no ice.

I'll have to get away from the university to make the hit, but first, I need to look into this Orson Lykoudis guy. And I need to get my damned matches to leave me alone, which means that starting now…I'm going to use Everett to make them jealous.

I don't want to draw attention to myself, so I can't go off the deep end to push them away. But I *can* use all the tactics on my list to get them on edge. And once I know their curses, I'll use those against them, too.

17

EVERETT

SILAS IS in a shittier mood than usual, which must be a world record of some kind.

He storms into my office, ripping through the standard magic wards for faculty offices, slamming the door behind him, and glowering at me.

"Where is she?"

I don't bother looking up from the papers on my desk. "Weird. Usually, Baelfire is the one throwing fits. Not handling our new keeper well, Mr. Crane?"

A warning pulse of magic kicks through the room, making me stiffen to glare at him. He doesn't back down, looming over my desk. And there it is—that slight twitch in his neck and the wild gleam in his eyes that makes him look completely insane at random intervals.

One glance at his hand tells me he's clutching his bleeding crystal.

"Get out of my office. Now's not a good time to pick a fight with me."

Not when my recent visit to the temple of Arati, queen of the gods, only left me more crestfallen than ever. Between that and the surprise burning pyres that have stirred up Everbound, it's all I can do to maintain an aloof, untouchable front when, deep down, I'm panicking.

And when I panic, I freeze shit.

I've never been very good at controlling my powers, so I've tried to do it by controlling my emotions. Which also doesn't always work, especially when Silas, Crypt, and Baelfire are annoyingly good at finding my triggers.

"I'll leave after you tell me where Maven is," he grits. His head whips to the side, glaring at a spot on the wall where there's…absolutely nothing.

Crazy asshole.

"Why would I know where she is?" I drone, trying to sound uninterested, even though just the mention of my keeper's name has frost blooming on my fingertips.

"You're her professed favorite," he snaps, dragging a hand through his hair. "And after she refused to let me heal her, I went searching the healers, and then I realized maybe she came to *you*—"

Healers? I sit up. "Why would she need healed?"

"Because she was—"

"Boo?" Baelfire calls, slamming open the door to my office once again.

I guess it's no surprise that they completely disregard the *by-appointment-only* sign hanging outside. He scowls at the two of us, though there's an underlying layer of panic on his face, and he's far more out of sorts than the Decimus's proud youngest typically puts on display.

"Where's that creepy stalking son of a bitch when you need him?"

Clearly, he means Crypt.

I roll my eyes. "You both *lost our keeper?* What are you two even —" I pause when I see the huge bundle of dead flowers in Baelfire's hands. "Why the hell are you carrying those around?"

"They're for Maven."

"Are you serious? You're giving her *dead flowers?*"

Gods on high, no wonder I'm in the lead, even fictitiously.

Anyone would think I was a playboy and these idiots had never had a real relationship in their life, even though the reverse is true.

"They're her favorite because they look like—" Baelfire cuts off with a huff. "You know what? I don't have to fucking explain it to you. And if you don't know where she is, then..." He trails off, glancing sideways at Silas. "He's about to attack your wall."

I look over in time to see Silas dig the crystal into his hand, lifting it as he glares at the wall with a vengeance. What the fuck is wrong with him?

"Si. Hey. Focus," Baelfire grunts, shoving Silas's shoulder and taking a swift step back when Silas whips around, features twisted into a vicious snarl. "Remember what I said? I won't, and the rest of us won't either."

I don't know what he's talking about, but that's not surprising. Whenever we were forced to spend time together as children, I was typically the odd one out. They've never understood how my life—how my *family*—works, or that my snubbing them was for the best. I excluded myself whenever I could, and there was no point explaining my reasons for it when they were so quick to call me a stuck-up dickhead.

When I saw that they would be in my quintet, I actually hoped things might eventually change.

But if I want things to improve between us...then for now, I have to keep icing them out—at least until we've all bound our hearts to Maven. Until then, there are just too many things that could go terribly wrong.

Baelfire mutters something else to Silas that I don't catch, and finally, the blood fae snaps out of it and drops his bloodied crystal onto my desk, ignoring the way I wrinkle my nose in disgust. He slumps into the chair across from mine, rubbing his face as if he's exhausted.

"I'll only ask one more time," I say coldly, glaring between them. "Why would Maven need to be healed?"

"Some asshole burned her during combat training." Baelfire looks down in regret and anger at the dead flowers in his hand...

which I still don't understand. "And then I went and made her day a hundred times shittier. Fuck, I just have to find her."

Before I can ask what he's talking about, yet *another* person knocks on my ajar door. But this time, it's a faculty member asking me to cover for Professor Haagen, who is apparently too busy helping investigate the burning pyres to teach his afternoon class.

"Professor Haagen is in the House of Arcana. Why would I teach casters potion crafting when I don't have that ability?" I point out dryly.

"I—it would be more to supervise than anything," the mustached lurch says quickly, glancing nervously at the glaring legacies in my office. He's equally uncomfortable with how I'm staring, judging by the sweat rolling down his forehead when he turns back to me. We're not the most welcoming group. "It's a lab day, so they'll just be crafting potions from grimoires and getting ready for the First Placement...where, you know, they're allowed to use anything they've crafted in class to try to survive—"

"Other teachers from the House of Arcana could supervise."

Besides, I didn't come here to *actually* teach lessons. I don't mind being a professor, but there were much bigger reasons to station myself at Everbound University. I don't plan on building a rapport with other instructors, not when the majority of them followed me around asking for an autograph during my first week here, claiming to be huge fans of my modeling, with one going so far as to show me a photo reel of their favorite photoshoots of me.

It was cringey and awkward.

The lurch wilts, looking ready to retreat, but then Silas fixes him with a stare that makes the man shiver. I get it. All blood fae have unnerving red eyes, but his are somehow worse.

"You said potion crafting?" he asks, sounding far too calm in comparison to nearly losing his shit a few minutes ago.

"Y—yes."

Silas glances at me. "Maven takes Haagen's potion crafting class."

I should still pass on it, but my mouth opens before I can control it. "Fine. I'll cover for him. Now get out."

The faculty member disappears, shutting the door gingerly behind him as if he's afraid that breathing wrong will set one of us off. Which honestly might not be too far from the truth.

Baelfire has perked up. "That's Maven's next class? She'll be there, then. I'm going with you, Snowflake."

Gods on high, I hate that nickname. I also hate him and the rest of the Decimus family.

But the gods must know something I don't, and I'm not about to insult them by freezing to death someone in my own quintet. Not even if it would be super satisfying.

Less than thirty minutes later, I'm eyeing Professor Haagen's potion crafting classroom, which is smaller than many of the vaulted, amphitheater-style rooms at Everbound. This one, in contrast, is just a room with one wall made of glass looking out over one of the fields leading to the forest. It's filled with tables set with many beakers, cauldrons, and other shit casters will need for potions. The opposite wall from the window is lined with shelf upon shelf of bizarre potion ingredients—everything from dried mosquito sacs to hawthorn berry oil to tiny jars of ectoplasm.

Students begin filing into the room, and several stop to gawk openly at me sitting at the front of the classroom behind Haagen's desk. Their reactions range from mild surprise at seeing an elemental professor in a House of Arcana class to the long stares of legacies who still see me as a supermodel.

Ignoring all of them, I study the contents on Haagen's desk. He's a bit of a slob, having left a banana skin to brown next to a pile of crinkled papers smeared with food of some kind. But I pretend it's something important I'm reading until *she* walks in.

And just like the first time I saw her standing on the stage at the Seeking, my heart almost stops.

Maven's dark eyes arrest mine for barely a heartbeat, but if she's surprised to see me in her class, she doesn't show it before walking to a table at the back of the room. She also has no reaction to the fact that Silas is already at the table waiting for her, his eyes tracking her every move with a possessiveness that would make anyone else flinch.

Baelfire is sitting at the table next to them, and the raw emotion on his face when he sees Maven makes me wonder what the hell happened earlier between them. He tries to say something to her, something I can't hear, and extends the bouquet of dead flowers.

Maven ignores him completely, just watching me like all the other students.

But her gaze is not just like the other students' stares, not for me.

No, knowing *she's* watching me has my nerves twisting into knots and my heart doing double time. Frost prickles across my palms, which I tuck into my suit pockets as I finally stand and address the class, pointedly not looking at her because the last thing I want is to fucking *blush* in front of a bunch of grad students.

"Professor Haagen had something else come up. Today, you will be—"

"Is it the investigation?" one of the students at the front cuts me off, eyes wide. "Is he helping clean up the corpses? What happened? Do you guys know if it was humans who did it?"

Voices explode across the classroom as legacies throw in their two cents, all talking over each other.

"As if humans could kill one of us, let alone four!"

"Didn't you see the way the corpses were dressed? They were supposed to look like the Immortal Quintet! Isn't that so fucked up?

"Why didn't anyone see them setting all that up?"

"Oh, relax! It was probably just someone pulling a stupid prank—"

The moment my patience runs out, the temperature in the room plummets sharply enough to crack the glasses of a mage in the front row, who yelps. Two light fixtures also shatter. Ice climbs up the walls while students draw in surprised gasps, the air pluming in front of their faces, huddling in on themselves and looking at me with wide eyes.

Most elemental students I teach come from highly religious,

devout families and would never bring shame to their last names by speaking out in class like that. They're too respectful and too aware of their own self-images.

Apparently, the House of Arcana is far more *lenient*.

"The next person to interrupt me will get to enjoy feeling their toes snap off due to frostbite," I say calmly, flipping open the old grimoire on Haagen's desk as an excuse not to look at my keeper just to see what her reaction to this might be. "Now. As I was saying, today, you will craft anything that you think will be useful during First Placement."

There are three Placements at Everbound. First Placement is a test at the end of the first semester for all legacies, matched or unmatched. It tends to be brutal and often results in several students' deaths, but the actual test changes from year to year. It's hard to tell what it could be, so any amount of preparation is useful. Second and Third Placements happen next semester among quintets to cement our rankings, active service assignments, and future careers.

After six years of waiting, I'll finally be participating in those.

Students exchange glances, but no one else speaks out of turn. I can hear Baelfire snort derisively at me in the back where he is completely unbothered by the cold, as dragon shifters always are—but Silas quickly slips out of his dark wool Chesterfield coat and offers it to Maven.

Damn it, she must be freezing. I'm an idiot. I'm tempted to apologize solely to her, but after she says something quietly to Silas that makes him scowl and set the coat in front of her on the table, she looks back at me and…smiles.

Smiles.

My stomach flips. I swear on everything holy that she is the most beautiful creature I've ever laid eyes on.

And now I *know* I'm blushing because my ears feel warm.

Looking away quickly, I try to unscramble my brain, but at least the other students have taken initiative and are now collecting potion ingredients from the shelves on the wall, whispering amongst themselves as they shiver and get to work on their potions. Some of them are still ogling me in the way I've forced myself to grow accustomed to, but mostly class is on a roll, and all I have to do now is not make a fucking fool of myself.

Which proves to be impossible when Maven approaches the desk where I sit.

Today, she's in a black sweatshirt with sleeves that go well past her hands and dark cargo pants that are far too big for her tucked into steel-toed combat boots. Her rich dark hair hangs loose around her, framing her face as she quirks a brow at me.

"Well?"

Formulating a sentence around her is so damn hard, but I clear my throat and look out the window, hoping like hell that I look indifferent…instead of how I really feel, which is eager to give her anything in the world she wants.

Seriously. As soon as we're bound together and curses are no longer a factor, I'm going to spoil Maven in every possible way. If she wants designer dresses, limited edition cars, first-edition copies of rare books, a big-ass mansion, a golden yacht—literally *anything*, I am going to be the one who gives it to her. I've always wanted someone to spoil and adore.

I just…can't. Not yet.

"Well, what?" I manage.

"You've had time to think about my proposal."

Right. Her proposal. Us getting close to make the others jealous.

Internally, I grimace. I don't want anything with Maven to just be for show. Although if that's all I can possibly have with her, I still want it because I'll take anything I can get from her. But even *that* is dangerous, with my curse hovering like a dark cloud over all my thoughts.

I can't let myself forget what's on the line here.

"No," I say quietly, even though saying that word to her makes my mouth taste like acid. "Go make your potions, Miss Oakley. Preparation is important."

Instead of obeying me, she rounds the desk to stand right beside me. I can practically feel the burning stares of Baelfire and Silas across the room, but I ignore them as my heart pounds painfully at the way Maven's eyes trace over my face.

The way she looks at me is different than the way others do.

They look to see a handsome face. Beauty. Another perfectly flawless Frost.

She looks like she wants to step inside my head and dance with all my deepest secrets and darkest fears, everything I've been hiding for years. And I would want her to if it didn't mean setting my curse in motion.

When she lifts a gloved hand to tuck hair behind her ear, it catches my attention as I remember what Baelfire said about her avoiding touch like the plague. A dozen questions are on the tip of my tongue for her, but no way in hell am I asking her about that while we're in a room full of other people. And from what little I've seen of my keeper, I doubt she would even spare my questions the time of day.

Maven leans closer. "Tell me how to bribe you."

"You—" My voice wavers, and I swallow hard. *You will never need to bribe me. Anything you want, it's yours.* "You're in class," I manage instead. "We'll discuss this more later."

I expect her to move on or roll her eyes or something.

The *last* thing I could have expected is her looking at my lips while licking her own. She's blatantly eye fucking me in front of all the legacies and gods and everybody.

Instantly, my cock hardens.

Shit. I absolutely cannot get a boner right now.

At the same time, something akin to shock and embarrassment washes over me when I realize that so many eyes are on us in this room and people are whispering. Knowing that we're being watched…is making me even *harder*. My ears burn, and when Maven notices my blush, she arches a dark brow at me.

I open and close my mouth several times before finally tearing my gaze away from her. "Go make potions," I repeat severely, mentally praying she hasn't noticed the hard-on I'm desperately trying to hide under the desk.

"If you insist, Professor," she murmurs, making her way to the back of the class again without so much as a sideways look at the students who are gawking at her.

Silas is immediately focused on Maven, stubbornly offering his potion to her despite the way she glares at him, and Baelfire—damn, he actually *winces* when she brushes the flowers he brought off her table onto the floor. It brings me a sick sense of triumph in a small way after everything his family has put mine through.

But at the same time, I feel bad for the guy. Whatever happened earlier between him and Maven, he looks miserable. That makes two of us since I know these next few months before graduation will be hell as I try to avoid my curse.

Silas looks increasingly frustrated as she rejects his every attempt to offer her anything.

Maybe Crypt is in just as bad shape.

One can only hope.

18

MAVEN

I'M MAKING PROGRESS.

Silas appears to be getting increasingly agitated, Baelfire looks like he might be sick every time I pointedly avoid looking at him, and Everett is ruffled.

I should be patting myself on the back. Celebrating.

Instead, I feel almost...guilty.

Which is asinine. Mistreating them is the surest way to get them to hate me, and the sooner that happens, the sooner they'll cut me out of their lives and quintet and move on. I have to force them to do that, so I must ignore the squeamish discontent writhing in my chest.

The moment potion crafting class is over, I try to bolt from the room. I leave Silas behind since he's still putting one of his many potions in a vial—he made twice as many as anyone else in the class, all for me to use during First Placement despite how flippant I was about it.

But Baelfire is immediately behind me as I stride through the halls, still determined not to look at him.

"Maven, wait. Please wait. I'm—fuck, I'm so sorry," he whispers so the other students eyeballing us on all sides won't overhear.

They're twice as whispery and nosy after my brief attempt to get Everett to flirt with me in front of the class. He'd blushed a bit but simply brushed me off, obviously annoyed with me. I only did it to try making Silas and Baelfire mad, but they seem far more frustrated with other things. Namely, Silas is still pissed I won't let him heal the burns, and Baelfire wants to talk about what happened earlier, which will happen over my dead body.

"You just wanted to try something, you only had *one rule,* and I massively fucked it up," he presses on, stopping abruptly to snarl at a random legacy who steps within five feet of me.

Admittedly, that's a massive perk of walking anywhere near my rejected matches: they don't let anyone else close to me. I'll miss that when they learn to hate me.

As soon as the legacy bolts away, the Decimus turns baleful golden eyes back on me. I'm pretty sure he could melt anyone with that look. It's so full of sincerity and heartache.

"Tell me how I can make it up to you. Want me to beg on my knees? I'll fucking do it right now. Just...please talk to me about what happened. Yell at me if it helps."

I pause, fully looking at him for the first time since I fled his room earlier. Considering his words, I lift my chin as an idea crosses my mind. "There is something you can do for me."

"Anything."

"Make me a blood oath."

That pulls him up short, and he looks surprised. "Blood oaths are...really fucking serious. Not to mention, illegal unless a priest or priestess is overseeing it."

"And?"

He studies me for a moment and shrugs. "And you're right, I don't give a shit about that. But what oath would you want me to make?"

"Promise to appeal to the gods for a different keeper and never speak to me again."

Baelfire recoils. "Are you serious?"

"Deadly."

"No. Fuck, no. Never going to happen. You're my mate, Maven Oakley. Mine."

His.

Ugh. Why must he be so gorgeous while making that declaration? It's far more challenging to ignore how attractive he is now that I've seen him naked and stroked his hot, thick, veiny—

No. Stop thinking about touching him.

I'll either throw up or, worse, try to do it again.

Given his track record, I knew it wouldn't be easy to deter Baelfire, but it was worth a shot. Turning, I stride away. "Just drop it."

I make it two halls over with him trailing along beside me like the most guilt-ridden person in existence before Kenzie's voice sings, "May! There you are!"

She prowls up to us with a smile, flipping coils of pale hair from her face as she throws her arms around the shoulders of the two legacies beside her—Vivienne and Dirk, who are both perfectly polite. "Wanna join us for a late lunch, you two? You don't have another class today, right, May?"

Damn her and her excellent memory of my class schedule.

"Fine."

Inside the vaulted eating hall, while standing in one of the food lines with Kenzie's quintet chattering happily and picking out the foods they want in front of us, Kenzie glances over her shoulder at me.

"I tried calling you, like, *ten* times. Seriously, you need to turn your phone off silent mode."

"That will be hard to do, considering it's at the bottom of a river."

"What?" She smacks her forehead. "Girl! We go to school in a fucking maze, and you disappear all the time on me! You know it freaks me out when I can't reach you, right? I mean, I think you're a total *queen*, and I'm sure you can handle yourself if you had to, but this place is full of some crazy competitive legacies, and now that you're matched with some of the strongest here—"

"*The* strongest here," Baelfire says smugly behind me.

"Whatever, Dragon Boy," Kenzie rolls her eyes but gives me a pleading look. "My point is, I'm worried about you, okay, Maven?

Promise me you'll get a new phone ASAP so I can send you dirty memes and check in a couple of times per day to make sure my bestie is still breathing."

She worries almost as much as Lillian. "Sure. I'll get a new phone."

"Get a cute case for it, too," she adds, squinting at my outfit. "And not just a plain black one again, you prude little monk woman. Make it sexy."

"Of course," I nod sagely. "Because phones can be sexy."

She grins. "*Anything* can be sexy with a little imagination."

"Especially your imagination. Plenty of ammunition," I smirk.

Kenzie throws her head back to laugh before sashaying to one of the tables with her quintet, leaving room for Baelfire and me to sit once we get our food. But when I turn to order, Baelfire is staring at my mouth with laser focus.

"Damn it, Boo. I want that."

"A smile?"

"*Your* smile. I've decided that's my new mission in life, so buckle up."

I pick out whatever foods look the most bland while I try to come up with the bitchiest thing to say. Because as much as it isn't sitting well with me, I have to make these guys decide I'm not worth all this hassle.

Before I can come up with a withering retort, he reaches beside me, carefully avoiding touching me, and piles more food on my plate, including a pile of hot wings. When I make a face at him, he winks.

"Gotta keep my mate well-fed. If you don't want it, toss it to me. I'm always ravenous, especially around you. Oh, and heads up? Your other stalkers are waiting for us," he adds, popping a mini roll into his mouth as he scoops up our plates.

Sure enough, Silas *and* Crypt are sitting at the table beside Kenzie's quintet, who look like they've lost their appetites in the presence of the Nightmare Prince and the notoriously cutthroat Crane. Kenzie looks like she's trying to lighten the mood as Baelfire approaches, but I can't hear whatever they're saying because a group of legacies passes by, cutting me off from them.

Someone taps on my shoulder, and my nerves go tight, but I calmly glance over my shoulder.

It's Harlow, who has swapped her nose ring for a diamond stud and styled her short purple hair into an array of spikes today. She has one hand on her hip as she looks me over, popping the gum in her mouth.

"You know, I thought you looked like a weak-ass pushover when I first saw you at the Seeking."

"Thanks."

She guffaws. "What I meant is, I was clearly wrong. I hear you mangled Sierra during combat training."

Is that what this is about? I suppose I should have anticipated Sierra's friends getting pissed off. I'm sure Harlow is just another legacy who would like to see me dead. She's probably approaching me like this to get a better read on me, trying to study me up close to decide a good way of killing me off later.

Good luck with that.

"Yes, I did. Do you have a problem with that?" I ask.

She surprises me by grinning. "Fuck, no. I respect the hell out of that. Any asscaster who can take on a high-ranked fire elemental and live to tell the tale is good in my book."

Is she…complimenting me?

"I mean, you're still *just* an asscaster and not worthy of your matches, but whatever," she adds.

There we go.

"Great talk," I mutter dryly, turning to go to Kenzie's table, where Silas and Baelfire are staring at us with frowns. Crypt has vanished, but I still sense him nearby, and I realize he's probably been listening in to this little chat with Harlow.

"Hold up, Oakley," Harlow says, stepping around me and extending a…blank piece of crumpled paper. She winks. "I'm sure you'll figure out what to do with this."

Gee, I wonder. Maybe throw it in the trash?

Before I can say that, she drops the crumpled paper into my hand and leaves the eating hall. Barely a second after she's gone, Crypt appears directly beside me, tipping his head.

"You mangled a fire elemental? I didn't get to see that," he pouts his lower lip.

"Odd, since stalking me seems to take up so much of your time."

"Not nearly enough of it, darling. By the way, what do you want in exchange for taking down those dreamcatchers? I haven't even tasted your dreams, and I already crave them."

I scowl at him. "You really do just pop in and out of existence like a case of bad acne, don't you?"

He laughs and drops back into Limbo as if to underline my point.

I'm starting to think he is a bit unhinged after all.

When I reach the table, Silas immediately demands, "Did that girl just threaten you?"

"Nope."

"Are you sure? What's on the paper?"

I hold his eye contact and tuck it into my pocket as I sit between Kenzie and Baelfire. "Not a damn thing."

That clearly annoys him, but his neck twitches, and he grimaces, shooting mistrustful looks around the room as if he expects shadow fiends to leap out any moment. Then he just stands and stalks out of the room, clutching his bleeding crystal. Kenzie is distracted chatting with Vivienne and Dirk, but I arch a brow at Baelfire.

"Is he finally going to leave me alone?"

He rubs his neck. "Nah. Silas is just paranoid. There's no way in hell he'd ever admit it to anyone, but it's getting worse, especially lately. He's probably leaving so he doesn't accidentally kill someone and tip everyone off about how unbalanced he really is. Doesn't want to appear weak."

That must have something to do with his curse. I frown at the arched double doors Silas left through, realizing that in the short period I've known him, he does seem hyper on edge sometimes, fingers twitching and looking ready to kill at the drop of a hat.

Suddenly I can't think about anything but the haunting pain in his red irises when he'd looked at me outside the greenhouse.

Most of them killed each other. Including my parents.

He was vulnerable in that moment, trying to connect with me by opening up about our pasts.

But he can't know about mine.

Shaking myself out of my thoughts, I make a mental note. *Paranoia for Silas.* I have no idea yet what my other matches' curses are, but as much as it eats at my gut to even think about…maybe making Silas suspicious of me and preying on his paranoia will be the final nail in the coffin where he's concerned.

And if I can get him to drop me as their keeper, I bet the others will eventually follow.

Kenzie's sharp gasp of dismay draws my attention to where she's gawking at Dirk's phone screen. "Gods, I heard it was bad, but that's…really bad."

Curious, I lean over and see that Dirk has a picture of the burning pyres, apparently taken by some other student before the faculty arrived. It's a graphic image of four headless legacies burning on makeshift wooden spires in a courtyard, black smoke ascending from the bodies dressed up to look like members of the Immortal Quintet—complete with each flag of the Four Houses hanging in shreds. Written in blood on the courtyard wall behind the morbid scene are five words: *Monster spawn deserve to die.*

Vivienne sees the picture, too, and clutches her stomach as she turns green. "Oh, gods. Is—is that someone's head on the ground? I think I'm going to puke."

Poor thing really won't have the stomach for combat after graduation.

Kenzie looks mildly disgusted, too, and Baelfire huffs at Dirk. "Put that shit away before you make my mate sick, too."

"Oh—sorry, I shouldn't have brought it up right now," Dirk says quickly, shooting me an apologetic grimace just as I take my first bite of mashed potatoes. "Sorry if that ruined your appetite, Maven."

I finish chewing and swallow. "Oh. Right. That's disgusting."

Bael's brows go up. "You're taking another bite."

"Because I'm hungry."

Now, he looks like he's trying not to laugh. "Strong stomach. You're kind of a psychopath, aren't you, Boo?"

Only out of necessity.

"I just don't understand why someone would do something like that, even if they're anti-legacy," Vivienne mumbles, still looking queasy. "Why focus on the Immortal Quintet? They've sacrificed so much for everyone, and they've always been kind to humans."

I almost choke on my next bite but manage to swallow. It's better to bite my tongue here. The last thing I want is more people here suspecting me of being involved in the anti-legacy movement, especially in the wake of the pyres.

Feeling Baelfire's eyes on me, I glance up at him. He frowns, opens his mouth to ask something, and then shuts it again. He shakes his head, leaning and dropping his voice so I'm the only one to hear him.

"You know…you can tell me anything, Maven. Literally anything. I'm always on your side."

"Pick a different side," I mumble, gathering my plate to leave.

Because there's no winning with me.

Baelfire, of course, tries to follow me from the eating hall, even though he's not done eating, but when I insist that I'm just going to the bathroom, he relents and waits outside. After trying to sense if Crypt is near, I decide I'm alone. Pulling out the crumpled piece of paper Harlow handed me and setting it on the counter, I frown at it.

If it's not trash, then maybe…

Drawing a deep breath, I chant the words to cast a small ember spell, the flame flickering precariously at the tip of my finger. This is truly one of the more impressive spells I've perfected, which is… admittedly pathetic.

Holding the flame under the paper so it will be backlit without burning it, I arch a brow at the writing that shows up out of nowhere.

Thursday. Midnight. Ruins in Everbound Forest. No outsiders.

Outsiders?

This is something I should just brush off. I'm already cutting it close with my mission here, and I've just added assassinating a wolf shifter into the mix, thanks to that demon's request. I'm hardly a reckless person, and a mysterious midnight meeting in the forest practically screams that someone is going to try to murder me there.

That, or they're just trying to scare me.

Either way, I can't wait.

Burning the paper, I snuff out my spell and glance in the mirror, sighing at my reflection.

"He's right. You are kind of a psychopath."

19

MAVEN

After two days of research, I've decided I'll sleep like a baby after assassinating Orson Lykoudis.

The name must have sounded familiar because he's one of the seven wolf shifter pack alphas—namely, the alpha of Northeast Pack located in Pennsylvania. He's also an idiot who doesn't know how to cover his shady tracks.

Though I'm hardly savvy on the internet, it didn't take me long to find articles about him taken to court over sexual assault charges, multiple incidents of wolf shifters dissenting from Northeast Pack solely because of his poor leadership, and a shit ton of pictures and videos of him on social media harassing human women at bars and strip clubs.

And, lucky for me, he leaves a massive virtual footprint to follow. I know what bars he frequents and even the names of the beta wolf shifters he usually brings everywhere. None of them are remotely a match for me.

All I have to do is slip in, snag a wolf shifter's heart, and bounce.

And hopefully, I'll return with enough time left before the winter solstice.

With a sigh, I shut my laptop—this is the first time I've found a use for it after buying it with Kenzie two weeks ago. It's seven thirty on Thursday night. Most legacies are bar crawling in Halfton, chowing down in the eating hall, or working their asses off getting ready for First Placement next week. That, or they're enjoying lots of bonding time with their new quintets like Kenzie is currently doing.

My quintet, on the other hand, is...problematic.

For the last few days, I've ignored them, made bitchy passing comments, and continued to smile at Everett every time I've seen him in passing just to rile up the others. Silas handed me a potion yesterday to use during Final Placement, and I smashed it on the ground and walked away, but did that stop him from following me around today?

Nope.

Crypt is constantly popping up, stalking me from Limbo, and meanwhile, Baelfire has walked me to and from every class, dished up my plate at every meal, and perpetually kept an upbeat, obsessive attitude. Even when I tried insulting the Decimus family, he just laughed it off and said they're not for everyone.

I pull out my *Make Them Hate Me* list and scoff. I've tried most of these tactics—boring, ignoring, mean, high maintenance...

That last one blew up in my face when I decided to try whining about not having a phone, and Silas left one at my door one night. A really expensive phone with a beautiful red cover and all my matches' phone numbers set to emergency dial—except for Crypt since he has no phone. The device definitely has some kind of magic ward on it to keep anyone else from trying to get into my phone.

He really is paranoid, but I haven't figured out how to use that to my advantage. Yet.

Besides Everett giving me a wide berth, my matches have been relentless. Legacies naturally part in hallways now to make way for me since Baelfire is still snarling at anyone who gets close to me, and Silas and Crypt are no less terrifying.

But even though the other legacies give me space, it hasn't stopped the whispers or the stares. And they've started to feel even more malicious than ever. Especially if Sierra is ever in the room—

she hasn't dared get close to me again, but she looks like she's ready to rip my head off at the first chance she gets.

I genuinely want to see her try.

Hmm. Maybe she'll get the chance tonight. She might be at my mysterious midnight meeting. It could be her and a dozen other legacies plotting to attack me, strike fear into my heart, and tear me to shreds.

I'm looking forward to that.

It just means I'll have to slip out of here at midnight without any of *them* being the wiser. Last I checked, Crypt was still hanging out outside my dorm, while Silas and Baelfire were finally, mercifully distracted with other things, like their own upcoming First Placement preparations.

I have three days left to get the still-beating heart to Melchom and get the nightshade root powder. After that, my only ticking time bomb is the winter solstice.

And if I fail—

"No," I whisper to myself, shaking my head. "You won't. You can't. They're counting on you."

I'll leave on Saturday to hunt down Orson. But to do that…

With a sigh, I call Kenzie.

"So? Which one do you think you'll fuck first?" She chirps without any preamble. She's found my attempts to repel my matches hilarious over the last few days. "Because my bets are on Everett. I know you said you're just trying to use him to make the others jealous, but I really think you have a thing for that hot—er, *cold* professor. Wait, is he actually cold to the touch? Because if he is and Baelfire is extra warm, then maybe you could get some back-and-forth temperature play action going when you're they're passing you back and forth—"

"Not happening."

She sighs. "You still haven't given up on making them hate you? Seriously, May, I think you have your answer by now. You've been unpleasant as fuck to them for days, and they're all hopeless over you. It's actually really cute, except I'm starting to feel bad for them."

Me too.

No. I can't afford to care about them at all because they will kill me if they figure out my secrets. It would be one nasty train wreck of a situation.

"Can I borrow your car for a couple of days?" I ask.

"Oh! Are you going on a road trip with them? That's adorable. I should go on a road trip with my mates, too. Hey, what if we all go together during the holiday break between semesters? Gods, that would be so much fun! I've missed hanging out with my favorite adorably gloomy caster as much lately."

I cringe. Not for the first time, I feel annoyed at myself for leading Kenzie on like this. I really tried not to get attached to her, but I'll feel like shit when she thinks I ghosted her next semester. Maybe I should do something nice for her before that happens to soften the blow.

"Yoo-hoo? May?" she checks. "You still there? You down for a holiday trip together?"

"Maybe," I concede, the lie tasting bitter. "But for now…"

"Sure, you can take Bluebell for a couple of days." That's her car's name. "Where are you headed, anyway?"

Shit. What would be a good excuse? "My adoptive father's very distant cousin is getting married in Pennsylvania. I was invited."

"Oh! Good opportunity for a wedding date. You should definitely invite your guys."

"For the last time, they are not *my* guys."

"Uh-huh, sure," she says, drawing out the word long and slow. "Just grab my keys sometime tonight and promise to have wild group sex, just maybe not in Bluebell."

"I'm not—"

She snickers and hangs up before I can finish my protest, and I scoff with amusement as I toss my phone back onto my bed. If I'm brutally honest with myself, I'm glad I have Kenzie here at Everbound. Although, if she knew the truth about me, she would also hate me.

That's enough to wipe away my smile, and I walk to the window, looking out over the snowy patches in the dark fields surrounding Everbound. There's a thick cloud cover overhead, meaning it will be nearly pitch black in Everbound Forest later.

Which means it will be more dangerous and time-consuming to go, you fool.

I've never been good at listening to myself.

So when midnight rolls around hours later, I finish tugging on my favorite black leather gloves, pull my dark hood over my face, and climb out the window. Using the door is a non-option since I can't be sure Crypt isn't still out in that hall somewhere or if he's out feeding on dreams. Carefully scaling down the side of Everbound Castle in the wintry night air, I drop silently to my feet and check to make sure no one is in this particular courtyard before setting off for Everbound Forest.

I know exactly where the ruins are. Rumor has it that a couple hundred years ago, another castle was built near Everbound as a backup fortress, but it was destroyed by an insane storm caused by some legacy's curse getting out of control. Everyone at the fortress was killed, and the ghosts still stand watch over what's left of the place.

Lifting a faint light spell in the palm of my hand, I study my surroundings in the dark, forbidding forest full of barren trees and mysterious shadows. An unnatural howling breaks out far in the distance, and I can hear rough growls echoing from another direction. The creatures in Everbound Forest seem to be more active at night.

The forest air is stirring with chill, spooky mist, and sinister fears that seem to delve under the skin like ghostly termites.

I love it.

Putting out my light, I arrive at the ruins and wait at the fringe of the tree line, looking for a hint of whoever else might be here. I'm armed to the teeth tonight, with my adamantine dagger tucked comfortingly in my boot and several other knives and weapons concealed on my person.

"That you, Oakley?" someone calls, stepping out of the ruins with a glowing mage light in their hands.

It's Harlow, and four other legacies are with her. None of them are Sierra.

Only five on one? I expected more. Maybe they have more friends hiding nearby. That would be fun.

"You can come closer. We don't bite," one of them laughs.

"What a shame," I reply as I approach.

It takes only seconds for me to analyze the best course for taking them out. Slitting two of their throats would take mere seconds, and the one on the left, who looks more physically intimidating, would be easy to take out with my adamantine blade. Harlow's neck snapped. The petite girl wearing the House of Arcana symbol on her shirt might throw out some impressive magic, but I still doubt I'll have a decent fight on my hands.

Disappointing, but it's time to get on with it.

The one in the House of Arcana shirt shuffles uncomfortably. "Um…before you attack us, could you listen to what we have to say?"

Fuck. Is she a psychic? I can't let anyone into my thoughts. Immediately, I empty my head of everything of substance as I've practiced countless times in my training.

Seeing the dagger already in my hand, Harlow snorts. "Girl. Relax. Monica isn't reading your thoughts, she's just an empath. And we're not going to kill you."

"Why not?"

"Because we're trying to *recruit* you, dumbass."

Blinking, I study each of them in turn again. It's dark aside from Harlow's dim mage light, but I realize everyone here is in the House of Arcana. Three women and two men, all looking at me with varying expressions of amusement, wariness, and curiosity.

But none of them with disgust, which makes me realize what this is.

"You're all atypical casters."

"Except me," Harlow nods. "But my mom was an atypical caster. Keep that to yourself, though."

Which means...

"This has something to do with the anti-legacy shit," I guess.

One of the guys grunts, scratching his beard. "Big conclusion to jump to. This is much more about being in each other's corners as the other legacies start turning on us when they start to get freaked out. I already had a siren threaten me earlier that if more so-called *real* legacies are found dead with anti-legacy threats, he's going to kill me first."

"I've been threatened, too," another of them groans. "As if it isn't bad enough that I have to spend the rest of my life around a bunch of dangerous legacies just because magic decided to pop up in my veins, now we'll all be targeted first if things keep going south."

Harlow folds her arms, looking me over. "And since you're already a prime target for so many legacies come next semester, thanks to your all-star quintet...you're in double shit now, Oakley. Face it. You're one of us, and asscasters need to stick together."

I don't *stick together* with anyone.

"So this is like a club for atypical casters. It has nothing to do with the burning pyres?"

"Not unless you want it to," Harlow grins.

Which answers my question. Maybe not all of them were involved with it, but she certainly was. The way she looks so smug about it is almost fucked up enough to make me like her. She's certainly done a good job of blending in with highly ranked legacies despite her moonlighting as an anti-legacy sympathizer.

"And you're the self-appointed president," I surmise.

"Hardly. After you handed Sierra her ass during combat, I realized you might be helpful. We're just in this to help keep each other alive," Harlow goes on, turning serious. "Checking in on each other, staying aware of what other students or professors think. And if they decide we're a threat just because we come from the human side of the tracks, we can go on the run together."

She means on the run from the bounty hunters that the Legacy

Council would send after us. They're the ones who hunt down and kill any legacy over the age of twenty-one that hasn't been officially registered with the Legacy Council.

As warm and fuzzy as it might make these guys feel to have each others' backs, it's still disappointing that this didn't turn into a frightening, bloodied brawl in the woods at midnight.

So much potential, wasted.

With a sigh, I sheathe my dagger into a hidden pocket. "I don't run, and I don't need any help staying alive. But if any of you are threatened again, invite me to the party. I enjoy spilling blood."

The bearded guy raises his brows. "Damn. You sound a lot more badass than you look. Not that you look bad or anything, just…uh, frumpy."

"Shut up, Evan," Monica sighs.

She looks at me with a sad sort of understanding. I wonder if she can feel how much I want to get away from her. As someone who purposefully ignores my emotions so they won't get in the way, empaths freak me out.

"I sense that you've been through a lot, Maven. We all have. Being a human in the world of legacies is…"

"Fucking terrifying," Evan mutters.

"Exhausting," another of them tacks on.

"A different world," Monica nods, smiling a little. "Just know we're a safe space."

No such thing.

"Good chat," I say flatly, turning to walk away before they think they can get chummy with me. "Don't bother me again unless there's someone to kill," I add over my shoulder before retreating into the shadowy forest.

20

SILAS

I'VE ALWAYS THOUGHT my curse would push me past the brink of insanity, but my keeper might beat it to the cut.

I'm at my wit's end.

Her behavior is erratic, and her personality is impossible to make sense of. One day, she ignores every attempt to get her attention and refuses to let me heal her, even though knowing her skin is stinging drives me up the wall. The next day, her tongue is like the barbed tip of a wyvern's tail, and every word out of her mouth is laced with acid. It's almost like she's actively trying to mimic every obnoxious person I've ever met.

But then, there are moments when I catch hints of the Maven I first saw several nights ago when she first dropped her facade in front of me. A taunting, intoxicating enigma, carefully concealing her true emotions.

I can't tell what's a lie and what's truth with her, but even when she's shattering potions that took me hours to make, ignoring any texts or calls, and stirring up the voices in my head…

Gods help me—I *crave* her.

By Friday night, after checking in on Maven throughout the day between classes only to see her bat her beautiful eyes at Everett at lunch while giving me the cold shoulder, I've decided I need alcohol to cope with the mounting urge to drag her back to my apartment, tie her to my bed, and tease her delicious body until she understands exactly how she makes me feel—dancing on the edge of a knife, mindless with curiosity, frustration, and newfound thirst.

I would never touch her without permission.

But that doesn't stop me from fantasizing.

Downing the remainder of my glass of bourbon mixed with fae mead, I rub my face and glare at the fireplace in my private apartment. Alcohol barely dulls the demons in my head. Still, it's impossible to focus on preparations for First Placement or my own magical experimentations when every moment is filled with the creeping knowledge that my keeper is in danger.

I *know* Maven is in danger.

She'll be targeted by everyone at this school when quintet rankings officially start. If I can't get closer to her before then—if I can't even get her to answer a fucking *text message*...our quintet is going to fall apart at the seams.

My attention drifts to the opened letter on the footrest before me, and I scowl.

I'm no closer to winning the wager with the others, but it's clear they aren't handling this well, either. It would be satisfying to see them miserable, except for the fact that I'm running out of time and need dragon scales. Perhaps I should start sabotaging the others somehow. They'll hardly be surprised if I fight dirty.

My phone vibrates in my pocket. I groan, standing to pour myself another drink as I answer.

"What?"

"Meet me and the others in our apartment," Baelfire huffs.

"Brotherly bonding will have to wait," I slur dryly, sipping more bourbon. "I'm not fit for company right now."

His growl crackles over the phone. "I don't fucking care. We all need to talk. It's about Maven."

That makes me go still. "What about her?"

"Just meet in the apartment in ten minutes."

Five minutes later, I throw open the front door of our shared quintet apartment—which, again, only Baelfire has been staying in. It's furnished and stocked, fully ready for our group to live comfortably, but no matter how many times any of us have brought up moving in with Maven, she just tells us to fuck off.

In the home theater room off to the side of the entry, Crypt is lounging on one of the large couches, watching a muted black and white horror film I've never seen before, while Baelfire is on his back, scowling at the ceiling. Even Everett is here, leaning against the wall.

He glances at me with disinterest. "Good. We're all here. Now you can spit it out, dragon."

Baelfire stands, folding his arms. "I overheard from Kenzie that Maven is going out of town tomorrow."

That catches Crypt's attention. He turns off the screen. "Not without me."

"Not without any of us," Bael says, lifting his chin as he regards each of us in turn. He has dark shadows under his eyes and looks like shit, proving I'm not the only one struggling with what to do about our contrary keeper. "We're all going."

Recalling every time Maven has rolled her eyes at me, walked away in the middle of me trying to talk to her, and generally metaphorically flipped me off, I grimace.

"She won't go along with this idea. She's been...*difficult.*"

"Agreed. Isn't she deliciously unexpected?" Crypt sighs.

I didn't think it was possible for him to care about anything or anyone, let alone sigh over them. It's hard to reconcile the Nightmare Prince I know with the incubus looking longingly at the door. I once watched him rip a man's eyeballs out for looking at him in a way he didn't like.

Being in his presence never fails to make me twitchy. Even the alcohol in my blood doesn't dampen my irritation.

"Before you go stalk her in Limbo and leave us hanging as usual, shut up and let Baelfire explain his plan," I grit.

"Touchy, touchy," he smirks. "I already have my own plan."

"No going lone wolf here," Bael snaps. "This is about bonding with Maven together for the first time since we've clearly been fucking things up on our own. As much as I'd love to wrap Snowflake in bacon and toss him into a hydra's lair—"

Everett looks heavenwards as if he's petitioning the gods for patience.

"—when push comes to shove, we need to start working as a team. After all, we'll be bound to the same woman for the rest of our lives. She doesn't deserve to be stuck with a bunch of fucking toddlers who can't play nice."

"I can play *very* nice if she'd only let me," I mutter.

Everett snorts.

Fine. Even I can admit that I sound like a petulant child.

Crypt pulls out his lighter, flicking the flame on and off impatiently. "Fine. What's the plan?"

Baelfire looks momentarily surprised, and he's not the only one. Crypt has never been a team player. From the start, I've assumed he would contribute very little to our quintet.

He's the oldest of us and I remember being fascinated by him when we all first met as children. After all, I'd heard so much about Somnus's bastard son from my mother, ever the gossip. To me, he had seemed stoic, unflappable, stylishly rebellious. But I'd quickly learned that he was a sociopath who lacked all empathy and would happily watch the world burn.

And that was before he messed up my family.

"The plan is to sweep Maven off her feet," Bael says, drawing my attention again. "I overheard Kenzie mention she's going to Pennsylvania for a wedding. We're going to hijack her trip and turn it into a fun getaway. Maybe she'll be more willing to open up to us in a human environment like the one she grew up in. We can do normal human shit with her, take her on a date or something. I'm sure adjusting to Everbound and the way legacies do things has been hard enough on her, and we've been making it worse by giving her no space to adapt."

For a beat, that sinks in for all of us. He's right. She only discovered she was an atypical caster weeks ago, and our culture and world are utterly foreign to her. While I suspected she might be trying to reject us because the idea of a quintet was odd to her, I didn't consider how her life must have turned upside down when she manifested her magic.

It makes me want to soothe her somehow, to hold her hand as she comes to terms with being lumped in with the legacies now.

But if I tried, she would probably tell me to fuck off.

Again.

"I'll book transportation for us and somewhere nice to stay," Everett mutters, studying the floor. For a fraction of a second, he looks torn. "I mean…I'll book somewhere for all of *you*, somewhere Maven will be comfortable, but I won't be go—"

"Shove it, Snowflake. We're all fucking going."

The professor scowls, loosening his tie. My brows bounce up when I see the silvery frost at his fingertips. That's a definite sign that he's panicking about something deep down. Whatever it is, there's little chance he would ever share it with the rest of us.

"Have it your way," the ice elemental finally mutters before leaving the apartment.

"Moody fucker," Baelfire shakes his head, and then he checks his phone and growls. "Not much time left before midnight. I'll be back."

No doubt he's going to go hunting to appease his curse.

Disbanding now is a good idea. The slight buffering of the fae mead I had is wearing off, quickly giving way to oily suspicions slinking through my veins. My head throbs and I walk out of the apartment before Baelfire does, intent on returning to my private dorm's uncontested safety before the voices in my head get too loud.

But my feet have a mind of their own, directed by the longing that's strangling the core of my being, and soon, I find myself standing outside of Maven's dorm, staring at her door.

The door that I warded to keep out everyone but her…

And me.

When weaving the spells, I gave in to the twisted temptation to be the only one with access to her space. After threatening both Baelfire and Crypt not to cross Maven's lines and to give her privacy…now here I am.

I'm a possessive, obsessed, fucked up hypocrite.

But I'm not sorry for it.

Laying my hand on the door, I can sense through the magic wards that no one is in the room. It's disappointing, and I'm immediately wondering where on earth she could be. Spending time with her lion shifter friend? Some secret anti-legacy meeting? Simply trying to avoid us?

The temptation to glean what I can about my keeper from her private space is far too potent, and I open the door.

It's minimalistic and extremely tidy. Some might see it as unwelcoming or not cozy, but I can easily picture Maven in this space.

My attention drifts to the minor light spells steadily warming several pots of indoor plants, all thriving and luscious, on her desk. I still have yet to see my little atypical caster actually *cast*, but I still smile at the thought of it and move closer, eyes sweeping over everything else.

Black curtains. Black sheets and blankets. Not a single display of decorations, pictures, or even our House banner to be found. The only colors come from the green plants and the blood-red dreamcatcher I wove for her hanging by her door. It fills me with gratification that she's using it despite the fight she put up.

Running my fingers over her dresser, I give in to my curiosity and pull out the top drawer. The only thing in here is gloves…and a notebook.

I shouldn't open it.

Oh, please.

As if you would stop your snooping now.

The voices are right. I'm already too far gone, too desperate to figure out my keeper.

Gingerly opening the notebook, I flip through several blank pages before finding any writing. Maven's script is a tidy, beautiful swirl of ink, but it takes me a moment of staring for the words to make sense because…what the fuck?

Make Them Hate Me

-Bore them to tears. (Easy. Just be yourself.)

-Be mean. (Again, easy.)

-Ignore them.

-Figure out how to be clingy and high maintenance.

~~*-Annoy them.*~~ *(Too time-consuming.)*

-Act like a bitch at every chance.

-Play head games. (Use Everett to make the other three jealous. See if Sierra's plan to seduce them worked, and if so, ~~*rip her apart limb by fucking limb*~~ *pretend to be heartbroken. If all else fails, try to stomach kissing Coach Gallagher to see if that finally pisses them off enough.)*

-Figure out how to prey on their curses. (Step One: Figure out what their curses even are.)

After reading the list and then incredulously reading it one more time, it finally sinks in.

Gods above.

All along, Maven has been *trying* to make us hate her.

She tried rejecting us, and now she wants to lose us. She really thinks we would ever give her up and appeal to the gods for a different keeper. Whether it's because of her involvement with the anti-legacy movement or some other reason I can't fathom, she is trying to make us hate her.

And the way she's been going about it, all these tactics and mind games, even going so far as to contemplate preying on our curses, has just been…

Diabolical. She's utterly vicious.

Fuck me.

A smile curls my lips, and my heart begins to pound. She intended to make us hate her, but now that I know she's possibly as cutthroat as I am, she's never getting rid of me.

"Game on, my vicious little minx."

21

CRYPT

When Maven leaves her dorm, I watch her every move from the end of the hall. She zips up her coat, pulling on dark leather gloves and tossing a wary glance over her shoulder—but not in my direction.

Over the last few days, I've carefully tested within what proximity she can sense my presence in Limbo. If I stay a fair distance away, I can still obsess over my keeper at my leisure without her being any the wiser. Though the fact that she can ever sense me at all in Limbo is intriguing. Not even other incubi can see or sense me most of the time.

Just another reason my darling is so fascinating.

As soon as she vanishes down the stairwell at the end of this hall, I launch up through the ceiling, passing through four stories of Everbound until I come out on the gabled rooftop where Decimus is sitting at the edge of a turret, legs dangling as he gazes out over the mist and snow-wreathed grounds surrounding the school. When I step out of Limbo beside him, his brows bounce up.

"Our pretty raven has left her nest," I confirm.

The plan is for me to follow Maven's road trip progress, unseen, while he flies ahead to where Crane and Frost already are. They traveled separately last night to Pennsylvania to get things ready. I must admit, when working together, we don't make an abysmal team.

Decimus pulls out his phone and shoots that update to the others. Crane ensured that I have a phone to use for this particular venture, too, since they'll be relying on me for updates. He used some overcomplicated spells on it to ensure it will work after going in and out of Limbo. It can't be used there, but it should be connected to my ability to walk between planes. Every other electronic or living thing I've tried to take into Limbo with me for any extended period of time has never survived the trip back.

Decimus stands and stretches before warning, "Don't you fucking dare lose track of my mate. And keep us updated so Everett will know when to—"

We've already been over this, and he's annoying me, so I shove him off the edge of the roof.

His shouted curse quickly morphs into a guttural roar as scales and talons explode into existence in a blaze of blue fire. Before he can hit the ground, golden wings flare out wide, and he swoops upward, wings punishing the air as he snarls in my direction with smoke rising from his nostrils.

I make a shooing motion, already fixated on the abandoned staff entrance that I'm positive Maven will come out of.

Growling, Decimus takes off, just barely gliding far enough out of sight before Maven's small, dark form slips from the very exit I hoped she would. She takes a hard left, quickly trekking through the wintry cold toward the parking area a short walk from Everbound Castle. I step off the roof just as I slip back into Limbo, gliding overhead and watching as she slips into a light blue Mustang.

It takes a moment before the car turns on. Her driving seems jerky at first, breaking and pausing several times before very slowly peeling out of the parking lot. Interesting.

Has she not driven in a long time? I find that idea bothers me—she is setting off on nearly a four-hour drive, after all.

For the first couple hours of her drive, I soar along after her in

Limbo, occasionally getting distracted by the glowing wisps that dance by in the murky, slightly warped dream world. Wisps are the ghosts of past dreams and are highly dangerous for anyone who isn't me, especially if they group together to break into the mortal plane of existence. But there aren't enough of them here to warrant any action, and I'm far more focused on Maven's progress.

Three hours in, she finally stops to refuel the car. I settle on the ground outside of the service station, watching in curious amusement as she studies the petrol pump like it's a monster she's never encountered before.

It takes her a while to figure it out, and I laugh out loud at the way her cute little nose wrinkles when she accidentally sprays the ground with gas while shoving it into the car.

Slipping around the back of the service station, I step back into the mortal world and slip the enchanted phone from my back pocket, along with a lighter and cigarette. Smoking reverium, which only grows in Limbo, helps my body relax after frequently swapping between planes. It takes a toll, walking between two worlds without the ability to call either home.

Crane answers on the first ring. "Where is she?"

Already, I can't stand not having her in sight, so I lean against the side of the building to catch a glimpse of where she's still adorably frowning at the pump. I want to smooth away the furrow between her brows with my lips.

"Fueling up in a quaint little town about half an hour out."

"Good. I'll tell Everett to get started. Just get her here before the—"

My spine goes rigid when a large human man in a baseball cap leaves where he's refueling his semi-truck and approaches Maven with a smile plastered across his bearded face. His aura is like burnt vomit. The way his eyes roll over her, glancing around to see if anyone else is here with her, has me ready to reach into his mind and rip it to shreds.

Even before I was old enough to understand the horrors they

daydreamed of, I made it my business to prey on predators. To show no mercy to those who turned their sick dreams into realities. After so many years of hunting down those predators, even without glimpsing this man's psyche or his dreams, I can see all the hallmarks of a sick pervert as he stops directly beside my keeper.

"Hey there, sweetie pie. You're lookin' a little lost. I'd love to help you," he drawls.

Maven ignores him, calmly observing the ticking numbers on the pump.

"Need a hand?" The man licks his lips, studying her profile and baggy clothes that leave so much to the imagination—and clearly, he's letting his imagination run rampant as he subtly adjusts himself in his pants. A dark daydream starts to color Limbo around his head.

"Fucking bastard," I growl.

My markings light up. I'm going to cut off his cock inch by inch. Should only take about three slices.

"Crypt?" Crane snaps in my ear, making me realize I've been tuning him out. "What's going on? Is Maven all right?"

The man gets annoyed with Maven ignoring him and reaches out to cover her gloved hand with his big, grease-stained one on the gas pump handle. At the same time, his other hand finds her back but slips down, seeking to brush over her ass.

My vision goes red, and I hang up, ready to rip this putrid human into a thousand pathetic, sobbing pieces.

But Maven reacts before I can even take a step forward.

In a smooth move that's too fast for me to comprehend fully, she yanks the gas pump out of the car, wraps the hose tightly around the man's neck, and shoves him against the petrol machine. He yelps and chokes on the hose, but after a moment, she lets go, leaving it slack. Her expression still hasn't changed.

"You bitch!" he shouts, trying to unwrap himself from the hose, which has already left a dark mark around his neck. "I'll beat your ass for this! What the fucking hell is wrong with you?"

"You don't want to know."

He snarls and finally shoves the hose off of himself, taking a threatening step toward her. I take a step forward, too, gritting my teeth as my hair and clothes begin to drift around me.

But she doesn't back down, and her voice turns chilling. "Get in your truck and leave before I shove that nozzle through your eye socket, pump your head full, and set it on fire."

The threat is graphic enough for the man, who pales and scrambles away, slamming his truck door and flooring it. The forgotten pump in his own truck yanks hard before popping out as he speeds away with screeching tires.

And I am left in rapt fascination as Maven snorts, lips curling up into a dark smile as she pays for her fuel.

She *enjoyed* frightening that man.

Knowing that makes my cock ache, and I slip back around the side of the station before she can spot me. Gripping my erection through my jeans, I lean my head back and hiss out a breath. Gods above, I wish she was the one gripping me tightly like this.

People are never more themselves than when they think no one is watching. Seeing that small glimpse into Maven's true personality has me grinning more to myself as I redial Crane.

He's seething. "If something happened to Maven, I'm going to—"

"Don't bother with an empty threat. I just had a lovely show of our keeper handling things on her own." Though I'll still track that bastard down and punish him later, in his nightmares. He won't wake up sane. "She's fine now, about to leave again. Have Frost ready."

Several minutes later, the time finally comes to officially hijack my darling obsession's little trip. Dark clouds have converged over this entire area, and snow has begun dusting from the sky so heavily that some cars are pulling off the highway, wary of the sudden blizzard.

Unfortunately, she doesn't pull over as we intended. But that doesn't stop me.

Flying low to her car, I slip through the roof of it and drop out of Limbo, directly into the passenger's seat of her friend's car. Maven inhales sharply, and the car swerves a bit, but otherwise, she just clenches her teeth and stares straight ahead at the quickly whitening road.

"Go away, Crypt."

I *love* how she says my name. Someday, I'll love her moaning it.

"How important is it to you to make this wedding, love?" I ask.

Her brow furrows, and then she sighs. "You overheard Kenzie talking, didn't you?"

"Unimportant. What *is* important is that you pull over and let me drive."

She rolls her eyes. "Why would—"

Someone in front of her breaks hard, sliding on the icy road and twisting completely sideways. I curse at them as I reach over to grip the steering wheel between Maven's hands, barely managing to navigate the car through the mess of parked vehicles along this stretch of road.

Maven huffs, blowing strands of dark hair out of her face. If she was panicked at all about the breaking cars, she doesn't show it.

"Let go."

"Let me drive, darling. You've never driven before, let alone in this kind of weather."

She side-eyes me briefly. "Is it that obvious?"

"Only because your driving resembles an electrified jellyfish," I grin.

The car suddenly loses traction, and for a moment, we slide slightly into the opposite lane—directly into oncoming traffic, where a minivan begins blaring its horn, its lights dim from the heavy snowstorm. Maven veers back into the correct lane, but I'm no longer grinning. I could slip into Limbo on impact and be fine, but the risk of her being injured grates on my nerves.

"Pull over. Now."

"Make me."

Fuck me, she's beautifully stubborn. Very well. She asked for it.

I adjust my grip on the wheel until my hands completely cover her gloved fingers. Immediately, I can sense her discomfort, and she pulls back, allowing me to pull to the side of the road where she brakes to a stop.

My hands are still on the wheel, so when I look at Maven, her face is close to mine. Her dark eyes are brimming with irritation as she studies me, but I'm using all my willpower not to lean forward and taste those tempting lips.

Finally, I force myself to focus. "Let's switch seats, shall we? Unless you don't mind being buried under a mountain of snow in this car with me for a couple of days," I add, enjoying the idea. "When the car battery dies, we can share body heat."

"You're an ass," she finally mutters, kicking open the driver's door.

I agree. Once she's in the passenger seat, brushing snowflakes off her nose and cheeks, I carefully pull back onto the road, adjusting the rearview mirror. She glowers at me, and I laugh.

"Something bothering you, love?"

"Stop calling me that. You know you're bothering me. Have you been following me since this morning?"

"Maybe."

She folds her arms when I take the next exit, following the directions I memorized earlier. "This is the wrong way."

"Nope," I say chipperly, popping the 'p.' "This is precisely how we get to our lodgings for the night. If you don't trust my word for it, call one of the others to make sure."

My little obsession stares at me for a moment before swearing with surprising vigor, glaring out the window. "You all planned this."

"Mostly, it was Decimus, but yes."

"And this storm…" She scowls.

"Frost's doing," I confirm, further amused when she flips me off for laughing.

Soon, I turn into the roundabout pull-in area for a large, beautiful inn lit up with holiday lights that glow in the thick snow flurrying around us. The luxurious inn is a fair distance from the rest of a nearby small town, set off the road with a backdrop of woods.

Maven takes it all in and huffs. "I'm not staying here."

"Then you'll accept being snowed in here with me?" I ask hopefully. "I can slip into Limbo to travel and bring back anything you want. Food. Blankets. Lingerie."

She gives me a dry look, grabs her bag, and gets out, slamming the door behind her.

It was worth a try.

I turn off the car and join her. As we approach the entrance of the massive colonial-style inn, Crane opens the door and smirks at Maven, who is carefully controlling her expression to look bored.

After days of watching the others interact with my keeper from a distance, I note that the way Crane is looking at her is different from yesterday. He seems far less frustrated yet even more possessive, with an edge of desire he doesn't bother to hide anymore.

Interesting.

"Welcome," he murmurs.

She walks right past him into the inn foyer, looking around at the impressive interior. I knew Frost would probably pick the most expensive, luxe option of this entire area, but I must admit it's a gorgeous place to stay with our keeper, all historic Colonial-style architecture but with a modern high-end touch. Glittering chandeliers, plush carpets, golden accents, and a beautiful staircase leading up to the second story.

But when I try to step through the threshold, I come up against an invisible wall.

Of course. Damn that blood fae and his obsession with protective wards. He's used magic to mark this building as an inhabited dwelling, so I can't enter without permission.

"Where are the humans who manage this inn?" Maven asks over her shoulder, jaw set.

"Gone for now. Everett rented the entire place," Crane says, nodding down one long hallway to our left. "The kitchen is that way. Baelfire is preparing an early dinner for you since Crypt never mentioned you stopping for food. I can take your bag—"

"What you can do is fuck off," she interrupts, glaring at each of us in turn. "How many times do I have to reject you assholes before you get it through your thick heads that *I don't want you?"*

Crane steps closer to her, a smirk twisting his lips as he leans down to whisper, "Keep lying to yourself if you want. But from now on, I reject your lies, *sangfluir*."

That's a fae word I don't know, but Maven does because she presses her lips together before finally sidestepping Crane. Even with the oversized cargo pants she has on, we both watch the sway of her ass as she ascends the stairs to find a guest room.

When she disappears around a corner, I look pointedly at Crane. "Invite me in."

"I think not," he shrugs nonchalantly. "We're all safer with you out there."

I offer a dark smirk. "You think so? Because even with all his many intricate wards and blood-drenched dreamcatchers, it only took me a couple of hours to get through to your uncle and infest his mind."

My taunt works. Crane is immediately on edge, his red glare pinning me, and I think we might finally get to draw blood for blood. But then Decimus appears from the hallway to our left, rolling his eyes at the two of us. As if we're ridiculous when *he's* the one wearing a frilly white apron.

"What part of *play nice* don't you two dickheads get? Just come in already, Crypt."

Immediately, the invisible wall disappears, and I step through the doorway, enjoying the way it makes Crane's eye twitch.

"With pleasure."

"Yeah, whatever, creep. Now, where's Maven?" Decimus asks impatiently, his draconic-gold eyes slipping to the stairs as his nostrils flare. "Is she—"

"Irritated? Very," I supply.

He pulls off the apron and shoves it at me as he passes, stalking up the stairs. "Don't let the pork chops burn," he calls over his shoulder.

I snort. "Yes, because an incubus who feeds on dreams and hasn't had physical sustenance in over a decade is the ideal sous chef for a romantic dinner."

Crane ignores me, following the dragon up the stairs. And since I would much rather observe my quintet trying to find our footing with our keeper, I toss the apron over my shoulder and follow them, slipping back into Limbo.

22

MAVEN

IT TAKES a lot to make me lose control. I've been through too much to be fazed by little things.

But they're. Fucking. Getting. There.

I step into one of the suites of the over-the-top inn and glare at the beautiful decorations, massive four-poster bed, sprawling marble hot tub in the corner, and the connected bathroom that could fit a herd of rhinoceros in the shower. Everything looks straight out of those luxurious magazines Kenzie reads, from the display of blood-red roses and glistening crystal ware on the suite's table to the kissing swan towels on the luscious bed.

Outside the large arched window across from the bed, wind howls and snow has turned everything white, obscuring even the trees nestled around the inn. It's a blizzard of epic proportions, cutting off the outside world.

Cursing the gods under my breath, I put my bag on the nearest dresser and blow my hair out of my face in frustration.

Until it calms down, I'm trapped in here with these idiots just as they intended. They plotted together to manipulate my trip, forcing me to spend time with them. Trapped us all together, even though I've been making them miserable for days. It's like they're all fucking masochists and can't get enough of me treating them like shit.

Ironically, that would *almost* make the gods right about making me their keeper since I'm something of a sadist.

This was supposed to be my chance to shore up my defenses against them, but now I don't know how long I can keep my cool around my rejected matches. On top of that, my mission to get Lykoudis's heart just got complicated.

I am nothing but deadly calm, I remind myself with determination. *I feel nothing else.*

But that does nothing to still the warm hum that washes over me when Baelfire knocks on the ajar door with a shit-eating grin when he sees me. Silas's gaze burns like he's seeing right through me. I can feel Crypt here, too, and I wish I knew where he was standing so I could flip that smug bastard off.

"There's my cute little raincloud," Baelfire greets warmly, tucking his hands in his hoodie pockets as he approaches like a conscious effort to keep from touching me. "How was the drive, baby?"

Exhausting. I never knew how annoying it was to drive on icy roads. Probably because Crypt guessed right about the fact that I've never driven *at all.* But I've seen Kenzie do it whenever we've gone to Halfton, and the controls were simple enough to figure out. I didn't crash into anyone, so I consider it a success.

"Peachy, until I was shanghaied into spending time with four assholes who can't fathom the concept of boundaries," I deadpan.

His smile is cajoling. "In my defense, boundaries suck. I want as few of those between us as possible, Boo."

I open my mouth to find some withering retort, but when I feel a twinge of pain in my chest, I quickly snap my mouth shut. It's slower this time, but definitely there—that familiar pain creeping out from my center, making my throat muscles seize.

Fuck. No.

My condition rearing its ugly head right now is literally *the worst* possible scenario.

This is bad. Genuinely fucking bad because there will be no escape from their questions if they see me like this, and they might figure it all out. Then I'd be stuck in this inn with four powerful legacies trying to kill me.

Typically, that would sound fun, but I really don't have time for this. I have to deliver an alpha wolf shifter's heart to a demon by midnight tomorrow.

Stay calm. Breathe through the pain.

"All of you, get out," I tell them. "Now."

Silas's gaze sharpens, and he edges closer, too. But when he speaks, his voice is unbearably gentle. "What's wrong, *ima sangfluir?*"

My blood blossom.

The damn man is giving me a nickname in his native tongue, one that holds too much meaning for a blood fae. Surely, they can't all have nicknames for me. That's just obnoxious.

The pain starts to mount. I need them out of here *now*. Putting on my bitchiest tone of voice, I roll my eyes. "What's wrong is that I'm allergic to pushy assholes who can't take a fucking hint. All I want is for you guys to leave me alone."

Suddenly, Silas is directly in front of me, leaning down so I can't turn away from his penetrating gaze. It's a wonder I'm not breaking out in a sweat, trying to keep the pain off my face. He's inches away, and I catch a light hint of bourbon and spice standing this close to him.

"What part of *I reject your lies* didn't you get? No more lying to me. Tell me what the real problem is so I can fix it," he commands, searching my face.

It doesn't help that Baelfire is on my other side, frowning deeply as he glances between the blood fae and myself. I think he's debating shoving Silas away, but he also wants to hear my answer.

But Silas can't fix what's wrong with me. No one can. I accepted that years ago.

Inhaling and exhaling evenly, I keep my poker face even though my chest *really fucking hurts.*

"I'm over this, Silas. I don't know what you want from me."

"Nothing less than everything. But to start, I want a chance to get to know you, the real you. Give all of us, including yourself, a sample of what our quintet could be. Give us one day before we… consider our options."

Wait. Is he admitting that they're finally considering appealing for another keeper?

Something unpleasant constricts my throat unexpectedly at that thought, but I ignore it just as much as I ignore the pain flaring in my chest. His words sink in deeper than I should let them go.

Letting them get to know the real me…

He has no idea what he's even asking.

The real me was broken years ago from the torture, isolation, and darkness. The real me is fucked in the head. Twisted. A monster who enjoys things I shouldn't.

But one day of not actively trying to make them hate me? Just letting go and being myself? It's too tempting. I'm so damn tired of rejecting them when deep down, no matter how wrong it is…

I want them.

You've always wanted them, you weakling.

The agony doubles in my chest, and I lace my fingers behind my back so they can't see me dig my nails into my flesh, desperate for anything to focus on but the torture in my torso. I just need them out of here. They can't see me like this. I'll agree to *anything* that gives me some privacy for a moment to let this episode pass.

"Fine," I say quickly. "You have one day with me."

Crypt suddenly appears to Baelfire's right, purple eyes glittering. "Pinky swear?"

"We're not leaving until you promise," Silas tacks on, eyes searing.

Gods, why are they making this so impossible? "I promise."

His lips curl up, and to my horror, I briefly get the urge to brush my lips against his mouth to see what that devious smirk feels like.

You're not thinking straight. That's just the pain talking.

"Hell fucking yes," Baelfire says, clapping his hands together and rubbing them conspiratorially. "Si, tell Snowflake to get back here. Maven, dinner will be—"

"Get. The fuck. Out," I grit, vision starting to blur despite how unreadable I've kept my face.

For the first time in my life, the gods seem to take mercy on me because Baelfire and Silas share a look I don't fully understand and leave. Crypt blows me a kiss and vanishes, but it's another few moments before I feel his presence leave.

The moment I know I'm really alone, I shut the door, lock it, and fall to my knees, slamming a hand over my mouth to desperately try holding a whimper of pain back because Baelfire might hear it.

Nausea barrels through me while the corners of my vision darken and fold. It takes all my strength to crawl to the desk where my bag sits. Desperately, I pull one of the dark vials I packed from the bottom of the bag and uncork it, downing it in one go.

Immediately, cold sweeps through me, and the darkness takes me away.

Images flicker through my mind. Most of them are too fast to register, but one of them sticks: A scene of me laying flat on my back, dark blood pooling on the tiled floor beneath me as a knife protrudes from my chest. A shadow stands over me, but I jolt awake before I can figure out who it is.

It seems only a few minutes have passed—the blizzard is still raging outside the bedroom window, the vial is still clutched in my hand, and I'm freezing where I lay coated in a cold sweat on the floor.

Giving myself a few moments to let the churning in my stomach subside, I groan softly and try to sit up. Something buzzes nearby, and when I realize it's not just a sound I'm hallucinating after that episode, I dig through the upended contents of my bag to squint at my phone.

Sighing, I answer. "Hi."

"Hey! Did you guys make it to Pennsylvania all right?" Kenzie asks. "And did you check the weather forecast before you left? Because I just heard that there's a *massive* snowstorm over there. It's supposed to get, like, really bad. Luka says—"

"Luka?" I cut in with a frown, still out of sorts.

She makes a sound halfway between a hum and a sigh. "Well... yeah. I know you said I was protecting myself by not letting him into the quintet too quickly, but over the last few days, he's been really nice. And I mean *nice,* nice. It's not fake. He's opened up a lot about some pretty terrible shit in his past that made him react the way he did to me, and he's trying to get to know me. We've had some long talks, and I think—"

As she talks, I stagger into the bathroom to splash my face with cold water, grimacing at how sallow my skin looks in the mirror. I look almost as exhausted as I feel.

"—and we all talked about our plans for the Matched Ball with him, and it was a good step in the right direction, so...gods, listen to me drag on. Back to what I was calling about. Are you and your guys safe and sound somewhere?"

"Until we ride out this storm," I grumble.

"I bet that's not the only thing you'll be riding. Good luck getting snowed in somewhere with nothing but four very horny, obsessed men to entertain you," she teases brightly. "Either you guys are going to play a crazy amount of Go Fish, or you're going to lose your virginity in every possible way multiple times."

I roll my eyes as I exit the bathroom. "Not happening. I'm still not going to be in a quintet."

"But *why not?"*

"Go fish."

Kenzie sighs. "Okay, well...maybe you won't be in their quintet, but you deserve to enjoy yourself for once. Let your guard down, let them actually get to know you, and maybe you'll see how perfect you all will be together. Seriously, May. Promise me you'll enjoy yourself and give them a chance."

I look at my gloved hand, flexing against the leather. "I promise."

And even if it will hurt like hell later, I mean that.

"And remember to use lots and lots of lube," she adds. "Especially if you do back door stuff."

Oh, my gods. "*Bye,* slut."

"Bye, monk," she snickers.

Tossing the device onto the oversized bed, I glance at the door. I'm tired, annoyingly affected by everything my matches do, and most importantly, I'm an assassin who can't complete her mission with four gorgeous legacy stalkers breathing over my shoulder.

I'll have to give them the slip eventually, but I can't right now with the raging snowstorm.

And then there's a growing part of me that just...doesn't want to give them the slip.

It's a bad idea to get close to them. I know that. I'm already on thin ice. If I let myself get attached to them any further, my thin facade will shatter, and everything I've been working towards will be ruined.

But if I already know how my story will end, would it be so terrible to allow myself one day? One chapter of good memories in a book of darkness?

Probably.

But right now, I want it. And for the next twenty-four hours, I'm done pushing them away.

23

MAVEN

I STEP INTO THE LONG, luxurious kitchen that gradually turns into an ornate dining room. One wall along all of it is solid glass. Maybe it normally has nice views, but right now it's a dark gray obscuring everything outside.

In the middle of the dining room is a table already set for dinner with crystal glass and burning candles flickering happily along the length of it. As soon as I walk in, Baelfire lights up with a smile in my direction from where he's tossing salad and...wearing an apron.

Who knew dragons could be domestic chefs? It's an odd sight, yet at the same time, somehow it also makes sense that he's comfortable in the kitchen.

Silas is on the phone in the dining room, facing the large window so I can't see his face, and his voice is too quiet to hear what he's saying. I can't see Crypt, but I can sense him somewhere in this room.

Baelfire uses his bare hand to reach in and retrieve two trays. Must be nice, being a heat-and-fire-proof dragon shifter. He shows me the sizzling offerings with a bright smile.

"I hope you like your butter-basted pork chops well done."

Damn. He's so proud, I almost don't want to pop his bubble.

Before I can decide whether or not to say something, Crypt

appears leaning against the wall by the fridge and drawls, "She's a *vegetarian*, you fucking buffoon."

Bael blinks. I can practically see the last few days rewinding in his head as he no doubt recalls all the times he piled food on my plate—usually meats I never touched. I didn't expect them to notice or care, but evidently, Crypt takes his stalking seriously.

"Shit. How did I miss that?" Baelfire grimaces and sets down the pans. "Is it because you have a soft spot for poor little animals? Because if so, I have some bad news. I hunt to kill, Maven. Like...a *lot.* So if you're one of those bleeding heart types..."

A morbid smile tries to pull on my mouth. "Nope. No bleeding hearts here."

His gaze snaps to my mouth. "I saw that. You just smiled."

"Barely."

"Still counts as getting you to smile."

I roll my eyes. "Want a gold star?"

His eyes heat and he rounds the counter to lean close without touching me, dropping his voice to a whisper that even Crypt won't hear.

"No. I want your praise. And just like you said, I'm going to fucking earn it."

Something greedy and curious pools low in my stomach at his hungry rasp. My eyes shift to Crypt leaning against the wall, and I expect to see him glaring at Baelfire, but when he catches me looking, he winks.

Why isn't he jealous? I would be. If I saw someone else with one of them like this...no matter how illogical it would be, or how *not mine* they are, I would be snapping more bones.

Wondering how far I can push it, I try not to think about what I'm doing and hold Crypt's stare as I stand on my tiptoes, pressing my lips against the corner of Baelfire's jaw under his ear. Bael exhales raggedly and cages me against the counter with his arms, still careful not to touch me.

But the Nightmare Prince doesn't look away as he smiles slowly at me, amused. "Taunting me, love? You should probably know I very much enjoy that. Edging. Teasing. The torment is delicious."

Well, then. That backfired.

"Maven…can I *please* touch you now?" Bael whispers.

Gods. He's so damn warm standing so close to me, and suddenly I'm having trouble thinking clearly, with these two looking at me like *I'm* the only dinner they want. But my lips are tingling from where they touched Bael, and suddenly I have to think about anything besides the fact that I just had his warm, bare skin against mine.

Not for the first time, I'm irritated at my inability to stomach physical contact. I don't enjoy being like this—the terror of feeling skin against mine, the familiar paralyzing sensation creeping up my spine and wrapping around my throat until I can't breathe. But even if I logically know that touching someone else isn't the end of the world, my body doesn't get the memo.

I'm a testament to how strong conditioning can be.

Even if I want to try touching them…I don't know how.

Baelfire sees the battle on my face and backs off immediately, smiling reassuringly as he opens the very overstocked fridge.

"So, pork is a no. Are you good with cheese? Do you like pasta?"

I didn't expect him to drop the subject. The fact that Crypt says nothing about it either is oddly comforting—as if despite the fact that they refuse to leave me alone, they aren't going to pry into anything that makes me genuinely uncomfortable.

They're not pushing me.

I watch Baelfire dice and sauté garlic, prepare other vegetables, and move through the kitchen with ease. I would offer to help, but I've never cooked a day in my life and even though I'm trying to hide it, the exhaustion from my recent episode is weighing on me.

Silas finishes his phone call and moves into the kitchen, focus trained on me. Something is different about the way he studies me, almost as if he knows something I don't and he enjoys it. That has me slipping back into a poker face in case he actually *has* figured something out about who and what I really am.

"Is Frost's tongue stuck to a frozen pole or something? What's taking him so long?" Bael asks, carefully plating a pile of cheesy pasta food that actually makes my stomach growl. The shifter hears that and grins at me. "*Bon appétit*, Boo."

"He'll arrive any moment," Silas replies, finally looking away from me as he and Baelfire get their own food and we move to the dining room.

Everett walks in a moment later, snowflakes dusted on the shoulders of his dark, photoshoot-worthy winter clothes and lingering on his skin, since it's not warm enough to melt them. The professor's gaze barely flits to me with an undertone of sheer boredom before he begins dishing up his own food.

Maybe he's annoyed with me for openly "flirting" with him at every chance even though he never agreed to help me make the others jealous. Or maybe he's just tired of putting up with my antics around him because he's dropped any semblance of enjoying my attention in front of the others.

I usually choose to be amused whenever people don't like me. It happens often, and there's something morbidly entertaining about rubbing someone else the wrong way.

But for some reason, the idea of him genuinely disliking me is... unpleasant.

Baelfire has been watching my face and his glare snaps to the ice elemental as a snarl builds in his throat. "You're not even going to fucking *greet* your own keeper? What the hell is wrong with you? You're the only one she *likes* and you're hurting her feelings, so get your head out of your frozen ass and—"

"Drop it," I cut in firmly. "My feelings are fine."

"Don't fucking tell me you're *fine*," he snaps. "I just saw you wince."

I did? Oops.

Since it's clear Baelfire is getting shifter-level angry, I offer him a distraction as I twirl pasta around my fork. "Maybe I was just reacting to the sizzling hot meat buffet in front of me. And I'm not talking about the pork chops."

That does the trick. He fumbles his own fork, blinking at me. "Did you just...*flirt*?"

The others are also staring. Crypt didn't get food—he never does, since apparently he just eats dreams—but he looks positively delighted with this new development. Silas arches a brow at me.

"I promised one day of the real me. Don't get used to it." I take a bite.

Everett sits down on my side of the table, several seats down, presumably so we won't have to look at each other. He clearly doesn't want to be here...but then why the fuck did he create this snowstorm and show up? Did they bribe him? I'm genuinely confused about his part in this forced group getaway.

As we eat, Crypt props his feet up on the table, lounging with his seat tipped back. When he pulls out a lighter and cigarette, Everett shoots him a dirty look.

"You can't smoke in here."

"Let's test that theory." The incubus lights one and draws deeply from it, blowing the smoke in Everett's direction. "Oh, look. Yes, I can."

The elemental's eyes narrow, and a thick sheet of ice suddenly crackles beneath Crypt's leaning chair, making it slip and sending him tumbling. But the Nightmare Prince vanishes into Limbo before the dining chair even hits the ground.

Silas rolls his eyes and uses basic magic to cast a protective charm over his food. It's something a lot of casters do, ensuring their food is perfectly safe...like from poisoning, for example. Seems excessive since Baelfire just cooked the food right in front of him, but that just further proves he truly has paranoia.

Baelfire snorts, catching my attention. "So. Growing up with humans, did you have shit like this happen at dinner? Neurotic fae, vanishing psychopaths, PMSing popsicles?"

"Shut up, dragon," Everett grumbles.

"You forgot the egotistical golden retriever." Silas lifts his glass of water like a toast. I don't know what magic he does, but it suddenly darkens into a dark amber mead that he sips.

"Golden *dragon*. Way more loyal than a dog and a hundred times sexier," Baelfire corrects.

"And so very humble," Silas rolls his eyes again.

I've tried to ignore my curiosity about their dynamic since we met, but if I'm letting myself relax slightly around them for the next day, I may as well ask.

"I take it you four grew up together?"

Crypt reappears in the chair directly beside Silas and grins wider when the blood fae glares at him. "Their parents hoped we would all become friends. I'm still waiting for the friendship bracelets."

Baelfire huffs as he pushes his already-empty plate away. I'm always amazed at how quickly shifters can put so much down. "We all come from pretty damn high-profile families, and legacies tend to try getting their children to befriend other powerful legacy children. They ran in the same circles, so we were around each other a lot as kids."

"But you're not friends," I say. It's not a question.

They exchange glances with one another, and once again, it becomes clear that there are past disputes lingering between them—Baelfire and Everett, Silas and Crypt. Though even Everett seems to dislike the Nightmare Prince, and Baelfire and Silas are a long shot from seeming like pals.

Silas sets down his drink and gives me a serious look. "No. We're not. But we promise our past altercations won't get in the way of us being a quintet you'll be proud to be the keeper of."

The others don't disagree, which tells me they've discussed this between themselves.

"We'll deal with our own shit. It will never be your job to break up any dogfights between us. And we'll try to keep the fighting over you to a minimum," Baelfire adds teasingly.

"Too bad. I enjoy spectating a good fight."

That seems to take all four of them aback, but Crypt laughs. "I like it when you're playful, darling."

Another thought occurs to me, and I study them. "Do you know each other's curses?"

That adds another level of tension to their shoulders, and I don't miss the way Silas sends a harsh look to Baelfire as if to remind him to keep his mouth shut.

"We know each other's weaknesses," Crypt says cheerfully, flipping his lighter on and off. "Whether they're curse-related or not is anyone's guess."

Baelfire leans across the table, curiosity written all over his face. "A much better question is…as an atypical caster, you don't even have a curse, right?"

It's true. Atypical casters aren't affected by the Legacy Curse at birth. Though I suppose my condition is worse than most curses I've heard of. Not that I'd tell them that, now or ever.

"Actually, I have four." I look at them each in turn meaningfully.

Silas's mouth curls up. "So you finally admit we belong to you?"

"Yes, in the same way a raging infection belongs to a leper."

I offer the insult sweetly before picking up my own glass of water. Before I can lift it to my lips, Silas waves his hand and mutters the same magic word he did earlier, and the liquid darkens into something rich and smooth. When I hesitate, he raises a daring brow.

"Fae mead," he explains. "For my favorite leper."

Everett stiffens in his seat where he's been picking at his food without really eating anything, and for the first time, he looks directly at me. "Don't drink it. It's always a mistake to drink anything at this asshole's whim. The last time I did, I nearly died."

"As if I would spike *her* drink with kraken ink," Silas rolls his eyes. "Fae mead is perfectly safe."

Kraken ink? Maybe their past issues with each other are more murderous than I realized.

Baelfire snorts. "Only if you have an iron stomach. Are you a lightweight, baby? If you are, don't even take a sip. That shit's heartless."

Maybe it's from watching their banter and finally letting my walls down bit by bit, but suddenly, the daring look Silas is giving me is irresistible.

They want to know the real me? Fine.

Tipping the glass back, I down it. All of it. The flavor is unexpected but pleasant, the alcohol warming me up from the inside out. By the time I'm done and I set the glass down, even Silas looks impressed but faintly alarmed.

Swiping a drop from my lips with my pinky, I pop it into my mouth and shrug. "So am I."

Bael's attention is pinned on my mouth. "Fuck me, that was hot."

Oh. I didn't think that through. Now, I have the undivided attention of four ravenous legacies. It doesn't help that the fae mead is spreading as a pleasant warmth throughout my system, relaxing my muscles and loosening my tongue. It's not as heady as the buzz I get from a kill, but this is still dangerous territory.

What if I let something slip in this state?

Better to retreat.

Standing, I grab my plate and walk to the kitchen. "I'm exhausted. I'm going to bed early."

"Wait." Baelfire hurries after me. "Stay a little longer. What about dessert?"

I want all of you for dessert.

No. Bad Maven. This is why I avoid alcohol.

Silas is suddenly on my other side, gingerly taking the plate from my hands to put it in the sink himself. "You promised to give us a chance."

"No, I promised a day of pretending we're a real quintet. Even though we never will be," I tack on forcefully because it's imperative that they finally grasp that.

"This was hardly a full day. Keep your promise and give us tomorrow."

I scowl. "I will not just play house with you four all day. I came here for a reason."

Shit. What was my excuse again? I can't think of it when they're both so close looking at me like this while the fae mead starts to kick in.

"Right. The wedding. We'll be your dates," Baelfire beams.

"Everett will get rid of the snowstorm once you promise we can go with you."

"No. I'm going alone."

Because there is no wedding, and I have a shifter to kill.

"We'll just follow after you," Silas challenges. "I hope your relative doesn't mind legacies crashing the party."

Gods, why are they such bossy, *annoyingly* attractive men?

"Unless you didn't come for a wedding after all. Perhaps you came to meet with...others." Silas's voice has lowered, and he's studying me like he would disassemble my mind to get an answer.

But I don't know what answer he's looking for. What *others* would I be meeting with? I can't think of a response to play my cards close to the vest. I'm too damn tired, thanks to that episode.

Crypt must have moved through Limbo because he steps out directly in front of me, studying my face as one corner of his lips drags down slightly.

"Let our girl go to bed. She's exhausted."

Dream-walking incubi like him can sense that. Usually, it would bother me that he can tell I'm dead on my feet, but I let it go because it finally gets Silas to soften, too.

"Just keep your promise of one day. Let us have tomorrow with you. No games."

I frown at him. He thinks I've been playing games? Since when? For the last few days, I've successfully driven him up a wall. Where did all that annoyance and frustration I've worked so hard to cultivate in him go?

"Fine," I relent, stepping around Crypt. "But if any of you try to bother me while I'm sleeping in, I'm gone."

Truthfully, I plan on slipping out early in the morning to kill Lykoudis and get his heart. Hopefully, the snowstorm will have calmed by then. Leaving them in the kitchen, I retreat to the guest room I picked and prepare for an early bedtime before dropping onto the luxuriously soft bed with a groan.

My phone buzzes on the nightstand. I scowl, picking it up to try to figure out how to turn off the vibration. I can never figure out phones.

The notification came from an email from Everbound University about the upcoming Matched Ball that takes place after First Placement. It's a big formal event that Kenzie has been ecstatic about.

I go to close out of it, but something in the email catches my eye. I quickly skim.

...our esteemed headmaster, Professor Hearst, has arrived back at Everbound and will deliver an address preceding First Placement to congratulate all legacies who have survived their first semester at Everbound University thus far.

The headmaster has returned.

Finally, some good news.

I just have to get through the next day without getting too attached to these assholes, and then I can get on with my mission. Clearly, getting them to hate me is hitting too many snags.

So maybe after I finish my mission here, I should just run. Never see them again.

No matter how that makes me feel.

24

CRYPT

"You want to tell us what the fuck is up your ass?" Decimus growls as soon as Maven is out of earshot, turning on Frost, who still sits at the dining room table.

The ice elemental sighs like he's resigned that his peaceful dinner is over and stands to face the rest of us.

"You told me to be here. I'm here. That doesn't mean I have to be happy about it, and she's too smart to buy any fake niceties I toss her way anyway."

Crane snaps at him about something else, and it leads to an argument that gets bigger and louder, but I don't join their little spat, content to sit back and watch. We all have such different auras, so it's no wonder we never meshed well as children like Maven was asking about.

Though I admit, I'm curious why Frost's aura is so soft compared to how icy and arrogant he has always acted. Of the three of them, he was the one I minded the least when we were younger, but he purposefully distanced himself at every chance. I suppose he's doing the same thing now with Maven.

I'm snapped out of my musings when Frost says something accusatory, and Decimus snaps, "I didn't fucking pressure her. She *wanted* to touch me, and it just...escalated."

Crane straightens, narrowing his eyes. "What do you mean, *escalated?* Did you fuck her?"

"No. She just..." Decimus rubs a hand over the back of his neck and looks uncharacteristically flustered. "She started teasing me, touching me, and I lost control. Came like a fucking geyser. And then..." He shakes his head again. "It wasn't sex. It's not like I won the wager. But I didn't fucking pressure her like *that*. I just strong-armed her into spending time with us here—"

"Hang on," I interrupt, my jaw tightening. "She stroked you off?"

He scowls. "It was a lot more intimate than you're making it—"

"I don't give a damn. My question is, did you get *her* off? Or did you take and give nothing in return?"

He grimaces. I can tell I'm not the only one that pisses off when Frost sneers, "And you're mad at me for not making progress with her? You're a dick, using her like that."

Decimus's temper flares. "I didn't use her. I wanted her to use me. She had me promise not to touch her—how the hell was I supposed to return the favor? And I was already way too damn close to snapping and fucking her rough and raw. I wasn't about to let her first time be with me out of control!"

Crane hesitates. "Maven is a virgin?"

"I don't fucking know," Decimus grunts, dropping into one of the island stools and rubbing his face. "She wouldn't tell me. But come on, what are the chances she's hopped into anyone else's sheets when she hates skin contact?"

Immediately, my thoughts skip back to Maven's dark eyes holding mine as she kissed the dragon shifter earlier. The way she was trying to provoke me. My cock hardens as I imagine what it would have been like for her to taunt me more, holding my gaze while her fingers trailed over someone else, driving me mad with need.

She didn't seem to hate skin contact when she wasn't solely focused on it.

"I have to wonder if that's one of her acts, too," Crane muses.

Frost looks at him sharply. "What are you talking about?"

"Our keeper has been fighting dirty."

I listen as he quietly reveals what he found in Maven's notebook. As hypocritical as it was for him to invade her personal space without permission when he took every measure to prevent me from doing the same, I find myself smirking when he's finished talking.

Decimus folds his arms across his chest, shaking his head. "Damn. She really has been trying to get rid of us, huh?"

"Once again, deliciously unexpected," I agree.

Frost is quiet, studying the marbling on the island counter. "If she really wants to get rid of us…"

The dragon shifter gives him a scalding glare. "Don't even fucking tell me you're fine giving her up. The gods picked her for us —we're *hers*, so whatever moody shit you're trying to justify, just let it go. Anyway, I'm relieved that not all of that was her actually hating me, but I want to know why the hell she's been fighting our quintet so hard."

I tip my head. "But that's obvious. If she's involved in the anti-legacy movement, being placed in a quintet with legacies like *us* would be completely antithetical to her beliefs."

It seems to take them a moment for that to sink in, and then Crane swears. "I hate to ever agree with you, but that might be it after all."

Decimus considers it and then shakes his head. "I don't think that's it."

"But if it is, I should report her," Frost mumbles.

"Report her, and I'll permanently mar your oh-so-precious model face," I warn.

The other two just glare at him, and he huffs before leaving the kitchen. Maybe he's going to finally go withdraw his power from wreaking icy havoc outside.

Crane tips his head as he gets lost in thought. "But if Maven is so anti-legacy—"

A nearby surge of subconscious terror pierces through Limbo and makes it into the mortal plane, making me tense. Sensing such a powerful nightmare would normally have my mouth watering, but my appetite twists when the aura saturating the terror is unmistakably Maven's.

I've been desperate to taste her dreams since the moment I laid eyes on her. No dreamcatcher keeps me from sensing her like this now—an oversight Crane must have made while preparing this place. So, whatever nightmare is playing in her head, I can keep it from hurting her.

Crane starts to demand what has me on edge, but I step into Limbo, so it sounds like he's speaking underwater. Kicking up, I quickly drift through the ceiling and walls until I stop in the guest suite, where my keeper is tangled in blankets.

That the sight of her asleep makes me breathless is something I fully expected.

But her sleeping form sending lust crashing through me? *That* is unexpected.

Thanks to my nature, I've seen countless people sleeping. Not once have I ever felt anything like this. But the desire to smooth Maven's furrowed brow, kiss every inch of her skin, and worship her resting body just as I've fantasized about pleasuring her in the waking world is suddenly consuming my every thought.

But my newfound hunger quickly takes a back seat when she whimpers in her sleep, stirring as the nightmare grows in Limbo.

"My dark little darling," I whisper, settling on the bed beside her and reaching for the nightmare to take the reins. "Show me what's causing you such pain."

Abruptly, I find myself standing in a dark room. The details of it are foggy, as dreams often are—but this is clearly a nightmare spawned from memory. There's too much real-world exactness for it to be something her subconscious is spinning.

And in Maven's memory, she's wrapped in nothing but a sheet as she sobs at someone's feet. The looming figure is faceless, as villains in nightmares so often are. This is a younger version of my keeper, perhaps somewhere in her teens. Her face is slightly rounder, her hips slimmer, and her cries wrench my heart.

"Please don't," she begs, tears dripping onto the stone floor. "Please. It was my mistake. Just punish me for it. Don't—"

Livid bile rises in my throat when the figure's foot snaps out, catching Maven in the face and sending her sprawling. Her head audibly smacks against the stone floor, but it doesn't stop her. She struggles to get up, still clutching the sheet around herself.

"*Silence*. You knew this would happen," a chillingly deep voice rumbles. "It is time you learned where loyalty always lies."

Someone else is screaming in the periphery of Maven's nightmare, and I can sense her horror and terror mounting as someone else is dragged into the room. Whoever it is, when she turns to look at them, I happen to be standing in the way. Sometimes, I conceal myself in dreams to watch them play out, but I haven't here, and her eyes snap up to me at once. My chest caves in when I see the blood dripping from her busted lip, the tears streaking down her dirty, stricken face.

She's covered in bruises.

The screaming reaches a fever pitch behind us as if someone is being ripped apart, and Maven's nightmare shakes around me. She's trying desperately to wake up, but it has her firmly in its grip.

But she's not begging the faceless monster anymore. She's begging me.

"Stop it. Please make it stop," my obsession pleads.

I do.

Whatever this memory is, whatever invisible scars it left within my keeper, I vow that she will never have to endure this in her subconscious again. Forcing my own subconscious to morph our surroundings, the darkness fades away, and my power branches out, spinning Maven a new dream in the blink of an eye.

She blinks at our new surroundings, sitting on a couch in a beautiful mansion facing a large window overlooking a moonlit lake. Stars twinkle outside, reflecting in the water, and now Maven looks the same age as she is in the waking world, cleaned of any dirt or blood.

It always takes dreamers a moment to adjust to the lucid dreams incubi can craft. But finally, she focuses on me, and there's a definite surge of *want* in the dream around us before she looks down.

"What am I wearing?"

The black lacy dress is dipping off her shoulders and clinging to her perfect hips. I was sorely tempted to dress her in nothing—but I haven't seen my darling stark naked yet, and even in her dream, I wouldn't dare try to fill in the blanks with the parts of her I haven't seen. I know nothing I could imagine will possibly be as mouthwatering as she'll actually be when I do finally get to see her naked.

Maven regards me, uninhibited in this dream state. Her brow furrows in concern again. "Wait. Wasn't I just..."

"There are enough demons to torment us in the waking world, darling," I whisper. "From now on, your dreams belong to me. I will allow nothing to hurt you here."

She's looking for the truth in my eyes, and she must see it because she visibly relaxes.

"Boo?" Decimus calls in the dream, joining us on the couch and pulling her onto his lap with familiar ease. He buries his face in her neck and inhales deeply. "This creep has been hogging you all day. My turn."

Creating projections of existing people is easy—especially when I know them well, from their mannerisms to what makes them tick. I've also perfected the ability to craft false memories within dreams for those whose subconscious I'm lingering in. The memories don't last past them waking up and don't affect their psyche in the least, but while in a dream, they're very believable.

Which is why, in this dream, Maven rolls her eyes with a smile and kisses Decimus.

In this fictional moment, we've been together for years, and the only thing she can't stand about our touch is how much she wants it.

"Getting started without me?" Crane asks, sliding in on Maven's other side. She breaks away from Decimus when the blood fae takes her chin, tilting her face to steal a deep kiss for himself.

"You're all so damn clingy," Maven says, pulling away with a smirk. But she reaches out to trail her fingers slowly through my hair.

I shut my eyes. Gods above, I want this to be real.

Frost is here now, too, leaning over the back of the couch to kiss her forehead almost reverently. "Don't pretend you don't love it, Oakley."

She studies him, then the rest of us as the dream projections exchange more banter. For a moment, I can feel her subconscious realizing that this isn't what she's used to. She's confused, but when I smile at her, she smiles back.

Breathtaking.

I normally weave nightmares, but I needed her to see this. Us. Everything we could be.

Because I couldn't care less if our suspicions about her are true. She can hate all other legacies but us. If she asks, I'll help her drive the world mad and watch her enemies rip each other to shreds. I have no loyalties to anyone but us. As long as I get to keep my dark obsession, the world can fucking burn for all I care.

Letting go of the reins of her dream, I watch, wondering what she'll unconsciously turn it into. If she genuinely wants nothing to do with us, I expect she'll snap out of this immediately.

Instead, she adjusts, straddling Crane's lap to lean over and kiss me briefly.

I can't breathe. *This is the truth. She wants us.*

When she pulls back, the depth and emotion in her expression is stunning. She traces the markings on the side of my neck curiously. "These markings. They're not tattoos. What are they?"

"Just…markings. From my curse," I manage.

Now her dream grows watery, a sure sign that she's starting to rouse from her sleep. But she hasn't shaken off the dream yet, and she frowns softly at Crane and the others. "How…how are we all together like this? Did I fail?"

"Fail what, *sangfluir?"*

"My purpose." Then she tenses, and I see the realization rush through her just as the rest of the dream fades away.

A moment later, I find myself sitting on the bed in Limbo as Maven's eyes flutter open. Her brow furrows, and then she sits up quickly, eyes narrowing in my general direction as she pulls the blankets closer around herself. She knows I'm here.

Slipping out of Limbo, I smile softly at her. "No need to be wary, love. I would never touch you without permission."

"You would just violate my dreams without permission."

"I'd hardly call it that. You were in pain. I needed to stop it."

She clenches her jaw. "What did you see in my dream?"

That memory clearly distressed her in the extreme. It's something private, something she wouldn't want me to know. I didn't get the complete picture of what was happening, but it doesn't matter—unlike Crane, I know not everything can be fixed. Invisible scars can't go away.

I understand that part of her more than she may ever know. I also understand wanting to keep a broken past as a secret.

"I saw nothing," I murmur. "I just sensed the nightmare and took it away."

I fully expect her to swear at me or kick me out of the room, so it's a pleasant surprise when she looks away, dropping the subject to frown at the curtains, which are letting in soft light. Time is warped in dreams, so it's unsurprising if her sleep felt bizarrely short.

"What time is it?"

"Mid-morning. Worried you'll miss the wedding?"

She pauses. "My father's cousin had planned an outdoor wedding. They postponed it due to the weather, so I'm not going after all."

Either she's a very smooth liar, or I must thank Frost for buying us even more time with our keeper.

"Then shall we lounge in bed for a few more hours?" I try, hopeful that she might be softening towards us after all.

Maven gives me a dry look. "Get out, Crypt. The fae mead left enough of a headache without you exacerbating it."

Obediently, I move back into Limbo, but this suite is spacious enough that she can't sense me anymore by the time I reach the front door. I watch, enraptured, as she rolls out of bed and immediately drops into a set of push-ups and other exercises. It's clearly her wake-up routine, though why she's pushing herself to do this when she told me herself about her headache, I can't comprehend.

I turn to drift through the wall and give her space, determined to taste her dreams once again.

But the next time I do, I want them to be sweet dreams. And someday, she'll be asking me to join her in her dreams every night. Someday, I'll make her just as obsessed with me as I am with her.

25

MAVEN

AFTER I SHOWER and go downstairs dressed in my typical baggy attire, a gorgeously sleep-rumpled, shirtless Baelfire serves omelets and fruit for breakfast. He makes small talk about his shifter-centric classes at Everbound while I fail to keep my eyes off all his golden muscles. Meanwhile, Silas keeps giving Crypt long glares. I don't know if he suspects that the Nightmare Prince took a joy ride in my subconscious last night, but he says nothing about it.

Neither do I. I'm still torn. On the one hand, the idea of anyone taking a look inside my head makes me want to tear out of my own skin.

But on the other…he stopped my most painful recurring nightmare before it got to the worst part. I haven't rested that well in a long time, even if I'll never admit that to him.

Still. From now on, I'm taking a dreamcatcher with me everywhere I go.

Everett joins us late for breakfast. The storm is no longer raging outside—instead, there's a crisp layer of glistening snow covering as far as the eye can see outside the ostentatious inn. I appreciate the macabre beauty of a world frozen over.

With no storm, I could leave to carry out the hit.

I just…don't yet.

They asked for a day, so I'll stay for a while and slip out later. I'll still have Lykoudis's heart to Melchom before midnight.

"So, Crypt says there's no wedding anymore," Bael says as he follows my self-tour of the inn. Silas trails behind us, and Crypt is invisible somewhere nearby. Professor Frost is keeping his distance elsewhere. "I gotta admit, I was really looking forward to seeing what you would wear to the shindig, Boo."

"This," I lie easily.

He blinks, stopping with me when I pause to examine yet another long hallway. "You were going to sit through a wedding while getting swallowed up by that long-sleeved shirt and pants that completely hide how perfect your ass is?"

"Not all of us can walk around half-naked." I look pointedly at his bare, muscular torso. The guy really is massive, and I'm starting to suspect he hasn't bothered putting a shirt on because he wants to test my limits.

"You certainly could when it's just us," Silas drawls. "Though I'd prefer you entirely nude."

"Agreed," Crypt teases, appearing at the foot of the entry stairs as I walk back down them.

Everett's impatient sigh from where he stands in the foyer with folded arms draws my attention. "We get it. You're all beyond horny, and you refuse to leave her alone about it. Moving on, have we decided on today's itinerary?"

Yet again, how unhappy he is to be here with me is oddly bothersome. The irony isn't lost on me that if all my matches had been as indifferent about me from the beginning, they would have already appealed for a new keeper. I would be well on my way to accomplishing my mission and moving on.

Baelfire bristles at the professor, but Silas studies me. "We're near a small town called Hope Falls. I learned they have an impressive display for the human holiday season, several historical sights…and an impressive greenhouse open to the public in the winter."

I wasn't lying when I told him I'm a botany aficionado. The greenhouse is genuinely appealing, especially because I won't be stuck here with four legacies that I can't stop thinking about trying to touch, thanks to the bizarre dream I had last night of the four of us.

Going to Hope Falls is a needed distraction from the lingering throb between my legs.

"Fine. Let's go."

I insist on driving Kenzie's Mustang despite Silas's attempts to take one of the two cars he and Everett brought. He doesn't seem to trust the baby blue vehicle. Unsurprising, since he doesn't seem to trust anything. After he lays a couple of protective spells on it, he gets in the passenger seat. Everett slides into the back, and Baelfire tries to, but it quickly becomes apparent he's built too big for the older car.

"I'll grab a change of clothes and meet you there," he winks.

Right. Because a twenty-five-ton dragon won't freak out the humans at all.

Crypt is invisible, but there's no doubt in my mind he'll be keeping up and watching, too.

Hope Falls is everything Silas said it would be. It's a tiny human community covered in glittering snow with festive decorations on nearly every building we pass driving into town. It's complete with an old clock tower atop a church, a town square filled with people chatting in earmuffs and puffy coats, and a collection of random historical New England monuments.

I park in front of a spot in the town square where there is an ongoing competition to see who can build the best snowman. As we watch, a massive shadow passes overhead, blocking out the sun before twisting midair. The sunlight catches on Baelfire's gleaming scales as he lands somewhere just out of sight to shift back. I can't help smirking as I watch a small child gawking so hard at the sky that she accidentally pushes her snowman's head off when trying to stick a carrot in it.

Crypt appears outside the driver's side door, opening it before I can. "After you, darling."

Baelfire catches up with us quickly, but it doesn't take me long to decide that strolling through the cheery streets of the cozy human town with them feels…odd.

For one thing, we don't blend in well. People's eyes keep shifting to us, lingering on the four disturbingly handsome men in my posse before looking away. Living so close to the Divide, I'm sure they see legacies often enough that we're not outright freakish to them, but they're obviously still uncomfortable.

But for another thing…I feel entirely out of place here.

They think I grew up somewhere like this, but it couldn't be more alien to me. Honestly, I can barely reconcile this cozy atmosphere with the brutal way I was raised.

Everything is so *wholesome*.

It makes me sick.

We stop to tour the fabled greenhouse, which is also decked out in holiday lights, and pictures of a fat man in a red suit, which I don't understand at all.

Silas glances at me as we pass a row of thriving orchids. "Did your adoptive father celebrate all the human holidays with you?"

Baelfire must have told him about that. "Not really."

Unintentionally, my attention slips to the glass wall at the front of the greenhouse. Everett opted not to come in, grumbling about not wanting to freeze their plants accidentally.

"Ignore him, love," Crypt murmurs, picking an orchid and offering it to me.

Immediately, a red-faced human woman bustles toward us, tucking a spade into her gardening apron with a huff.

"Hey! The signs very clearly say *no picking the flowers*."

The Nightmare Prince doesn't bother looking away from me. "And I very clearly don't care."

She stomps toward him, ripping the orchid out of his hand and wagging it in his face. "I don't care if you're one of those monster spawn keeping this area protected! We work damn hard to keep this greenhouse nice, and your tattooed punk ass is about to get thrown out!"

"My ass is not tattooed."

The woman splutters and looks at *me* accusingly. "Don't think I don't know how you monster groups work! You must be the whore they keep as a plaything. Get them out of here before they cause real problems, or else."

The snarl that rips out of Baelfire's throat is so threatening that she drops the orchid and steps back. Silas gives her a chilling stare-down while Crypt flickers and disappears, making her yelp.

This whole situation is oddly amusing to me. "Or else what?"

The woman blinks at me. "What?"

"You were trying to threaten us. At least make it creative. Maybe something like *or else* you'll take that spade and shovel out our innards to fertilize the greenhouse," I suggest helpfully.

Baelfire makes a choking sound. Silas laughs darkly.

The woman turns a delightful purple shade as she steps back. "Ugh. Get the hell out of here, you fucked-up little *freak*, before I call the bounty hunters to come check if you're legal!"

"Since you asked so nicely," I shrug, turning to leave.

As soon as we're outside, Baelfire snaps, "I know we're not supposed to harm humans, but that bitch was begging to be roasted."

"Her neck looked extremely breakable," Silas agrees in a low tone.

Everett looks between them like they've grown extra heads. "What the hell is wrong with you two?"

I can't help it. I laugh.

Baelfire gawks at me. "Did you just…fucking *giggle?* I can't tell if that's the most adorable thing I've ever heard or if I should be worried about your sense of humor."

"Why can't it be both?"

Uh oh. Was that flirtatious? It felt flirtatious. Being like this with them, not bothering to hide my expressions or contain myself, is unnervingly easy. A broad smile spreads over Bael's face, and I scold myself for the way it warms my neck.

"Gods, I can't get enough of you. Come on, Boo. I saw a hot chocolate stand with your name on it."

The rest of our hours-long tour of Hope Falls is uneventful, aside from the fact that Crypt reappeared later to hand me an entire bouquet of orchids that he most certainly took from the greenhouse out of spite.

The more time I spend with my four rejected matches, the more I can't stop thinking about that scene in my dream last night. The ease between us. The…comfort.

That's not for you. Snap out of it.

But even if I can't have that long-term, maybe Kenzie is right. Maybe I can enjoy myself with them just for this one day without causing trouble. I won't let them get in the way of my oath and my mission. Besides, I won't be at Everbound much longer, anyway—and the thought of never seeing them again makes me feel an emotion I've never experienced before.

I'll never get that dream I had in real life. But I have a few more hours of pretending I could.

As we drive back later, Silas observes me from the passenger seat as we approach the inn. Everett has been silent in the back. He's said nothing to me all day.

"You're deep in thought. I have a question for you," Silas says.

"I probably don't have an answer."

"Do you agree with the woman in the greenhouse?"

I arch a brow but keep my eyes on the road. "About me being a fucked-up freak? Of course."

Everett scowls viciously behind us, and suddenly, the car's interior is frigid. "She said *what?*"

Silas ignores his confusing outburst. "No. About keepers being playthings. You come from a human background, so I understand if the dynamics of quintets are…opposite your beliefs. You're clearly not keen on the fact that we're a quintet."

"We're *not*. I rejected all of you."

It's like talking to a wall for all the reaction they have to that. Anytime I bring up my rejection of them, they ignore it. Fucking cocky high-profile legacies.

"Whatever your beliefs are, *sangfluir*...we're still yours," the blood fae says quietly.

His words have a hidden meaning that I try not to read into. I don't know what he suspects, but I can't afford to let it distract me. I need to slip away within the next three hours and go hunt down Lykoudis before the deadline, so even if he starts to get an idea of who I am and what I'm here for, now is not the time to worry about it.

Forty minutes later, I sit at the kitchen island again, pushing my now-empty plate away. It's almost annoying how good Baelfire is at cooking. He's trying to impress me, and it's working. For dinner, he made some kind of potato casserole dish, free of meat but hearty and satisfying. Silas eats beside me, and Crypt sits casually on one of the counters, where he appeared a few minutes ago from Limbo.

Everett also finished dinner, and he's now scowling at something on his phone as he leans against a nearby counter. I'm still not sure why he's here, but I'm sure he will be the one to mind the least when I make my getaway very soon.

"And now for dessert," Bael says smugly, pulling out a tub of... white stuff.

He shovels it into some kind of edible dish, handing me the first one. Dubiously, I try the foreign dessert.

Oh.

So this is what love feels like.

"What is this? The nectar of the gods?" I ask, a grin breaking over my face before I can stop it.

They say nothing, and when I glance up, they're all staring at me in confusion and amusement—even Everett.

"What do you mean? You said vanilla was your favorite," Baelfire points out, laughing.

It takes me a moment to remember what he's talking about. But then it hits me. *Ice cream*. This is ice cream. Duh, Maven. I should have figured that out sooner.

"Oh. Right."

Too late. Silas tips his head and studies me far too intently, and I get the unnerving feeling that he knows more about me than he's supposed to.

"Tell the truth. This is your first time eating ice cream. Isn't it?"

"Perhaps." I take another bite, enjoying the way it melts in my mouth.

Everett scoffs. "What? It's *ice cream.* Why haven't you had it before, or at the very least seen it? Were you raised in a cult or something?"

When I don't respond, the amusement drops away from their faces really damn fast. They have questions, and I can see that they're about to start asking them, so I hold up a hand.

"Let it go."

"*Let it go?* Fuck that. We don't know anything about your past," Baelfire argues, scowling as he practically tosses the scooper into the tub of ice cream. "Look, it doesn't take a genius to figure out that something doesn't add up with you, Maven. I need to know more about my mate's life before all this. Why the hell are you—"

"I said *drop it,*" I snap, fixing him with a fierce look. "My past is none of your business. Don't bring it up again."

Baelfire scowls at me before finally looking away. "Fine. I'll shut up about it *for now,* but only because I don't want to spoil our romantic getaway."

I almost choke on my next bite of ice cream. "Romantic? That's what you think this is? You're kidding."

Everett snorts as if he agrees. I hadn't even realized he was paying any attention.

"We'll all return to Everbound tomorrow morning," Silas says, studiously spinning an empty cone on the counter like a top. "Tell me. How do you want us to spend our last night here, Maven?"

Unbidden, that same sinfully tempting fantasy I had of them days ago comes to mind. Them surrounding me, whispering and groaning and worshipping my body. Only now, that fantasy includes…*touching*. All over. I want them all over me.

Oh, gods.

My stomach churns even as my thighs clench of their own

accord, trying to stop that damn throbbing at my core. Baelfire's head snaps up before his golden eyes turn molten. Shit. He can definitely scent what my thoughts just did to my body.

"Fuck, baby. How about we—"

"Movie night," Everett surprises us all by interrupting to suggest. "We can watch her favorite cheesy rom-com."

"Cuddling optional but highly encouraged," Baelfire adds, biting his lower lip and still not looking away from me.

He's making it impossible for me to brush my arousal under the rug, and I really can't have him alerting the others to this newfound problem.

And a romcom? Gag me with a knife.

Crypt sees my nose wrinkle and grins. "You'd much prefer a bloody, gory slasher film, wouldn't you, my dark little darling?"

He's one hundred percent correct.

But far more importantly, I have to find a way to ditch these four gorgeous assholes soon, and sitting in a dark room with them nearby me to watch a movie is not going to help me get rid of the fantasies still playing out in my head. No matter how I fight the curiosity about what would happen if I actually tried to touch them, it keeps popping back into my head.

Maybe you'll enjoy their hands on you.

No. Even now, my hands start to shake, so I quickly hide them under the counter's edge. Thinking about skin contact is a rookie mistake, and I try to shove it from my mind altogether.

"Pass," I mutter, standing as I prepare to make my escape.

Silas studies me thoughtfully. "There's a large cemetery nearby. We can all walk through the graveyard under the light of the full moon."

I hesitate. Full moons and cemeteries are two things I love.

"Come on, Boo," Baelfire urges, eyes trailing hungrily over me that belie his lighthearted voice. "That's right up your alley. Admit it, you wanna go on a creepy midnight hike through a bunch of dead people with four monsters. Well, three monsters and a Popsicle in a tweed jacket."

"Fuck off," Everett rolls his eyes but glances at me. "The cemetery, then?"

Damn it. They're starting to get a feel for my macabre delights.

I plan to shut this down, claim I'm tired, and walk away, but my attention snags on Silas as he rolls up his sleeves, cuffing them to scoop his own ice cream. The muscles in his forearms are flexing as he glances over, catching my eye. His ruby irises darken immediately as if he's noticed a shift in the room's energy.

Crypt tips his head, his dreamy eyes tracing over me as he slides off the counter with graceful ease, tucking his hands in his leather jacket. It again draws my attention to the intricate, swirling pattern of markings on his skin, and I suddenly want to see how much of him they cover. Some are dark like tattoos, while others are pale.

"Something you want, love?"

No. I can't want them. Bad, bad Maven.

I'm so godsdamned horny.

"No," I say quickly, feigning ignorance to how they're all fixating on me now.

Even Everett's cool blue eyes have me pinned, and I swear my body heat is slowly mounting. For the hundredth time, I internally curse the gods for matching me with men this damn gorgeous. Why couldn't they have been homely, unhygienic, body-odor-laced perverts with unkempt facial hair? Instead, my body is being torn between my conditioned fear of touch and the bone-deep burn of attraction.

Finally, I can't take it anymore. I have to get out of here immediately.

"I gave you a day, and I owe you nothing else. Put on a movie by yourselves if you want, but I'm done here. From now on, I want all four of you to stay the hell away from me," I declare before turning and practically bolting from the room.

26

MAVEN

I NEED to call Melchom to update him on where to meet me for the beating heart. That will take my mind off of how fucking wet I am.

I shut the suite door behind me and blow out a breath, covering my face. But my panties are damp with neediness. It's ridiculous that just the thought of them with me like that incites this kind of reaction from my body. It makes me squirm, huffing at the arousal that I already know I can't get rid of by touching myself because that never fucking gets me there.

Before I can track down my phone and call the demon, Crypt appears directly in front of me. I inhale sharply and take a step back, but that's just as the door opens, and I suddenly feel body heat at my back, though they don't touch me.

"You and your lies," Silas whispers in my ear. His breath against my neck, stirring strands of my hair, sends goosebumps skittering to my toes. I can smell that same hint of bourbon and spice on him. "I told you, *ima sangfluir.* No more lying."

"I am not—" I start to say, but my voice is far too breathy.

"*Godsdamn,* your arousal smells so fucking good, baby," Baelfire groans as he steps into the room, inhaling deeply.

Heat flares in my neck at the gravel in his voice. I step away to distance myself from all of them, but when I turn to face them all, my gaze drops to where Silas is adjusting himself in his pants. Baelfire is tenting hard, and I quickly look away.

Oh, my gods. They're as keyed up as I am.

This is bad. I need to get away before I fuck up. I can only resist temptation so much.

They'll kill you. If they figure you out, they'll kill you, I try to remind myself.

Unfortunately, the threat of death doesn't faze my body much anymore, so it's like white noise. When Crypt hums softly and steps forward, slowly backing me toward the bed like a tiger on the prowl, the heat starts to build low in my stomach.

"I saw you squirming with need, darling," he rasps. "Tell me. How soaked are you?"

"Get out," I whisper, the backs of my knees bumping against the bed.

"Why?"

Words start to slip out. "Because I don't—I *can't* want..."

Fucking gods, they're making this impossible, all crowding closer bit by bit. Crypt is suddenly on the bed behind me, still not touching me but near enough that I can hardly breathe.

"Why can't you want this?" Silas challenges. The ruby red of his irises won't let me look away again, and frustration mixed with hunger makes his voice rough. "Just tell the truth. Tell me why you've been pushing us away. Why did you try to make us hate you?"

How did he...

Shit. It takes only a moment for it to click. After all, he's the one who put down the damn spells.

"You snooped and saw my list," I grit. "You're an asshole."

"I'm not sorry. I will be as much of an asshole as it takes to keep you, Maven, and I need answers. If you really don't want this quintet to work, give us your reason why."

"I promise that whatever it is, it isn't fucking enough to keep us away," Baelfire adds, his eyes burning me.

All the frustration and need building in me explodes in a rush of angry words. "You guys have no fucking idea how bad it would be to be bound to me. I'm *protecting* you idiots."

"From what?" Crypt demands.

I can't tell them that. Gods, I can't tell them *anything*. How dare they try to corner me like this when I can't think straight through the cloud of arousal in my head? They're close enough that if I try to sidestep one of them, I'll brush against them—and if I touch any of them, I have no idea what will happen. Either I'll climb their bones like a lioness in heat or break out in hives and have a panic attack.

"You're our keeper. *We* get to protect *you*," Silas says forcefully, bracing his hands on either side of the bed railing but still not touching me. My body starts to react as if he did, though, a restless need pulsing through my muscles and my breath stuttering. "So spit it the fuck out. What's stopping you from letting us have you?"

"I made a blood oath," I snap.

That makes him recoil, as does Baelfire. Crypt is still behind me. And when I glance over Silas's shoulder, a shock rolls through me when I see Everett leaning against the wall in the hallway outside the room, a frown on his face as he glares at the floor. He clearly heard me, too.

"What sort of blood oath?" Crypt asks softly.

The sort of blood oath that means I can never have a normal life. The kind that means my story is already written in stone as a tragedy —but I *had* to make that oath. Even if I could go back now and change that moment, watching my blood trickle down my fingertips and infuse with dark magic that took a bit of my soul with it, I wouldn't. This mission had to happen, and I was the only one left who could do it.

Blood oaths are the highest order of binding magic in existence. They supersede the gods and carry on into the Beyond. Anyone who tries to break a blood oath or find a loophole to get out of it is wiped from existence. Extinguished.

"It doesn't matter what I swore to do," I shake my head. "I refuse to drag you four down with me."

The gravity of my words has Silas reaching out, but he stills his fingers before they can brush against my cheek. His brow is furrowed, his dark curls mussed over his forehead as he tries to understand me.

"Or maybe we can help you. Tell us what you swore to do."

I finally break the eye contact. "I can't. You'll kill me."

Baelfire growls and breaks my rule again, reaching out to gently grip my chin and force me to look at him. The contact makes my skin flush and my breath stagger.

"Is that what you've been so afraid of? Us hurting—gods, *killing* you? That's never going to fucking happen. *Never*. It doesn't matter what terrible thing you swore to do or how much you try to make us hate you—none of us will hurt you, Maven."

Please. I'm well acquainted with pain, and I know it's delivered best in prettier packages. There are so many ways they could hurt me…and they would.

They'd have to if they knew who and what I am.

Crypt senses my disbelief and reaches out to remove Baelfire's hand from my chin before gingerly brushing my hair away from my face, careful not to touch my skin.

"This oath. Has it anything to do with the anti-legacy movement?" he asks. "Is that why you think we can't be together, love? You're in opposition to the Legacy Council?"

The anti-legacy movement? That's…

Huh. That's an easy way out.

Why didn't I think of that sooner? If I tell them that I made a blood oath on behalf of the people who hate the legacies—if I say *I'm* one of them…won't that be enough to make them decide we aren't going to work? No legacies would want a keeper who is actively petitioning for their kind to be killed off or sent back to the Nether.

Yes. This cover should work.

I nod, not trusting myself to speak when they're watching me so closely, and I can't calm my body's reaction to them. I can feel Everett's piercing eyes from outside the room. As a professor at the university, I'm sure he's going to flag me as a dangerous student or something.

It doesn't matter. I'll be done with my mission and long gone by the time this fake confession could possibly catch up to me.

The knowledge that I'll soon disappear from their lives makes my chest ache with hollowness.

"Then I hardly care," Crypt whispers, his fingers twisting a strand of my hair.

Surprise floods me.

Silas nods. "Good. Then we're all in agreement."

"You know what? I don't care, either," Baelfire huffs, eyes fierce as he moves even closer. "Like I said, I'm always on your side. Hate legacies all you fucking want—that doesn't mean we can't be together. Believing different shit doesn't mean you're my enemy, Maven. There's no way you can make me hate you."

Damn it. My brain and body can't agree on the best next course of action. I *needed* them to accept that lie and choose to reject me for it finally. Yet, at the same time, I'm...relieved. If they'll get over a fake problem of that magnitude, could they possibly get over the actual truth?

No. That's like comparing them forgiving a finger prick to ripping their hearts out.

"You should hate me," I argue, glaring at each of them to try to get the point across one final time. Even Everett, who is still in the hallway, arms folded now. "Because if you don't hate me now, you *will* hate me later. It's inevitable. Being with me will be hell for you because nothing will keep me from what I need to do, not even you four. We're fighting for such different things—"

"Says who?" Silas cuts in. "Let me remind you, Maven Oakley, that just as we know little of your past, you barely know us. Don't be so certain that we subscribe to everything you hate about legacies. I am many things, but not loyally blind. The Legacy Council is corrupt. So is the Immortal Quintet. I'll bleed them dry if that's what you ask of me."

"I'll burn whoever you ask me to," Baelfire murmurs.

Crypt lifts the strands of hair in his hand and kisses the tips.

"Make us your weapons, darling, and no one will stand a chance against our quintet. Let us be yours."

Well. That was annoyingly unexpected.

I'm speechless. I've never actually been speechless before, but I don't like it. I need to find some new barrier to put up because all my defenses are failing. How am I supposed to keep rejecting them if they rip down my walls and make me feel this way—as if maybe the obstacles looming between us are scalable?

As if they're really on my side.

As if I'm worth fighting for.

Damn them. I'm reaching my breaking point when I *know* that the only person who will ever really fight for me is myself.

You're on your own. You need no one. You are nothing but deadly calm.

But the mantras in my head are just more white noise when they're here, determination and hunger in their eyes as they finish ripping down any chances of saving them from me. My chest aches, and my soul has been fucking *starved* for any kind of connection like this for as long as I can remember.

I've never wanted anything like I want them, and now I squeeze my eyes shut as the rest of my walls slip away.

Fuck it. Fuck all of it.

I stop fighting for once and give in.

27

MAVEN

I DON'T KNOW who's more surprised when my lips brush his, me or Silas. But emotions explode through me when he immediately takes control, commanding my mouth with his, coaxing me to open to him until his tongue slips lightly against mine.

Yes. This.

But the moment his hands move to cup my face, I wrench back as the familiar pinpoints of horror dance over my spine. He immediately drops his hands, but the lust swirling in his red eyes remains.

"*Sangfluir…*"

"Hey," Bael says quickly, concern on his face as he gently takes my gloved hand. "Talk to us. What's going on in your head, baby?"

"I don't know how to…" I shake my head, struggling and frustrated at the way my body is starting to react. Exhaling on a rough scowl, I cover my face. "Gods, this sucks. This is another reason you guys should find someone else because I'm too messed up to—"

"There is none but you for me," Crypt quietly warns over my shoulder.

He wraps some of my hair around his fist and pulls slightly. The possessive action only adds to my wetness, and now my body is even more confused.

"You're not messed up," Baelfire says, leaning down to catch my eye.

My laugh is sharp. "Yes, I am. You have no idea. Another keeper would be—"

"Nope. You can go ahead and forever scrap the idea of us looking for someone else because it's not fucking happening. Just tell me yes or no. Do you want us to make you feel good?"

Crypt gently tugs on my hair again. "No one here will touch you unless you want it. If they do, I'll skin them alive and douse them in acid. You have my word."

Silas's fingers trail down my sleeve, tugging at the fabric as he holds me hostage with his intense gaze. "No lies. Tell us what you really want."

I swallow down the residual fear, mooring myself to how ravenously they seem to want me. They won't hurt me, not right now. I just have to convince my body that their touch isn't the end of the world.

"I want you to touch me, even if I can't stand it," I whisper, reaching down to tug off one glove. Then the other. I feel so damn naked without them, and I know I'm shaking, but I reach up to brush the tips of my fingers against one of Silas's curls. It's so *soft*. "Get me out of my own head. I need to be overwhelmed until I lose myself."

Just for tonight. Until I run and you never see me again.

He melts, pressing his forehead against mine. "Let go. Lose yourself in us."

And then he's suddenly kissing me hard, taking my breath away. Just as my body starts to catch up to what's happening and stiffens, Crypt's hands slide along my waist, giving a sudden tug that has me abruptly on my back on the bed, looking up at his upside-down smirk from where he sits behind me, cradling my head. He leans down and kisses me, too.

I expected the Nightmare Prince to kiss like the psychopath they say he is, rough and demanding. But his lips are unbearably tender as his hands slip into my hair, tangling and twisting it until he has my head at exactly the angle he wants to consume me slowly.

But I can't focus on only that because Silas slowly lifts my shirt and starts kissing his way across any exposed inch of me. It sends shocks of skittish sensation through my core, and suddenly, I can't breathe. I will him to kiss higher and higher.

At first, it feels incredible.

But all those years of conditioning pull my nerves taut until my veins flood with warning. I squeeze my eyes shut.

"Wait."

Immediately, Silas's touch disappears, and Crypt pulls away from the kiss, his violet eyes like a distant galaxy. His sweet leather scent envelops me. "You want us to stop, love?"

My forever-neglected pussy throbs with need. I'm so frustrated with my own body's responses that I groan, squirming on the bed to try to relieve the ache between my thighs.

"No. Don't *stop*. Just..."

"You're still stuck in your head," Silas murmurs, moving to the side of the bed so his warm, sinful mouth can resume his kissing along my exposed hip. "Baelfire, occupy her."

My gaze flicks to the gorgeous, giant dragon shifter when he groans brokenly. He grips his huge, hard length through his pants and swallows, meeting my gaze.

"Please, can I touch you, baby?" he begs.

I realize he's triple-checking because he's worried about a repeat of what happened last time. Needing more, I wordlessly lean up to grab his big hand, dragging it to the apex of my thighs instead.

"I need your touch here."

"*Fuck*. Yes."

Suddenly, he's dragging down my pants. He falls to his knees at the end of the bed, and I almost jump out of my skin when his face presses against my soaked panties. He moans and kisses me through the fabric, nuzzling my thighs open wider.

"Fuck, baby. I need to see the hot little cunt I get to spoil for the rest of my life. I'll be so fucking good for your sweet pussy."

Oh gods. He has such a mouth on him.

"Shirt," Silas commands Crypt, and they work together to shuck the huge long-sleeved shirt off my upper half. The air in the room is crisp against my newly exposed skin, making me suck in a gasp as my nipples harden into tight peaks. Instinctively, when I feel the cold, my attention skips back to the doorway.

The professor is still there. He isn't taking his eyes off me, but frost is blooming across the hallway wall where his hand is firmly planted. A muscle in his sharp jawline pulses.

They're doing enough to distract me until suddenly, Silas tenses, and his finger softly traces the pale, jagged scar between my breasts.

"What is this, *ima sangfluir*?"

The others snap to attention, and Baelfire growls up from where he's poised between my thighs. "Who the fuck did that to you?"

"A doctor. It was a heart surgery when I was a child. It's nothing now." I've told this lie before, so it slips easily from my tongue as I squirm again, shutting my eyes as my body begins to tense from the lack of stimulation.

Before panic can sink in about their skin all over mine, magic flares from Silas's fingertips, and my bra snaps open—and then his hot tongue drags slowly across one of my nipples. I gasp and arch at the delicious sensation. Crypt swears softly above me, and even though my eyes are shut, I know it's his fingertips that begin toying with my other nipple.

"Stunning," he breathes. "You're handling this so perfectly, darling."

"I need more," I plea.

My panties are ripped off, and Baelfire curses softly, his fingers slipping through the wetness there, sending my back arching again.

"Holy *gods*, you're so pretty, Maven. I can't wait to fucking devour this. You smell like fucking heaven."

Immediately, Silas's touch vanishes again, and I'm left panting on the bed, disoriented but awash with need when Crypt slips into Limbo briefly to rejoin them at the foot of the bed, and they all groan at the sight of me now completely naked.

Their reaction makes me feel powerful, and I bite my lip to keep from grinning as I trail my fingers down between my breasts.

Silas's mouth curls up darkly, and he licks his lips. "She is *soaked*."

The Nightmare Prince hums, agreeing with the blood fae. "Should we give you what your body is weeping for, love?"

He appears suddenly beside me again, but this time, he leans over to bite my nipple.

Not nip. *Bite*.

"Fuck," I swear, twisting his hair violently in my fingers as the red-hot sensation sinks in.

He hisses in pleasure, licking away the sting around my nipple. And I don't have to worry about my haphephobia kicking in because that's when Baelfire's tongue greedily laps at my entrance. His moan of delight echoes my own, and suddenly, I'm awash with sensation as Crypt slides his hands over my jaw and kisses me demandingly.

They're both devouring me, just in different ways. The pleasure has been building in my core slowly, but when Baelfire sucks hard on my clit, sweet release finally—godsdamned *finally*—ricochets up my spine, and I cry out, stars spotting my vision as my breathing stutters.

Oh. My. Gods.

He doesn't let up, and it's suddenly so overstimulating that I jerk away from Crypt to try to push Baelfire's face away.

"Stop. G—give me a moment."

Bael nips playfully at my fingers, his eyes shining with a profound hunger as he licks my wetness off his lips. Silas is also grinning sinfully at me from where he sits on the bed beside me, his fingers trailing softly up and down my side. Crypt kisses my temple.

"*That* is what it feels like?" I finally manage, blown away.

No wonder Kenzie is a slut. I might also take up that hobby in pursuit of a release like that.

Crypt stills. "You never had an orgasm before?"

Baelfire grins broadly. "Hell fucking yes. I just made my mate come for the first time ever. But if that was your first one, we need to get you caught up as soon as fucking possible. Spread them wider for me, baby."

He tries to dip his head back, but I grip his hair, forcing him to look at me.

"Kiss me." He's the only one who hasn't, and suddenly I need to know how his mouth feels on mine.

Baelfire obeys immediately, crawling over me on the bed, bracing his arms on either side of me as he claims my mouth with his. I shut my eyes, only letting myself focus on the sensation of his soft nips and low groans. He kisses down my neck while Crypt reaches between us to toy with my breasts, and soon, I can feel the coiling sensation building inside of me again.

Surely I can't come a second time. I've tried and failed so many times to get myself to finish even once that I'd almost decided I wasn't even capable. Is twice possible?

I want to find out, and I *need* this to go on. I need their groans and whispers as I come apart at their touch, fingers tangling in their hair and dragging over their jaws at every chance.

"More," I demand breathlessly. "Give me more."

Silas doesn't hesitate. His lips press softly over my clit, and then he pulls back. I hear clothes shuffling, and then a shock jolts down my spine when something warm and *really hard* grinds in exactly the right place.

I fist my hand in Baelfire's hair, the other gripping the sheets. Desire rocks through me when Silas slides his cock through my wetness again.

"*Yes*. Fuck me. Hard. Now."

His hands squeeze my hips so tightly I bet they'll bruise. "I have to go slow, Maven. It…will hurt at first. If you've never—"

"I'm not a virgin. Just fuck me."

He groans something in fae before he pushes into me. And I have no idea how I resisted them this long. Why on earth would I deny myself this? The pressure and stretch, the warmth, the shockwaves of pleasure? It's dizzying. Silas thrusts all the way in and seems to lose all semblance of control, slamming into me at a brutal pace as I cry out.

My cries are quickly captured by Baelfire as he takes my lips again.

"Gods, look at you. So fucking gorgeous and greedy. My perfect mate," he whispers against my jaw.

The pleasure coursing through me reaches a fever pitch, and I groan, needing that release again. I need something to push me over that edge.

"Bite me," I whisper.

I want that. Their marks on me—the soreness around the nipple Crypt bit, unintentional bruises on my hips from Silas losing control, and Baelfire's bite.

And…Everett. I want something from him.

Where is he?

Baelfire growls in a sound that is more draconic than human, and then his teeth sink into my shoulder. It's not hard enough to break my skin, but the pain gives all the pleasure one final push.

I gasp, my core seizing tightly as euphoria sweeps through me.

That sets Silas off, and he swears before burying himself in me as deep as he can go, his cock jerking until he's left panting against the side of my calf. I was so overwhelmed by everything happening at once that I don't even know when he lifted it that high.

The chill in the air slowly brings me back to earth, but this time, when my attention sweeps back to the hallway, the ice elemental is gone. And somehow, that makes me feel…incomplete.

Which is fucked up. Because they don't belong to me. I've made that very clear, so I can't now be wishing I could look into his glacier-blue eyes and see warmth instead of indifference.

Silas bites his lip as he pulls out. I feel warmth drip from me, and I don't miss the way his eyes flare watching it.

"Gods damn me, I may have bruised you," he rasps.

I hum, still not fully recovered. "Thanks."

Baelfire laughs quietly and maneuvers me on the bed until I'm cradled against his chest. He's still fully clothed. They all are, except Silas's lack of pants. He slips into the attached bathroom, where I hear water running briefly.

But even though I feel the massive erection he's sporting, Baelfire doesn't try to rock against me or press me for more. He just nuzzles his face into the crook of my neck with an infinitely pleased groan, kissing the spot I know shifters mark their mates.

"You're not about to hex me to shit thunder for a month, right?" he teases.

"You gave me my first orgasm, so your ass is safe. For now," I murmur, more relaxed than I've felt in…I don't even know how long.

Baelfire kisses my neck again. "You're so damn perfect."

Crypt catches my eye and settles on my other side, propping himself up on one arm. I blink when he places a light kiss on the tip of my nose, his expression dreamy as he gazes at me.

This moment feels…nice. Intimate.

Far too intimate.

Just like their skin. All over mine.

My breathing turns shallow, and I swallow hard. Cold sweat slowly breaks out over my body as memories from years ago come flooding back, washing away the delicious afterglow and triggering my gag reflex.

Rotting flesh. Oozing innards. Hands on me as I tried to stifle my cries. The pain and conditioning and the cold stone rough against my fresh wounds as I cried myself to sleep.

Shit. My system is starting to freak out. I need to distract myself, but I'm freezing up.

Baelfire tenses and sits up, brow furrowed. "Boo? What's wrong? Why are you—"

"Excuse me," I whisper hoarsely, and then I run to the bathroom, barely making it to the toilet before dropping to my knees and heaving. Gentle hands pull my hair back from my face, and finally, I shiver and wipe my face.

Silas's face is steely when I glance over my shoulder, but his irises burn with the questions I know he wants to ask. Baelfire looks stricken in the doorway, and Crypt appears murderous—not at me. Just in general. As if he wants to strangle whatever is haunting me.

But some ghosts are all in our heads.

"Relax. It wasn't you guys," I mutter, standing and remembering I'm *very* naked. I'm grateful when Silas quickly hands me a white bathrobe. It's fluffy and soft and makes this awkward moment slightly more bearable.

Baelfire reaches out to fuss over me, but I step back quickly on instinct because I genuinely can't handle anything else right now. A flash of hurt crosses his face, but he covers it quickly with a small, encouraging smile.

"Would a hot shower and buttery popcorn help? We can set up that freaky slasher movie night while we wait for you to get back," he offers.

He's giving me space to process.

It's sweet. *Bitter*sweet, because when I glance at the bathroom windows, I estimate that I only have five hours to get the beating heart to Melchom in order to get the nightshade root powder. But…I followed Lykoudis's social media updates earlier today, and I know generally where he is. Demons travel fast. I could easily make this hit in two hours.

Which means it's my choice to leave now or stay for the movie. Do I want as much as I can get with them before I have to disappear?

Yes.

I find my mouth turning up in a small smile. "Pick something extra gory."

They mention setting up the movie night in the suite Silas stayed in several doors down and file out. At least, Baelfire and Silas file out. Crypt slips back into Limbo and lingers longer than he should while I turn on the shower and watch the steam start to rise. When I flip off the general void around me, Crypt slips away until I can no longer sense him.

Slipping out of the bathrobe and under the warm stream of water,

I shut my eyes and breathe deeply. My story will end badly, but those moments with them earlier…

I get to keep those.

Now, I just have to ignore the temptation to try to keep *them*, too.

28

EVERETT

*G*ODS ON HIGH, *please help me endure this.*

My cock throbs in my pants.

Leaving that hallway did little good. I was trying to put distance between us to prevent myself from going in there and ruining everything, but my pulse pounds in my ears, and it feels like the world is melting around me as I make my retreat. Swearing, I shut myself in my guest room and immediately brace against the wall, pulling out my steel-hard cock and squeezing the base of it hard.

Dear *gods,* the sounds she made. That soft panting and the way she whispered what she needed. Seeing that pretty little pussy on display and glistening, and her soft gasp when Silas pushed in.

I need to fuck her like that. With an audience so they'll see how much she's mine.

Oh gods.

That mental picture is too much to take. I pump my dick hard until I come with a harsh groan, burying my face in my arm against the wall to try to muffle the sound. But as soon as the pleasure ends, I turn and slump against the wall, glaring at the ceiling.

This is hell. Whichever god or entity designed my curse is a damn sadist. I have never been as turned on in my life as I was in that hall. But as always, it was me outside looking in. Aching and so damn lonely.

Get over yourself. You have to be lonely.

Cleaning myself up quickly, I catch a glance in the mirror as I leave the room. The flush is still fading from my cheeks, but otherwise, I look the way my family always wanted me to.

Collected. Cold. Unfeeling.

But the truth is, I feel *everything* far too deeply. Especially where Maven is concerned.

I return to the kitchen downstairs, pacing in front of the long window overlooking the darkening twilight outside. I shouldn't have come here in the first place. It's dangerous. The others would have tried to strong-arm me into it if I'd resisted more, but the truth is? I couldn't fucking stay away from her.

I'm weak.

And since I can't trust myself to stay away from her, maybe I need to take a page from her book and *push* her away. The idea of hurting Maven kills me, but that's a hundred times more preferable to what my curse will do if it gets triggered.

"You look cold."

Her voice pulls me up short, and I turn to face her quickly, slipping my hands into my jacket pockets so she won't see the frost that continuously blooms there in her presence. Maven stands in the kitchen dressed in her typical attire. She studies me thoughtfully, her face carefully composed as it usually is. My fingers itch to weave through her dark, damp hair. She clearly just showered.

"I've never felt cold," I assure her stiffly, desperately putting on the aloofness I wear like a shield.

She smirks, which makes my heart do somersaults. "Physically. Metaphorically, you don't strike me as someone who's felt much warmth."

Maven is perceptive. I watch as she grabs a glass to fill with water, her movements lithe and smooth. There's an unstudied grace to her that makes my cock start to harden again. I'm trying to think of something to push her away, but she glances back at me.

"The movie night is in Silas's room. Your cuddle buddy candidates are Baelfire or Silas. Crypt already announced he'll chop off the dick of anyone who isn't me on his lap."

I think...she's trying to make me feel included. My chest melts even as panic starts to take hold. Even just a second alone like this between us is dangerous. I need to push her away. I can't let her have moments like this where she's subtly trying to cheer me up. It only heightens the risk that I'll end up destroying everything I ever wanted.

I turn back to the window and scoff, "I won't be joining. I'm already not looking forward to hearing their argument."

Maven hums thoughtfully. "I suppose you're right. They could end up fighting over anything. Apparently, none of you get along."

Forcing out the next words takes effort, but I deliver it in the exact asshole tone I need to. "I meant, I don't want to hear them argue about who won the bet after that show back there."

She's quiet for a moment, but the mysterious little caster is smart. I know she's putting it together, and it fucking kills me knowing that I'm about to hurt her.

But if I don't...if I mess this up and my curse takes hold, I'll never forgive myself.

This is for the best.

"Bet?"

Her voice is quiet. She suspects it. All it takes is assuming a dry tone that would make anyone feel stupid.

"Yes, the bet about who would fuck you first. We named our prizes for the competition. We thought getting you in bed would be a challenge, but here we are. One day of fawning over you, and it opened you right up. Now that it's done, we just have to decide who won their prize."

Every word out of my mouth tastes like bile.

Unable to bear it anymore, I turn—and see *pain* on Maven's face. Just briefly. She hides it so fast under the blank slate expression she's perfected, but I still saw it, and it's fucking agony to know she's hiding her emotions from me right now.

I thought this was the best tactic. Coming clean about the bet and trying to create distance any way I could. But seeing that brief agony on her face is a thousand times worse than I expected, and I choke.

"I take it back. I'm sorry—"

"Stop talking."

She turns and begins to walk out, but it feels like my heart is being yanked from my chest so I move to follow after her, the frost on my hands spreading to my forearms as my emotions spiral.

"Maven, wait. Please, I—"

There's a thin whooshing sound, and all my instincts go haywire a second before a dagger cracks into the cabinet directly beside my head. I halt, blinking at the weapon that nearly just killed me. My eyes snap back to Maven, who keeps her chillingly blank expression. It's like she just switched off her ability to feel, and all warmth has disappeared from her body. She moved so quickly that I didn't even see the dagger.

Without a word, she turns and leaves.

It takes significant effort to remain rooted in place instead of rushing after her to try to soothe the sting of my words. But I just hurt her. She doesn't want to see me, and this way, she isn't in danger of my curse. If it means I'm miserable and feel like the scum of the earth, then that's what I'll fucking deal with because it's better than the alternative of my curse getting a hold of her.

I just hope that maybe she'll forgive me when the time is right. When I can finally adore her the way I can't afford to right now.

Dear gods, I hate this.

My phone buzzes. I ignore it. If it's a family member, they can be pissed at me later, and I definitely don't want to answer it if it's one of my quintet members.

Sure enough, not ten minutes pass before Silas walks into the kitchen. "Where is Maven?"

"Not here."

Crypt materializes behind the blood fae, who instinctively whirls and lifts his hands that glow with red magic. The Nightmare Prince doesn't even spare him a glance as he frowns at the room.

"Her aura is here. She was just here. Where did she go?"

"You're her invisible stalker, you should know," I mutter, making my way to the wine rack and glasses. I need something to dull the sharp edges cutting up my insides.

Silas's blood-red gaze sharpens on me, and the anger is already in them. "When she was in here, what did you say to her?"

I pour myself a large glass. The moment my fingers curl around the wineglass, the glass frosts and the wine chills, ice fractals swirling on top. Now isn't a good time for them to get pissed at me, but then it never is.

The hulking dragon shifter sweeps into the room next, and it's no surprise the brute is somehow shirtless again. He glances at the rest of us. "What's going on?"

"Everett. What did you say to her?" Silas repeats carefully, still focused on me. Something about the fae has always reminded me of a shark. Any amount of blood in the water, and there's no shaking them. Plus, they're equally ruthless. It's been a while since I got on his bad side, so I guess I'm overdue anyway.

"Just the truth. She deserved to know a bet has been motivating you hypocritical assholes all along."

For one second, they're all silent. Then all hell breaks loose.

"You fucking *idiot,*" Silas snarls, storming toward me.

Crypt beats him to it, going from zero to a hundred in a fraction of a second. Before I can take a sip of my wine, I'm suddenly crashing through the wall of glass, shards of it raining down into the snow as he pins me by my throat to the ground outside the inn. His swirling markings are glowing, and his glare is unhinged.

"How dare you hurt what's mine?" he seethes, gripping the broken wineglass beside me like he's barely holding back from cutting up my face.

He probably is. But even if he wants to kill me, I'm in Maven's quintet, too. None of them is going to actually kill me.

They'll just grow to hate me even more than they always have.

"Get. Off. Me," I bite out, unable to stop the thick, ominous ice that starts crawling up Crypt's hand planted on the snow beside me.

"No surprise that it's the *Frost* who screwed everything up," Baelfire snaps as he exits through the broken window. The look he levels me with is all disgust before he turns, runs, and leaps off the hill the inn is perched on, shifting and expanding midair until he's a golden dragon. His wings beat the air, creating a swirling draft that stirs the snow around Crypt, Silas, and me as he takes off with a roar.

I glare up at Silas, who is glowering down at me. "You found out Maven was playing games, and it changed your perspective. She had the right to do the same thing. You should have told her sooner or called the bet off entirely. It's not like she would have never found out—I just made sure it happened sooner than later. Now that it's out of the way, we can pick up the pieces and make *real* progress with her."

His jaw clenches. He also looks like he wants to kill me, but the blood fae can't argue with what I'm saying. Because it's true. There is no keeping secrets from a keeper, and the bet was always going to make Maven doubt our intentions with her.

"Forget about progress," Silas says darkly. "You just ruined any chance at *anything* with Maven. None of us will ever forget this."

He stalks away, and Crypt drops the broken glass to deliver a brutal punch to the side of my face. I shout, and instinctively, a wicked-sharp blade of ice forms in my hand that I drive through the wrist of his hand still wrapped around my neck. Blood gushes from his wound onto my face, and he finally sneers at me, clearly deciding that locating our betrayed keeper is the priority.

"Sleep with both eyes open," he warns before vanishing back into Limbo.

I'll be sleeping with a dozen dreamcatchers standing guard. No one wants to face Crypt's wrath in the dream world. I've never been through that myself, but I know what happened to Silas's family, and I don't want a taste of that.

Wiping his chilled blood off my face, I stare up at the sky. The first stars are starting to come out, and the night is growing colder by the second as the aching loneliness starts to influence my power.

I would never admit to the others how much their hatred has

always hurt. Legacies like us are all about power and strength, and showing any kind of weakness is like an animal baring its throat in the wild. Even in our own families, it has always been fight or die. Especially mine. Which is why I have desperately wanted anything that is truly *safe* in my life.

Like Maven. Being in her quintet, all of us watching each other's backs and bound together by the mercy of the gods...that would be safe. Then, I could finally open up to someone else and be vulnerable for once. I'm so damn *tired* of keeping up my cold facade.

I want our quintet more than I've ever wanted anything.

But that's exactly what my curse will ruin.

Although...maybe Silas is right. Maybe I did just permanently ruin any chance at the only thing I've ever wanted. And even if it does work out, I'm not sure they'll ever get over hating me.

The prophecy I got from the gods never specified that.

I mutter a prayer to Pheli, the god of the dark sky above me... who is also the god of hope and change. Maybe he'll have mercy on me when nothing else seems willing to.

29

MAVEN

THE CLUB PULSES with light that hurts my eyes and music so deep it rattles my skull. I slip through the throng of humans grinding on one another, carefully avoiding contact with anyone as I keep my focus trained on the dark VIP doorway.

When I reach the door, a large human bouncer steps in front of me, folding his arms in a futile attempt to appear more menacing. He glances over my baggy clothes and expressionless face and snorts.

"No smile? You could at least try flashing me your little tits. If they're good enough, I'll think about letting you in. Otherwise, get lost. Only prime meat gets admitted."

Ew. I'll never understand misogyny.

Normally, I might offer him another chance, but I'm far from a merciful mood.

I'm pissed off, and he's in my way.

So when he reaches toward me to manhandle me, I break his hand in four places, punch his throat to collapse his trachea, kick him aside, and leave him crumbled on the ground, fighting for breath while I snatch the security card from his pocket and slip through the VIP door.

It leads to a dark upstairs section that overlooks the rest of this club with one-way glass. The only people occupying this sultrily decorated space are my wolf shifter target, two of his pack betas, and three human women who are having a terrible time.

One of them is clearly trying to hold back tears as a shifter gropes her chest, not letting her off his lap. Another half-naked woman is on the alpha's lap, staring off into space in a way that tells me she's mentally checked out to get through tonight, while the third is stripping for the leering male shifters with trembling hands as they wait for the party to get started.

Assholes.

I step out of the darkness, and the shifters glance my way. The fact that they left nothing but a human bouncer down there and don't even get up when they see me tells me their survival instincts are severely lacking. But then, I suppose that's the point of me. I'm not supposed to tip off anyone's danger senses until it's too late for them.

Lykoudis's nose wrinkles. He has dark skin, scars all over one half of his face, and a voice dripping with annoyance. "Who let your ugly ass in here?"

I glance at the stripping woman. "Dress yourself and leave. Take your friends."

She hesitates, visibly trembling as her attention flicks back to the shifters. She knows how dangerous their kind is, and she's only human. All three girls in this room seem hyper-aware of the power imbalance and the fact that these wolf shifters could snap their necks and get away with it.

Lykoudis scoffs. "Well? Take the rest of it off, slut. And you, bitch? Get the fuck out of—"

Before the words are out of his mouth, I slip a large silver dagger from my sleeve and send it straight into the forehead of the third pack beta. His neck snaps backward, head hanging at a broken angle as the blood gurgles from his face, his body twitching.

Instantly, a buzz fills my veins, and I take a deep breath.

This is what I needed. Something dark to help me ignore the hurt. Something to remind me what my reality is. Not the daydream I let myself have for a day.

The women scream. It's not the kind of screaming I enjoy because they're innocents. But at least it gets them to listen to me as they grab their clothes and scramble from the room. The two shifters snarl and leap to their feet, now assessing me as a real threat instead of a minor annoyance.

"What the hell?" Lykoudis roars. "You'll fucking pay for that!"

I should make this quick. I could have his heart and be out of here in a couple of minutes, but my anger needs to go somewhere, and it's been too long since I got to blow off steam by watching someone bleed and cry.

Which is why I don't kill the other pack beta right away when he launches toward me. He shifts midair and bares his teeth at me, but I slide beneath the leaping wolf and stab another knife into his flank, exactly where his joint is. He howls and drops, unable to heal quickly thanks to the silver.

Lykoudis bares his teeth with a snarl he probably thinks is impressive. "Do you even know who I am? How dare you fucking attack me! I'm going to—"

"Less talking. I'm getting bored."

He finally shifts and attacks just as the beta rips the dagger from his flank and comes at me again. Fighting off two oversized wolves from the same pack should be tricky since they should communicate telepathically and work together to take me down. Instead, they fumble, bumping into each other, snarling, and going for my throat at the same time.

I plunge a second silver knife up into the beta's neck as I roll to the side, and when Lykoudis leaps on top of me, I finally tap into the rush of new static in my veins. Dark tendrils of magic explode from my fingertips just as they make contact with his big furry frame, and a pained yelp knocks from his throat as he crashes against the wall of the darkened room.

The beta is already dead.

Sad. I wanted to see him cry. It might've made me feel a bit better.

I rip my second silver knife from his throat and stalk to where

Lykoudis is writhing on the floor in agony, thanks to my unique type of magic. Slipping a tiny bottle from another hidden pocket, I uncork the potion and force the entire thing into the alpha wolf's thrashing snout.

He chokes, and abruptly, the potent wolfsbane concoction forces him to shift back. I can't help the sick smile that blooms over my face when he spits the bottle back out with wide, fearful eyes, his back against the wall. His nose is bleeding profusely, which is satisfying.

"S—stop! Whatever you want, I'll give it to you!" he sputters, spittle flying. "Is it the location of my pack? They're stationed right outside of—"

"Shut up," I sigh, jamming the silver knife into his thigh.

When I yank it back out, the spurt of blood goes everywhere, and he yelps again. He tries for a punch, which I easily dodge, and since his hand is already there, I whip out my adamantine dagger and sink it through his forearm. Immediately, he screams as it starts to turn his blood into acid, eating him up from the inside out.

"You're really a pack alpha? Yikes. I thought this would be a fun fight. But I suppose any alpha who would willingly sell out the weaker in his pack is truly a coward at heart. Speaking of which…"

I trace the silver knife around his torso and down to his crotch, amused by the wet spot that's soaking through his pants as he starts to twitch.

"I—I have money. Is that what you want?"

"If I wanted money, I would have it already."

"Then what do you want?" he explodes hysterically.

I study the pathetic shifter, finally letting the pain and loss in my aching chest wash over me. The buzz from my kills was nice but not enough to push down the emotions still slicing through me.

"Dead men tell no tales, which means I can tell you anything, and it will go straight into a grave. So it won't hurt to answer your question. You want to know what I want?" I lean over and whisper into his ear. "I wanted *them*. More than I've ever wanted anything in my life, which is a hell of a fucking lot, by the way. But now, I need to forget I ever wanted them. I need to forget I was ever stupid enough to fall for competitive, heartless legacies."

He whimpers and clutches clumsily at his bleeding arm, which still has my dagger impaled through it. "The fuck are you talking about?"

"The fact that I should be immune to heartbreak, but here I am," I mutter. Then I shrug. "But back to the matter at hand…I want nothing except what I came here for."

"Then just take it! Stop terrorizing me and take whatever shit you want!"

"If you insist."

I peel off my right glove, and darkness flares to life around my hand as I whisper the forbidden words. When my fingertips first breach his chest, the wolf shifter goes perfectly still and looks down, his jaw hanging open. The blood drains from his face as I wrap my hand around his beating heart and pull it straight from his body—slowly, to see the agony last a little longer.

But my spell works, and he's still alive, choking in horror as I lift his heart with a triumphant grin. It pulses rapidly in my hand, reflecting his ongoing terror.

"I—I'm…still alive?" he whispers, limbs twitching uncontrollably as the adamantine starts to wreak havoc on his system.

"For now. Don't worry, that only lasts twelve hours. Unless your heart is returned, which it won't be. In the meantime, enjoy hell on earth."

He'll be in agony as a living corpse until the spell fades and his heart stops. The adamantine has already nulled all his powers, so he's a nonissue now.

Less than an hour later, I sit on the curb outside a gas station on the route back to Everbound University. Snow falls softly from the night sky, and a brisk wind blows, but I ignore the cold and glare into the dark distance as I wait.

"Devils and dicks, look who it is in the flesh. You're a mite smaller than I expected, *telum*," Melchom says as he steps out of nowhere using dark transportation magic and hunkers down beside me.

I spare him a passing glance. He has a strongly hooked nose, beady eyes, finely groomed facial hair, and that same malicious sparkle in his black eyes that all demons do. And, of course, he wears a hat over his long black hair to hide his horns in the mortal realm. His tail is tucked away unless he went the extreme route and cut it off to try to blend in with mortals better. Some demons do that.

When I make no reply, he snorts. "Yikes, you're a lot more lifeless in person than you were on the phone."

I stare at him.

Melchom blinks and then throws his head back in a sharp, resounding cackle. "Wow, sorry—insensitive much? But really, you look like you just went through some shit. What's got your gooch? Wanna talk about it, *telum?*"

As if I would confide in a demon.

Changing the subject, I ask flatly, "Who's Kevin?"

He blinks several times. "What?"

"You mentioned a Kevin on the phone."

The demon huffs. "He's the cuntfaced asswipe who stole my girlfriend."

"I thought your girlfriend was out of town."

"Yeah. With *him*. Lying bitch thinks I don't know, but I do." Then he tips his head. "Gotta say, I didn't think you'd be the type to get into the nitty gritties of someone else's personal life."

I hardly care about his personal life. Or his life, for that matter. I just want any kind of distraction from the pit in my stomach that's only gotten worse since I made my exit from the inn earlier.

Ever since before arriving at Everbound, I knew legacies were grossly competitive. In their world, might is right, and brutality is rewarded. They do what it takes to survive and excel. So why the hell didn't I put it together sooner?

Of course, my rejected matches had ulterior motives. That should have been my first thought when they refused to let me go after I rejected them. No wonder they were so hard to shake—they weren't after me at all. They were after their prizes. They were interested in besting one another, another chapter in their long list of spats since their childhoods. I was an object in their game, nothing more or less.

Why should I be surprised? I always knew quintets were bullshit.

Letting them in, even briefly, was my fault. And now I'm paying the price of naiveté.

It won't happen ever again.

The intimate, beautiful moments I thought I had with them are like acid in my chest, so I quickly distract myself by reaching into the bag at my feet and withdrawing Lykoudis's still-beating, still-bloody heart. It pounds steadily in my hand, and Melchom's brows shoot up.

"Infernal *hells*. You really did it. Not that I ever doubted you," he adds quickly when I arch a brow. "That's just…damn. Ever thought about joining the black market? You'd make a killing. Pun intended."

"Shut up and give me the powder, Melchom."

He makes an inhuman hissing sound and darts his gaze around. "Stop, stop, stop. No more using my name, okay? Here, here's the fucking nightshade root powder. *Over* a gram, I might add."

He clearly expects me to be impressed as he hands me the tiny bottle of violent fuchsia powder. I'm not. I'm just tired and want to get out of here before any of *them* manage to track me down.

I look the demon in the eye. "If I find out this shit isn't real, I'll hunt you down and reach down your throat to pull out your heart instead."

Melchom takes the beating heart from me, studying it with fascination. "Huh, that's not a bad threat. D'ya mind if I steal that one the next time I talk to good ol' Kevin?"

"Knock yourself out."

"Good doing business with you, *telum*. If you need anything else—"

"I won't. Don't cross my path again."

He takes my dismissal without argument, offering a mocking little bow before vanishing once again using his dark magic. It leaves a pungent scent in the air, and I glare down at the bottle of powder in my hand. This ingredient will make fulfilling my mission a breeze. Then, I just have to disappear…and move on to the next one.

And never see them again.

Make us your weapons, darling, and no one will stand a chance against our quintet. Let us be yours.

Damn them for using such pretty words to ruin me like this.

I need to move on quickly.

30

MAVEN

I SLICE the blade across my palm and watch the dark blood droplets drip.

This kind of forbidden magic is therapeutic.

Once enough of my blood is in the bowl full of rare ingredients, I sprinkle in the tiniest bit of nightshade root powder. It singes against my skin and scalds my nose, but I cover my mouth with one of my long sleeves and wait until the concoction finishes sizzling.

And then I dip my adamantine dagger into the bowl and wait. Everbound Forest is dark and forbidding around me, with the distant sounds of strange creatures and haunting whispers sending delicious chills skittering down my spine. Dawn is half an hour away, and I haven't slept.

I don't have time for sleep. I could be done with my mission and hundreds of miles away before any of *them* return to the school.

Let go. Lose yourself in us. Let us be yours.

I shake my head. I need to purge any trace of them from me and do what I came here for.

My pocket vibrates as I wait for the blade to absorb the deadly spell. I groan. I haven't figured out how to turn it off, and it's been exploding for the last couple of hours with dozens of calls and texts from Silas and the others. I'm sure Silas is mad he can't track the device, since I asked for Kenzie's help in disabling that feature immediately after he gave me the damn thing. I've also gotten dozens of texts and calls from the rest of them, even from Crypt.

I'm sure he's finding it impossible to track me down in Limbo, thanks to the potent concealment spell I placed on myself. It took a lot of magic, but it was worth it. Once I'm done here, they'll never see me again.

I can't comprehend why they would try to talk to me at all. They got what they wanted from me already. They should go argue about their bet and let me slip away forever.

When it buzzes again, I grit my teeth and yank it from my pocket before squinting at the unknown number. I try to hang it up, but my technologically impaired fingers somehow end up answering it.

"Shit," I mutter, annoyed.

"Hello? Minerva? Are you there?" Luka demands through the phone. His voice is urgent.

Ugh. This is probably about lifting his hex. He'll have to find someone else to lift it. Preferably someone whose name he actually knows.

"Where the hell is K—" he starts to ask, but I finally manage to hang up. Then I smash the phone to pieces under my foot and bury it under a clump of dirty forest floor snow with the toe of my boot.

There. Now I won't be bothered.

Thirty minutes later, I finish scaling the side of Everbound Castle to the headmaster's office. The sun is just beginning to rise far in the misty, wintry sky, and the school is going to start coming alive for a new Monday morning. Which means Headmaster Hearst will be in his office soon.

I'll assassinate him quickly and silently. Then I'll disappear.

I stand on a thin lip of stone to the left of the headmaster's office balcony, my back pressed against the cold side of the castle and my hair moving softly around my face with the light breeze. It's frigid out here. I'm dressed almost head to toe in black, my mouth and nose covered so my warm breath plumes against my face.

Waiting gives me time to plot.

I know the room's general layout thanks to my study of the interim headmaster's office. He'll enter, and I'll wait for him to sit. I'm sure he'll be keyed into dozens of protective magic wards on the room, but that's where the rest of my magical store will go—to disabling them.

Once I can slip in unnoticed, he will sense me and try to attack. As a mage and a member of the Immortal Quintet, Hearst is a highly formidable target. In fact, he's known as *unkillable*, thanks to a rare amulet he bonded his soul to which he always has on him. He can wield ridiculous amounts of magic, but he's no match for me in physical combat, especially when I have the element of surprise.

And once I stab the amulet with the nightshade root powder that nulls its powers, I'll end him and be done with it.

Inside the office, I hear the faint sound of a door opening and closing.

They're relying on you. Don't fail. You were literally made for this.

Carrying out this hit is a stepping stone to fulfilling my blood oath. There's no backing down, now or ever.

I breathe deeply, clearing my head of anything that could distract me from the next few fraught minutes. Placing my right palm against the wall behind me, I silently release the holds on the dark magic that is stored inside my veins. It seeps out of me slowly, corrupting the existing spells, wilting all existing wards so gradually that it won't tip off Hearst until it's too late.

At least, it's not supposed to. But I tense when I hear him shout inside the room.

My throat tightens, and I stop breathing, waiting for him to throw open the balcony doors and unleash hell on me. But there's just a tiny garbled sound that I can't understand, and it goes completely silent again. An odd feeling sinks into my gut—a feeling I'm very used to.

Death. Someone just died nearby.

My curiosity mounts until I quickly slip in through the balcony doors since this room has no more magical protection. I'm silent as I slide out of the drapes and step into the large, ornate office, but the scene in front of me makes me freeze.

Headmaster Hearst is supine on the floor, dead, with his eyes unfocused on the ceiling. Blood is quickly pooling around his head, which has a gaping hole in it somewhere. The amulet hanging from his neck is shattered, seeping a dark red liquid.

The unkillable mage is dead.

But I didn't do it.

What the fuck?

Before it can sink in that someone *else* just killed my target, my ears pick up on the soft *whoosh* of something at me, and I dodge on instinct. A gnarly-looking sword embeds itself into the headmaster's desk, and I whirl to face—

Surprise hits me square in the gut.

"What are you doing?" I whisper.

The lion shifter makes no sound as she withdraws another sword from her back. She's dressed similarly to me, a cloak half-obscuring her face—but it's definitely Kenzie's face.

Which makes no sense.

Her expression is unlike anything I've ever seen on her normally cheery face, dark with undivided focus tracking my every movement. She moves toward me smoothly, but something about it is *off*.

This entire situation feels off.

But I don't waste time with more questions since she's clearly about to try to kill me.

When the sword swings toward me, I roll to the side and withdraw two plain knives from their hiding places.

"I don't have to hurt you. I'll leave. Just tell me why you did that."

I nod toward the dead mage, but she ignores him and lunges toward me. I've seen Kenzie fight before in combat practices. This is entirely different.

It's *brutal*.

Momentarily taken off guard by the way she knocks aside one of my knives and simultaneously lands a kick to my upper thigh, I stumble back. It buys her time to take a swipe at me, and I hiss when the sword glides smoothly through the flesh of my stomach. An alarming amount of blood gushes from the long injury at once.

Kenzie tries to capitalize on my pain, leaping forward again.

She doesn't move like Kenzie.

The feeling that something is off magnifies as I cartwheel away from the attack, my stomach on fire. My eyes snap to her face again just as her hood moves slightly. And that's when I get a clearer look at her eyes.

Oh.

This isn't Kenzie at all. It's a changeling.

It's odd, running into this rare monster here, of all places.

My moment of hesitation evaporates, and all my training kicks in at once. The next time it moves for me, I counter it smoothly. For a moment, we're caught in a silent, deadly dance as the creature tries to angle the sword to nick me again, and I block and avoid its every attempt.

Killing it would be easy, but I need it alive for questioning. If it's wearing Kenzie's face, then it already got its hands on her. Which means she might be in danger.

Or she might be dead.

That thought sends anger through me, and I bury a dagger in its arm, forcing the changeling to drop the sword. It clatters loudly to the tiles, but I don't have time to worry about someone in the faculty hall overhearing us right now.

It swings for me, but I duck and grip the arm over my head, using the creature's momentum to send it crashing to the floor. Before it can right itself, I straddle it, ignoring the agony curling through my system from my gaping stomach wound, and pin its other arm to the ground using a silver dagger from my boot. I cover its mouth to muffle its scream.

Its voice is Kenzie's, too. That pisses me off.

"Where is she?" I hiss, ripping down my mouth covering.

The changeling struggles beneath me, trying to dislodge its pinned arm as it glares up, a disturbing mirror image of Kenzie.

Except for the pupils. That's one giveaway of a changeling—slightly square pupils. Most people don't know to look for that, but this is not the first time I've crossed paths with this kind of monster.

Someone knocks on the office door, and Mr. Gibbons' voice calls out, "Headmaster? Are you in there?"

Shit.

I go still while muffling the face of the creature. It bites my palm deeply, drawing blood. As if that would get me to release it. When it feels my blood ooze into its mouth, it starts to choke on the liquid and thrashes in a panic while I smirk quietly down at it.

But I don't hear anything else from Gibbons, and soon I withdraw my hand, trying to wrestle the monster off the floor quietly.

It puts up a fight, which is inconvenient because I'm starting to get lightheaded from blood loss. When it manages to dig an elbow into the gash across my waist, pain ricochets down my spine, and everything goes blurry for a moment as my body briefly goes into shock.

And in that moment of weakness, I can't fend off the creature as it grapples at my chest, drawing out the dagger that was just visible in one of my concealed pockets. I'd had it at the ready to take out the headmaster, but all at once, the adamantine infused with nightshade powder penetrates my chest—aiming for my heart.

I can't stop the cry that escapes my lips when the ice-like agony explodes across my body. My veins bulge and thicken beneath my skin with a sensation like a thousand needles pricking every inch of them. The nightshade root powder makes it unbearable.

Suddenly, I'm lying flat on my back beside the dead headmaster, unable to breathe or move as my life saps away. My blood pools onto the tiles beneath me.

It's the exact scene from my last episode.

The changeling stands over me, and just as my vision blurs, I see the creature's eyes and hair darken. Its face morphs slowly, changing from Kenzie's, and just before nothingness claims me, I'm looking up into my own face.

And then I'm gone.

31

CRYPT

THE ONLY THING keeping me semi-sane while I search for my missing obsession is fantasizing about how I'll kill Frost if she's as hurt by his words as I suspect she might be.

First, I would break his mind, of course. He deserves to suffer intensely, keenly. Just as I am, the longer I float through the void of Limbo without any trace of Maven's aura or any hint of her existence in sight.

What if she's crying somewhere, alone, thinking we were only interested in her for sex?

I'll murder someone if I find her in tears.

Again, it will likely be Frost.

I have no idea where the other two are. Possibly they're working together to look for her, but I'm far more efficient working alone. Though, I'm beginning to get frustrated. There was no trace left of her leaving the inn, her phone goes straight to voicemail, and now I'm floating through the walls of Everbound University, searching every nook and cranny.

She has to be here. I saw her friend's car parked in the parking lot, though there was no lingering hint of her essence anywhere near it. Just how long ago did she return? The fact that she returned so late at night, sleepless and exhausted, puts me on edge. What if she had crashed that damn car? And what if, at this moment, she's in her dorm room, trapped in a horrifying nightmare? I'm unable to reach her there, thanks to the dreamcatcher.

But I didn't see remnants of her beautiful aura in that hallway.

So my darling must be somewhere else.

Wherever she is, wherever she may ever go, I'll always find her. I thought I was well and truly obsessed before, but seeing her guard down, hearing her moan softly and cry out in pleasure, watching her eyes soften as she studied me in that bed…

I need to carve her into whatever remains of my broken, blackened soul.

Where is she?

Just as dawn starts to color the world outside, I drift through the faculty hall, internally stewing that Frost lumped me in with the rest of them when he told Maven about their asinine little wager. Now she thinks we only worked so hard to get close to her just to win prizes when in actuality, nothing the members of my quintet could offer would ever remotely interest me. I ignored their wager from the beginning and thought nothing of it until Frost *hurt* her with it.

Gods above, I really might kill that convoluted ice elemental.

A door clicks, and I freeze in place, shocked when a dark figure shaped like Maven exits one of the rooms. I launch toward her in Limbo, eager to get a glimpse of the hooded figure's face, but then I pause, frowning at its aura.

A pungent mass of swirling muck, like all colors blended together.

Not my keeper.

But the door is left slightly ajar to the office they just left, and I drift closer to peek inside curiously.

Horror and denial flood me so fast that Limbo shakes around me. Before I realize what I've done, I'm tearing into the mortal world, incognizant of everything else in the room rising from the hold of gravity and swirling in a topsy-turvy mess as I drop to my knees beside—

Maven.

Unmoving. Cold. Staring up with unseeing eyes at the ceiling.

With a dagger through her heart.

A raw cry rips from my throat, and I pull her against me, panic streaking through my system when I see the blood soaking her chest, her hand, her stomach—gods above, it's *everywhere.*

She's dead.

She's *dead.*

How am I supposed to exist now? I'm going to destroy the entire godsdamned world for taking her away from me. I'm going to watch them all rip each other apart so their blood drowns out my tears. I'll curse the gods and follow her into the Beyond to be with her if I have to.

No, no, no, no, no—

My eyes snag on her hand, floating limply like everything else in this room. Limbo is still seeping into the world here, distorting everything in a confusing haze, but when I see the bite marks—fucking *bite marks*—on her hand, the breath catches in my throat.

They're mending.

The room calms as my confusion overshadows my grief, and finally, we're both solidly in the mortal world as I gawk at Maven's hand. Soon, there's no hint of injury left behind. Unable to stop myself, I gently lift the edge of her ripped, baggy black shirt. My eyes widen in shock.

This was a fatal wound. There is enough blood that I'm sure of that. Yet now there is nothing but blood-streaked, perfect olive-toned skin surrounding her belly button.

My fingers shake as I shift the shirt further up until my attention zeroes in on the wound that's attempting to close around the strange dagger embedded there, right where her pale scar bisects her beautiful chest. Not daring to breathe, I grip the dagger's hilt and slide it out, tossing it aside and remaining wholly fixated on the hole that quickly closes up.

She's dead. Yet she's…healing.

Maven's chest rises slightly with a shallow, ragged inhale. That inhale sounds pained, but I barely restrain the relieved sob that tries to break free from my chest.

Alive.

Somehow.

It makes no sense, but she's alive, and that's all I can think about.

Voices and footsteps sound in the hallway. I gently set my beautiful, *confusing* obsession down to shut and lock the door. When I return, she's still breathing. All I want is to smooth the hair from her face and kiss every inch of her as she warms back up, but I refrain. If she wakes and feels me touching her, it might set off that sickening terror she has of skin contact.

But as the color starts to return to her face, sweat beads on her forehead, and her brows furrow softly in pain. A whimper so soft I almost miss it rises from her throat.

"Darling," I whisper hoarsely, aching to soothe her somehow. "Where does it hurt? Who did this to you?"

Whoever it was, I'll rip them to pieces in every possible way. I'll end them and feed whatever remains of their carcass to the monsters in Everbound Forest.

Maven's eyelashes flutter, and her dark eyes open, but she can't seem to pinpoint where I am. She grimaces and rolls her head from side to side.

"Dammit. I'vegot…tokillthem," she whispers, her words slurring together.

She's fighting the effects of something. A poison, maybe?

I glance around for any sign of what may have done this to her and blink when I see the dead headmaster half-draped across his desk with blood drying all over his sliced-up face. My loss of control in Limbo must have put him in that position.

Hearst.

He is—or *was*—in my father's quintet and beat me regularly growing up. We resented each other equally, so seeing the corpse of the so-called unkillable monster is nothing but a tiny bit of joy before I move on, far more concerned with the way Maven is groaning softly.

Someone knocks on the door.

I ignore it, gently brushing hair from my keeper's face without touching her skin. "Keep breathing, love. Gods above, *please* keep breathing. I'm taking you to the healers, and they'll take the pain away. And if they don't, I'll kill them and find someone who can. All right?"

Her eyes flutter again, and she swallows hard. Her speech is still staggered and broken. "No healers. Ineedto kill them…now that they…know."

My voice is strained since my attention keeps flicking to her pained expression and the way she's clutching at her chest. Was that dagger poisoned? That must be it. Every instinct in me is going haywire, desperate to take away her pain and rain hell down on her enemies.

"Now that they know what, love?"

"My secret," she murmurs faintly, her eyes shutting in defeat. She's not in her own mind right now, so far gone to whatever poison is pumping through her that it has loosed her lips. "That…my deaths don't stick."

My deaths don't stick.

I stare at her, perplexed and shell-shocked.

But she's exhausted. She's *hurting*. Whatever she's really trying to tell me will wait for another day.

The person outside the door pounds on it again, far more insistently. With a silent scowl, I start to move, but Maven's hand gently brushes against mine. My heart skips and I halt, looking back at her.

"Whatever happens…do *not* let anyone try to heal me. No one," she mutters, and then I can sense her slip into unconsciousness, Limbo crowding around her there.

The person outside loses their patience, and the door is kicked in, splintering into dozens of pieces that rain across the room. I whirl around, positioned protectively in front of Maven and ready to kill.

But it's Crane, Decimus, and Frost.

And the moment their panicked eyes fall on us, speechless horror overtakes all three of them. I look down at Maven, too, a disturbing new theory surfacing in my mind.

Because it's clear that our keeper has bigger secrets than we ever could have suspected.

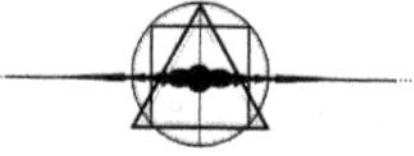

Enjoying the story? Feel free to share your review for Blood Oath on Amazon or Goodreads for others.

If you want to join a Facebook reader page to chat about the Cursed Legacies series and other why choose romances, feel free to join Morgan B Lee's Why Choose Fiends.

Thank you for reading!

ABOUT THE AUTHOR

Morgan is a certified nerd who loves long bubble baths and big, bad, OTT possessive sexy cinnamon roll book boyfriends. When she's not busy reading spice or lint-rolling cat hair off of her yoga pants, she writes to her little black heart's content while daydreaming about the before-mentioned cinnamon roll book boyfriends.

www.ingramcontent.com/pod-product-compliance
Lightning Source LLC
Chambersburg PA
CBHW070613310726
48982CB00001B/74

* 9 7 9 8 9 9 3 6 3 2 4 0 7 *